BLIND EYE

BLIND EYE

ANNA M HOLMES

The Book Guild Ltd

First published in Great Britain in 2021 by
The Book Guild Ltd
9 Priory Business Park
Wistow Road, Kibworth
Leicestershire, LE8 0RX
Freephone: 0800 999 2982
www.bookguild.co.uk
Email: info@bookguild.co.uk
Twitter: @bookguild

Typeset in 12pt Adobe Jenson Pro

Printed and bound by CPI Group (UK) Ltd, Croydon, CR0 4YY

ISBN 978 1913913 458

British Library Cataloguing in Publication Data.
A catalogue record for this book is available from the British Library.

To my partner, Hubert Kwisthout,
a founder member of Forest Stewardship Council (FSC).

1

Cockroaches, rats, humans. All of them pests. And forget rats and roaches, it's humans that are destroying the planet. Linda took a breath to still her shaking hands then opened the web portal and began.

DAE.org/Blogs/Linda

Just imagine, it's hot, sticky, can't wait to hop in a shower and you could kill for a cool beer. Maybe you're thinking this trip was a bad idea and you should've stayed home. I had one of those moments earlier.

The day started well. We were in the forest when I heard thrashing in the top branches, looked up, and there she was: Mom with a baby clinging on to her tummy, swinging to the next tree. Awesome. Take a look at this **video**. See how caring she is? You can't help but feel the connection between our species. But that's it for the cute bit. I want to tell you what happened later when we saw a different mom and babe. She was clutching a branch on a solitary tree and keeping hold of her little one. Long story short: Mom fell from a great height, missed the darned net they were trying to catch her in, and it took a long time for her to die. These guys were trying to *save* her, move her to a protected area. Huh! Sickening to witness.

Linda winced, recalling the thud of that massive orange bundle of fur connecting with the hard earth. Goddamn humans! If she had known then what she knew now, she wondered whether she would have had kids. But she loved her two – both decent human beings – and she was getting used to being a grandma. Not a hands-on granny, but her daughter understood. Whatever time she had left was going to count. Linda interlocked her fingers, cracked her knuckles and continued.

If you've a strong stomach, click on this **link**. The babe you see survived. Another one for the sanctuary. Let's stop shit like this happening!

To find out what Direct Action for the Earth is doing to save our planet and how to get involved, go to our **Campaigns**. Check out our **Membership** schemes and don't log off till you've clicked through to **Donations**.

She dispatched her latest blog post into cyberspace.

Ben pedalled steadily, dodging traffic on Westminster Bridge and along Millbank. London's toxic air probably cancelled out the benefits, but cycling was a matter of principle. He secured his bike, checked there was no chain oil on his good chinos, raked his fingers through his hair and headed towards the Department for International Trade's Whitehall office.

After he passed security, he made his way deeper into the functional part of government. He knew the way, but he followed a junior staffer to the second secretary's office where she knocked and showed him in.

'Mr Ahearn, Doctor Fletcher's here.'

Connor Ahearn looked up from whatever he was working at on his laptop. 'Thank you, Grace. Good to see you, Ben. Thanks for coming.' He stood, a welcoming grin on his face. 'How've you been?'

'Fine.' Ben nodded noncommittally as they shook hands, and settled into a chair across the desk. So it was to be just the two of them then. That informal.

He hadn't spoken with Connor for over a year. Now, following Connor's text suggesting they meet: '*...an informal meeting – would like to sound you out on something*', his curiosity was piqued.

Governments changed and trade secretaries were shuffled, but Connor seemed to have a knack of remaining "a stable hand at the tiller", as he had said to Ben often enough. Ben glanced around the room. Nothing much had changed since he was last here: ring-binder files on the shelves, a new laptop, a wall-mounted TV. Connor hadn't changed either: well-cut suit, stylish hair – a hint of a bald patch these days – and that confident smile that had served him well.

'Good match at the weekend. Ireland's win over England was deserved, don't you think?' Connor asked.

Ben shrugged. 'I don't follow it.' That was true, and he didn't feel like small talk.

Connor cleared his throat. 'I want to share something with you – an initiative we're working on with the Indonesians. Right up your street, and thing is, we could do with your input.'

'Oh?' Ben left his question hanging.

'A Positive Partnership Initiative. Us and Indonesia. A forest project in Kalimantan to our supply outlets here. Trevor Arnott is—'

'As in Arnott's furniture and so on?'

'Yes, with local partners out there. He's joining the green brigade, taking a lead.'

Ben scoffed. 'The king of the edge-of-town retail parks? Since when was he a leader in anything other than putting profit first?'

Connor continued: 'It's an industry-led initiative. They're developing their own certification—'

'A double turn-off. We've got globally recognised organisations they should work through. Why set up another?'

Connor held his eyes. 'That's why I didn't email the details. You'd have pressed delete before opening and reading. Come on now, hear me out.'

Ben raised a hand in submission, deciding to let Connor hang himself with his own rope. He had no time for Mickey Mouse forestry initiatives. They both knew that.

'The minister's taking a keen interest in Arnott's project. In fact, the prime minister's keeping a close eye. It'll make a good headline project for the trade summit.'

'Ah.' Now he knew where this was heading.

'We need an environment-friendly good news story. Or two. We'd like your input: evaluate how it's doing and consider the potential.'

'Potential?' Ben guessed they'd be wanting some sort of overview report. Nothing to scupper the good news but with the right amount of authoritative rigour. He could do a job like this with one hand tied behind his back, but he didn't like the sound of it.

'Look, Ben, it'll be a great opportunity to get this to the top of the agenda. It's a major summit. A chance to get your name out there.' Connor paused and Ben wondered if he had been tempted to say "*back* out there". Connor turned his laptop around. 'Take a look.'

A *Guardian* online article: a photo of a baby orangutan clinging to a white woman, a group of younger Indonesians surrounding her.

Ben frowned. 'Yeah, I've read it.'

Even with a protective mask covering her mouth and nose, Linda Smith was immediately recognisable with her spiky grey hair, fierce eyes staring defiantly at camera and raised welts visible below her T-shirt sleeve. Twice their paths had crossed, the last time at a conference in Thailand when she had hijacked the floor, loudly criticising the presentation he was giving. She wouldn't shut up and had been escorted out. The woman who had founded Direct Action for the Earth had to be one of the most radical, determined people he had encountered – and that was saying something. He didn't approve of her, or DAE's, methods: risking lives, not compromising.

He glanced at the article headed *Habitats Destroyed*. The investigative report had uncovered illegal forestry in Borneo. 'Another chunk of pristine forest destined for palm plantations,' Ben offered, then skim-read the bit about the chain of wood handlers being traced to companies in the UK.

'Look, Ben. The orangutans do it for the media – and the public. Pulls the heartstrings more than number-crunching tree clearance stats or banging on about importers operating without due diligence. Trevor didn't like being lumped in with this. Don't write him off. What can be bad about that?'

'Plenty. Current reckoning suggests at least half of Indonesian timber is illegal. You think Arnott's sources will be different?'

'Why not?' Connor revealed another tab on the internet; he had obviously lined them up ready. Arnott's homepage filled the screen, with its photo of Trevor Arnott, a florid-faced man in his fifties, standing proudly in front of one of his stores wearing a two-tone shirt and striped tie. Connor brought up a screen proclaiming: *We're Going Green* with images of tropical forest and wooden garden furniture.

'You sure about this?' Ben looked dubious. 'He's not just greenwashing?'

Connor leaned forward, hands clasped, gaze challenging. 'Why shouldn't Arnott and his partners out there have a way of making it work? He says it's working. Better be! Go out there. Tell us what you make of it and report back before our September summit.'

Ben eased back in his chair. 'Remind me. How many reports have I done for you?'

'Enough so I know you're the one to do this. I assure you it will be read. Taken seriously. It will make a difference.'

'I've heard that before. I barely recognised my last report it had been so heavily edited—'

'Nonsense. Your last one—'

'Was meant to prove the worth of my unit! My staff!' Ben pushed his chair back and jumped up. The forest research unit he had assiduously built up had been cut from under him. It still stung. Lives had been upturned, his own among them. Connor had no idea what it meant to work freelance, to always be looking for the next contract. As far as Ben knew Connor had been in a secure job since leaving university.

Connor was attempting a sincere look, a slight furrow between his brows.

'It's a pity what happened. You know I fought your corner—'

'Did you?'

'Yes. Restructures. Cuts. You know how it is.' Connor half rose, held out his hand, indicating the chair. 'Please.'

Ben hesitated. He was not one for dramatics, for making a scene. He sat down.

'Look, Ben, this summit's a big deal. Pick a good team you know you can work with and turn this around.'

'I'm not sure—'

'If it doesn't interest you, or you're too busy, I'll reach out to someone else.'

Ben could tell Connor was trying to bait him. For all he knew Connor might have got his staff to check if he was working on something right now. He wasn't, but did he want to work for this government again? A new research opportunity was in the pipeline at the Oxford Centre for Tropical Forests which would allow for extensive fieldwork. That was what he loved: being out in the forests, out in nature, with limited time in a fusty lecture hall. But he wasn't sure when this Oxford post would be advertised, and he might not be appointed…

'So?' Connor's eyebrows formed perfect arches.

'All right. Send over what you've got, and I'll get back to you.' Should he add *thank you for thinking of me?* Ben gathered his backpack and stood.

'Good man.' Connor looked genuinely pleased. He came around his desk and gripped Ben's hand firmly.

Angling his bike into the lift, Ben pressed the button for the seventh floor. His tiny one-bedroom flat south of the Thames was not in a fashionable area, but even so he struggled to afford the rent. Once inside, he leaned his bike against the wall. Anyone who owned one – and he hadn't noticed many cyclists in this block – had to do the same. Bikes wouldn't survive the night chained outside in this jungle.

He by-passed cardboard boxes and plastic containers with partly unpacked belongings, his eyes sliding off camping equipment dumped in a corner. His stuff. Most of the useful furniture had been Sarah's, which of course she had now. He had moved here a few weeks ago after short-term arrangements with friends, but found he was reluctant to commit to the place. It was soulless compared with the home he and Sarah had shared. Months had passed since they split, yet he was irritated to find his heart pounding at the hurt of it all. He should unpack, but if that Oxford job materialised he would be moving. Tossing his jacket on a chair he headed to his desk.

In contrast with the rest of the room, this was neatly ordered. Shelves lined with books and official documents on forestry, fair-trade and global economics were carefully catalogued: Greenpeace and the Environmental Investigation Agency reports among them. Everything was e-published these days, but some of the older reports were useful for reference. He picked up a specialist book, just delivered and ready to dive into. He had hesitated before ordering it, knowing how low his bank balance was, but when a new title caught his eye, he couldn't resist buying it. He opened his laptop and began reading what Connor had sent through on the Positive Partnership Initiative. Once he had got beyond the jargon-filled political aspirations, he settled in his seat. The multi-partner ambitions for the project (worthy, but were they realistic?); the partners (some suspect, in his opinion); statistics of forest cover lost (well documented elsewhere); timescale for the scope (always too short); the fee (not bad at all…).

A project like this was exactly where his heart was. Where his head was. Connor had been right to say it was up his street. He should have voiced his thanks, should have said, 'Good of you to think of me,' but he wasn't ready to forgive the international trade minister's senior dogsbody yet. He turned to see splodges of rain on the windowpane, the steel grey sky beyond. It had been a dismal spring and early summer, while in Indonesia it was the dry season. His personal life had taken a hit, and an academic appointment he had thought might interest him had turned out to be tedious; he found he hadn't the stomach to supervise student work, even at post-graduate level, so he had left. At thirty-six he was at a crossroad.

He idly rocked back and forth. So, a trade summit in September. A perfect platform to promote an innovative forestry project – if it could be shown to be viable. And it could provide a fillip to his work profile.

Connor could wait a day for his reply; he didn't want to appear too keen. Unpacking his worldly possessions could wait as well – he wouldn't be settling in just yet.

DAE.org/Blogs/Linda
Still in Indonesia. We were about to leave when I got the heads-up about stuff going on where stuff ought not to be going on. Couldn't resist a nosy.

This is what a **log landing** looks like and it shouldn't be here. See how it has eroded the bank, made the water muddy? That stack of logs by the edge of the river shouldn't be there either. I would love to stick around, but Rob got the jitters and I need to keep my guest safe. His fans would be down on me like a ton of bricks if anything happened to him!

I'm being asked to take fewer photos of trees and orangutans and more of Rob. So here you go, check these **pics**. I'm not normally a fan of those man-bun thingies, but it suits him. That's my goodwill gesture for the day, yours is to read on and take action.

To find out what Direct Action for the Earth is doing to save our planet and how to get involved, go to our **Campaigns**. Check out our **Membership** schemes and don't log off till you've clicked through to **Donations**.

Linda paused to read over what she had written. Should she say more before the bog-standard paragraph she always ended with? There was a lot she could say but she was too angry, so she was going for a light touch today. For sure Rob's fans would love the photos and maybe put some money in the kitty. She meant to milk his presence as much as she could.

Direct Action for the Earth's Sydney co-ordinator had forwarded Rob's email. He was looking for a "jungle experience to tag along on". Linda hadn't had the slightest idea who Rob Gilmore was. Her son soon put her right, screeching down the phone, 'Far out, Mom. You can't say no to Rob. He's *massive.*' Her daughter teased, 'If he's coming, can I tag along too? He's up for grabs after that bitch dumped him.' So Linda got a crash course in what was what and who was who in the world of popular music, and figured a celebrity could help Direct Action for the Earth get their message across. The most Linda had emailed to Rob was, 'Get good travel insurance, bring your mosquito repellent, get yourself to Samarinda, Kalimantan – look it up – and we'll take it from there.'

And they *had* taken it from there. While Rob was nothing like she had imagined a rock star to be – so grounded, so likeable – he was a millstone around her neck all the same. For "got the jitters" read "frigging petrified".

No one in authority was giving her the time of day, but she had heard about a government-backed monitoring project happening elsewhere. Perhaps she would stick around. Perhaps she could think of a way to bend their purpose to suit her own.

She dispatched her blog with a staccato tap of her middle finger.

2

THE WHINING OF THE TWIN ENGINES OF THE SIX-seater Cessna was hypnotic. Ben rested his forehead against the plexiglass window, looking out at the sun's rays reflected off a wing edge. Far below the small craft, he traced a river meandering through patchy forest. Smoke rose from fires billowing vast grey clouds. Each year during the cutting season, Indonesia suffered from a haze of pollution as hundreds of thousands of hectares were burnt. He expected to see this, but even so it hit him in the pit of his stomach. Looking closer he could make out small roads running like veins, and the unmistakable grid pattern of palms in massive plantations: monocultures detrimental to wildlife.

A decade earlier, when he had first visited Kalimantan, the natural forest had been much more extensive. And people whose memories were longer than his own recalled flying over an unbroken green canopy of pristine rainforest, or travelling for a week on a boat on clear rivers with trees right up to the edges, to reach distant destinations in the heart of the forest. Those days were gone. But he could play a small part in halting the destruction, even turning it around. Why not? A world without forests was unimaginable. He took up his camera, waited for the aircraft's wings to dip so the reflection disappeared, and began to take photos.

Ben had selected his team, two men he'd previously worked with who were, thankfully, available to put aside other commitments for the coming weeks: Doctor Ardhi Durmali, a forestry economist in his early thirties, from Jakarta, and Rick Wilson, a seasoned forester from Vancouver, who must be in his mid-forties.

In Jakarta, Ben and Ardhi had been briefed by officials from the Ministry of Environment and Forestry as well as from the Trade Ministry, and had been impressed by their determination to be thorough in monitoring this shared industry initiative. Afterwards he and Ardhi took an internal flight to Samarinda, Kalimantan, where the two of them had visited a flooring and furniture manufacturer. This was the company making products from certified timber harvested from the forest they were heading to. All had been in order. After this, they had met up with Rick before transferring to a small plane for the final hop into the interior: the Malinau Regency.

The pilot dipped into a descent, touched down and taxied along the bumpy airstrip to where a SUV waited.

As Ben stepped out of the plane into the glaringly bright day, the heat felt almost thick enough to lean into. Within a short time his light fabric travel trousers and casual cotton shirt would be soaked with sweat. He had a love-hate relationship with the tropics: always happy to be here to work, enjoying the change of climate and unexpected flora and fauna, but content to return to England.

Each of them shouldered their backpacks and small bags and headed towards the Indonesian driver opening the back of a dusty four-wheel drive Mitsubishi. Behind them the pilot was already turning his craft ready for take-off.

Ardhi greeted their driver, offering a cigarette. The two of them leaned against the vehicle chatting, inhaling the strong-smelling tobacco. Rick set about doing ungainly stretches, grunting as he tried to touch his toes, then twisting his trunk right and left.

Their flight had been delayed an hour waiting for Rick's transfer – his third flight from Vancouver – and Ben wanted to arrive at their destination before the reception party he understood would be greeting them.

'C'mon, let's get going.' Ben slid into the front passenger seat. The driver stubbed out his cigarette and climbed in next to him, Rick and Ardhi in the back.

They travelled through the countryside, past mile upon mile of regimented oil palm plantation, farmland and through occasional tiny settlements with paint-peeled wooden houses surrounded by garden patches. Their driver honked repeatedly at two motorcycles up ahead, one carrying a family of three, the other managing to squeeze a child between father and mother with another child perched precariously at the back. There was more honking, and somehow the driver found a gap sooner than Ben would have wished.

Behind him, Rick was well into his tree-themed puns.

'How do trees get online? ... They just log in.'

'How did the tree get lost? ... It took the wrong root.'

Ben opened his window and raised his camera.

'Hey. Close it, will ya?' Rick tapped his shoulder. 'You're disrupting the aircon.'

'Sorry, won't be long.' Ben made a gesture of apology. He had treated himself to the Nikon a few months earlier when money wasn't so tight. Through the lens he focused on local farmers – men and women alike – carrying piles of firewood on their backs, or watched as they strained to pull loaded carts. Life was tough here. He clicked and clicked, with half an ear on the conversation in the back.

Rick was sharing family photos stored on his phone. Ben could imagine a teenage boy decked out in ice hockey gear. On the rare occasions he and Rick connected for work, Rick shared his family life – overshared, in Ben's opinion.

'He's doing good. Seem to spend all our weekends driving him some place. His team won the regionals.'

'I got married two months ago.' Ardhi sounded shy, but proud, as he shared his news. Ben could hear Ardhi fiddling with his own phone. 'This is my wife.'

'Nice! She's pretty. Where was my invitation, heh?' Rick teased. 'Fletch? Wanna see?'

Ben closed the window, dutifully looked at the images and mumbled, 'Lovely,' before handing the phone back.

'So, how's Sarah?'

Ben flinched. There was no reason why Rick shouldn't ask. It was a polite question and Ben had mentioned Sarah many times in the past. 'We split.'

'I'm sorry to hear that.'

There was an expectant silence, but Ben didn't want to go into the details. It had been painful – still was. He and Sarah had been together more than ten years, five of them married. It had been a shock when she announced she was leaving. He truly hadn't seen it coming.

Travelling towards them, a pole trailer logging truck laden with roundwood logs took up the centre of the road. Horn blaring, the oncoming vehicle forced them to swerve, their own driver cursing and honking in a futile gesture of defiance. The logging truck thundered past, the company logo, AZTAR, clearly visible on the door.

'Woah! Our guys, right?' Rick caught Ben's eye.

'Yep, 'fraid so. Agus Zumran along with Trevor Arnott.'

'I hope Agus is keeping his nose clean on this one,' Ardhi said. 'His extended family has form when it comes to logging.'

Ben sucked his teeth. 'Don't we know it?' The Zumran family tentacles extended through Asia and deep into the Pacific and Africa. Before Ben had signed the contract with Connor, he had checked with a number of organisations who kept tabs on such things, and Agus did appear to be keeping his nose clean.

Ben swivelled his head and watched the logging truck retreat. All should be well.

At the edge of the village that would host them for the duration of their fieldwork, the driver slowed on the dusty red earth road. To either side, large-leaved banana palms and high stalks of maize were intercropped with other vegetables: beans, chilli peppers and cabbage, and the inevitable cassava, those long carbohydrate-rich tubers that Ben had found were used in so many ways.

They passed shingle-built houses raised on wooden stilts, some with steps leading to porches, others with a simple plank ladder up to an open door. Roofs were of wooden shingle, or corrugated iron. Older-style dwellings constructed of plain wooden planks sat next to newly built brightly painted houses. Several homes doubled as small businesses, selling produce from the porch. Washing hung on lines, motorcycles and a few trucks were parked along the road. To the left they passed a solidly built hall: 'The Council room,' Ardhi said; and Ben spotted a school set back from the road.

Chickens and crowing cocks scratched in the sun-baked mud beside the pot-holed road, or perched on old oil drums, while mangy-looking dogs had sought out shade. The settlement now had a rough road, but the river flowing to one side had been the main transport link to the wider world for generations.

This Dayak subtribe straddled the old world and the new, wishing to keep as much of their old ways of life as possible and still participate in the modern world. Always a dilemma. How could this community benefit from the forest on their doorstep? Exploit it without destroying it. Ben sincerely hoped this project they were assessing would deliver this objective for them.

Just ahead, in the village compound, Ben spotted an official car parked and a small crowd gathering. 'Damn. The reception party's here. I'd hoped to freshen up.'

'You look fine.' Ardhi appraised him. 'And you Brits are famed for your charm.'

'Yeah, practise your schmoozing, Fletch. See if you can winkle more money from them for a deeper scope.'

Ben looked around, mentally ticking off those he expected to be here. The government official was easy to spot in his business suit, along with an underling who was fussing about him, tidying his tie. The official had brought a cameraman with him, videocam at the ready, and a camera for stills slung around his neck. Ben identified the forester from his uniform, and the rest were locals: men wearing shorts, light trousers and cotton button-through shirts or T-shirts, bare feet or flip-flops; women in faded dresses or loose trousers.

At the far end of the compound, beyond the welcoming party, an open-sided hut with plastic tables and chairs provided somewhere to eat and drink. His eyes probed the shaded interior trying to pick out who was there, and spot the cause of the merriment among a bunch of jabbering kids clustered round a table.

Rick prodded him gently in the small of his back, following with Ardhi at his side.

The government official walked forward, placed his hands together in greeting and gave a small bow before offering his hand to shake. 'Doctor Fletcher? I hope your journey was bearable.'

'Yes, thank you.'

The official held out his business card, and Ben reciprocated with his own: *Dr Ben Fletcher. Consultant Sustainable Forest Economy.*

'May I introduce my team? Doctor Durmali from Jakarta… Mr Wilson from Canada…'

More exchanges of cards, and yes, Ben assured the official, he and Ardhi had been well briefed in Jakarta.

'Doctor Fletcher.' The official turned his head slightly towards the camera focused on him and launched into his prepared speech. 'On behalf of the Indonesian government, welcome. Our Positive Partnership Initiative between your country and ours demonstrates we take good care of our forests. Your report will show the world that solutions are possible—'

'Indeed, I very much *hope* so.' Ben cleared his throat. 'We are looking forward to starting our work.'

'Of course. May I introduce Balan, the headman who has so kindly agreed to host you in their village.'

The official beckoned to a middle-aged man who stepped forward wearing a long-sleeved faded shirt, long trousers, his feet bare. The official continued. 'Balan will meet with you later, with an interpreter.'

Ben was about to ask who that was when the government official beckoned to the forester. 'Mr Manapo, our head forester, will be assisting you.'

Mr Manapo shook hands, saying, 'Pleased to meet you.' It seemed the forester would be acting as interpreter; there was no problem with his English.

'You have my card, Doctor Fletcher, in case you need to contact me, and, ah…' the government official offered Ben another card, 'Inspector General Sartano, police chief for this region. You will be in safe hands.'

He bowed, about to back away, then hesitated. 'Ah, yes…'

A Chinese-Indonesian woman detached herself from a group of local women and walked towards them. She wore a floppy sun hat, neat blouse and knee-length skirt, and Ben judged her to be in her thirties.

'May I introduce, er…' The government official hesitated.

'Yulia.' The woman bowed slightly.

'…who as you know will be joining your team.'

'Pardon?'

'Ah!' The government official looked uncomfortable. He took out a clean handkerchief, dabbed his brow, repeating, 'Ah!'

Yulia smiled politely, her eyes on the official, wordlessly enquiring whether she should speak. He waved her forward, looking relieved.

'Doctor Fletcher, I work for an environmental sustainability organisation. In Jakarta. We do consultancy and partnership work.'

'Yes… And?'

'I assisted this community in the initial consultations with Mr Zumran. In a non-official capacity. The government have kindly amended your brief to allow me to follow up. Officially.'

Ben spun around to face his team, but Rick and Ardhi looked as flabbergasted as he felt. He'd often found himself with unexpected "extras" such as official bag carriers or cooks, but he had never had a key member join the team without the courtesy of anyone liaising with him. He didn't want to make a scene in front of the government official – or at least be caught doing so on camera – but he couldn't help staring at Yulia, waiting for her to explain.

'Umm...' Yulia looked a little anxious now. 'And as I am reasonably fluent in the language, money that would have been spent on an interpreter can be for me and my work.'

'I believe you have received an update? An email?' The government official looked hopeful. Ben shook his head. 'Ah... Ah... It will be with you shortly, and when you read—'

'I'm sorry. I wonder if—?'

'Doctor Fletcher, please wait and read the revised brief, and if you have any questions, any at all, please refer to London or Jakarta.'

The official bowed and backed away towards his parked car, followed by his assistants and the cameraman, who was hurriedly stowing his equipment. Ben felt the heat rise in his face as he glared at the woman standing demurely in front of him. *Who the hell are you?* he longed to ask. Instead, remembering he represented the British government, he forced a smile and said: 'Perhaps you would like to explain?'

'Doctor Fletcher, surely you agree it's vital to take on board the rights of this community?'

'Naturally. Have you studied our brief?'

'It focuses heavily on economics. I believe it would benefit from more emphasis on social—'

'For God's sake!' He had meant to stay professional, but he was irked. Although she lowered her eyes, she did not appear submissive and Rick seemed amused by the situation.

'Let's see what that email has to say, Fletch. With any luck, this will be a straightforward add-on.'

Fair enough, Ben thought, and turned to the local forester, who had been waiting patiently.

'Your English is very good.'

Mr Manapo smiled. 'Thank you. I worked in Australia for two years.'

'Might we—'

'Hiya, folks!' A woman's voice. American. Ben's head snapped around.

Linda Smith was heading towards him. The faded T-shirt atop her old cotton trousers and sensible sandals bore the distinctive Direct Action for the Earth logo. Trailing her was a white man in his twenties, long dark hair tied back in a ponytail. And trailing him, a bunch of village kids vied for his attention. *What the f…*

'I'm Linda. This is Rob.' Linda grinned at Ben. 'Remember me?'

'What are you doing here?'

'And hello to you too!' Linda raised an eyebrow. 'Heard you guys were due, so decided to hang around.'

'Uncle Tom Cobbley…' Ben muttered.

'We're not here to bugger things up. It'll be sweet.' Linda's companion offered this warm thought. Hearing an Australian twang, Ben looked closely at him. His face was somehow familiar.

'Have we met before?'

'This might trigger a memory.' Rob began playing air guitar, singing, '*The story's in your eyes… Read it like a dream…*'

'A pop star—'

'Rock!'

'—on a crusade to save the planet!'

Before Ben could say more, Rick had leapt forward to pump Rob's hand.

'Hey! Xcalibur, right? I know your music…'

Linda chuckled. 'Yep, with millions of others. It's one way to get a message across, so fine by me. You should see how many followers he has on social media. Remind me?'

'Oh, a couple of million.' Rob looked chuffed. 'And being here is so inspiring. I'm working on new material for our next album.'

A disparaging noise rose in Ben's throat.

'C'mon, let's grab a drink and I'll tell you what we've been up to.' Linda pointed to the open-sided hut. 'The Shack. That's what we've named the local watering hole.'

'And I've seen you too somewhere.' Rick squinted at Linda. 'But you're not a rock chick or groupie.'

'Nope, but I get around.' Linda threw her head back and laughed. 'Come on.'

Linda shepherded Yulia, Ardhi and Rick away, both men lugging their bags, then she drew Mr Manapo into her fold. 'You joining us?'

All Ben wanted was to find a quiet place to open his laptop, read the fresh proposal – if it was a proposal and not a command – and begin to exert his authority over the mission. But it would be churlish not to join them, and he was longing for a drink. He wondered if beer was sold here, or if this village followed the no-alcohol rule common elsewhere. He hadn't thought to research that. God. He hoped this was not a dry village. The sound of the government official's car made Ben start. He waved as it passed by, scattering chickens and children in its wake. He figured they must have gone to considerable effort to get out here, and now had a long journey back to – perhaps? – a regional airport.

He shouldered his backpack, picked up his hand luggage and followed the chattering group towards the Shack.

3

THIS SMALL VILLAGE WAS WELL OFF THE BEATEN TRACK and didn't cater for ecotourists. Ben supposed there must have been a scramble to sort out places for Rob and Linda, and now Yulia. He, Ardhi and Rick were being accommodated in what was, notionally at least, a health centre. It had been built a year earlier, Mr Manapo told them, as he led them to it, but was "currently unused". Ben eyed a diesel generator whirring gently under a rain shelter beyond the single-storey building. Good, there was electricity at least.

Inside he saw what looked like medical notices pinned to the wall. Beds had been set up for them, and they had a table and wooden chairs. A door with female and male symbols attached indicated the toilet.

'This looks great,' Ben assured Mr Manapo. 'Why isn't it being used?'

'I'm not sure. So, if you are comfortable, I will leave you. I've set up an office in a small room in the council building. Six o'clock tomorrow morning?'

'Thank you.' Ben accompanied the forester to the porch then turned to Rick and Ardhi. 'Let's see what Jakarta have to tell us about, er…'

'Yulia,' Ardhi reminded him.

He scanned the updated brief, fearful the mission's scope might be eroded. Ardhi peered over his shoulder. 'Yulia's been busy lobbying other ministries: Human Rights, Culture…'

'But why wasn't this discussed with us in Jakarta?' It didn't make sense.

Ardhi shrugged. 'Maybe our officials didn't know at the time. These things happen. Someone higher up decided it was a good idea.'

Rick glanced at the screen. 'Yep, she's snuck in on this one.'

She surely had. Ben focused on the plus side. Yulia could focus on community rights and cultural preservation, allowing him more time in the forest. Her intermediary role as translator was about to be put to the test as they had been invited for dinner. He hoped she was up to the job.

Cooking aromas greeted Ben at the door of the headman's house, and he realised how hungry he was. He removed his footwear at the entrance and crowded in with the rest of the visitors: Yulia, Rick and Ardhi. Hearing Yulia speaking the local language with Balan, he was relieved to hear she sounded relatively fluent.

Balan's wife stood by an open stove in an adjoining outhouse, slowly rotating thick bamboo poles over the flames. Yulia beckoned her, introducing her as Asung. The woman bowed, thick-fingered hardworking hands pressed together, her cotton dress as worn as her husband's outfit. The children came next: a pretty teenage daughter named Bai, and two younger boys Ben had seen following Rob earlier. He didn't catch their names. Too much detail – things he didn't need to remember, at least not right away.

Balan, having carried out his official welcoming duties, was now at ease in his own home, proud to host his guests as they settled to Asung's chicken and rice meal prepared in the traditional way. And Yulia was useful, Ben decided, bridging the gap between them, sometimes chatting with Bai and Asung, whose hands covered their mouths when they giggled; translating something into English that Balan or Asung said. Balan's wish, according to Yulia, was "that the village could go on as it had in the past but be in the present too"' Nicely put, Ben thought. Ensuring they benefited from the forest was part of his brief.

'By the way,' Ben said, 'why isn't the Health Centre used? It looks brand new. We're staying there.'

Yulia asked Balan, then Ben watched his face become animated and his hands gesticulate as he talked. Yulia "mmmed" then translated: 'One of the things that hasn't worked out.'

I bet. It would have been a promise made by the logging company, AZTAR. 'This is your area, Yulia, please look into it.'

As the day shut down Ben was reminded how swiftly the transition from light to dark happens in the tropics. He felt his muscles relaxing, his tired brain letting go. The shared meal was pleasant, but situations like this where every word must pass through an intermediary were a strain. He was desperate for time alone.

Early next morning Ben waited as Mr Manapo unrolled a large-scale forest map on a table in his temporary office; a small fan circulating stuffy air threatened to blow it away. 'Here.' Rick placed his phone at one corner, and each of them followed with their own.

Blue meandering lines marked streams, and brown lines the logging roads and tracks.

Thick drawn borders marked boundaries of logging concessions where the government had granted selective logging rights to companies.

Mr Manapo waved his hand over a far-away patch of green. 'No logging here. It's protected. Orangutan habitat.' Then he traced a finger around a marked-off patch of forest close to the village. 'The boundaries of AZTAR's concession you are evaluating.'

'Yes, agreed,' Ben said.

'We have a vehicle for your use – it will take an hour or more to reach the outer boundary. I'll be driving you to the audit sites so you get your, um…'

'Bearings?' Ardhi offered.

Mr Manapo nodded. 'And if I am needed elsewhere, I will arrange another driver. At least till you know the routes. They've selected and taped off three one-acre sites for you to inspect: two uncut, one that's been logged.'

It was usual for companies to select the sites, but as this had government backing Ben needed to be sure. 'AZTAR? And you're content these give a fair representation?'

Mr Manapo affirmed.

'And this. What's here?' Ben pointed to a marked-off section of forest abutting the area they were assessing.

'Another company is logging that,' Mr Manapo explained.

'Controls in place?' Rick's question was casual, but after a pause an edge crept into his voice. 'Well?'

Sensing the forester's unease, Ben caught Rick's eye. 'Leave that.'

'Just asking.' Rick shrugged.

'Let's stick to the job we're here for.'

Ben didn't want to get side-tracked and they had a tight schedule. He turned to Mr Manapo. 'Are we ready to leave?' Picking up his phone Ben took a photo of the relevant part of the map, then they gathered equipment and followed Mr Manapo out to his mud-splattered forestry jeep.

Deep in the rainforest, Ben was surrounded by the thrum of cicadas and unfamiliar bird calls high in the canopy. He, Ardhi, Rick and Mr Manapo were surveying one of the sites allocated for future harvesting. His long-sleeved cotton shirt stuck to his skin and his lightweight trousers were soil-stained. All of them wore canvas-sided jungle boots with trouser legs tucked into socks. Leeches were a persistent pest, mosquitoes more so, and he had doused himself in repellent.

For hours they measured circumferences of trees due to be felled; recorded species composition and tree frequency; assessed harvesting ratios. They would be monitoring the direction selected trees were to be felled to limit damage to surrounding growth; checking ease of access to forest tracks – again to protect smaller trees – and would report on any nearby water courses and pollution that might be caused from extraction. This scoping exercise was not as deep as the full audit Ben would have preferred, but it allowed him and his team to be satisfied everything was in order, and showed potential to scale up.

He brushed drops of sweat from his nose and swiped off ants with a vicious nip which had already got the upper hand, reminding him this was their territory. Not a bad idea to check for leeches that might have found their way under his clothes. So sticky, so humid. Even so he could appreciate the beauty of the place, grateful to play a small part in helping preserve such magnificence. He touched the trunk of a yellow meranti tree. Feeling its rough bark and seeing it towering high above reaffirmed the reason he was here. From his day pack he took out his camera, focused on the play of light among branches and clicked the shutter again and again. He could spare a minute to capture the splendour of nature. The movement of a butterfly caught his attention, green marks across black wings like a tiny bird. He had seen a few of these, and others with bright red and blue markings: fleeting shots of colour against the constant green. He would look up their name when he got back.

Their work done for the day, Ben emerged onto a rough red-dirt track where the forester's vehicle was parked. Four loggers worked nearby, using a mobile grapple to load stacked crosscut logs onto an AZTAR pole truck. Ben laid a staying hand on Mr Manapo's sleeve. 'Come. You can translate.'

Leaving Rick and Ardhi to finish loading equipment – callipers and increment borers, along with their spreadsheets – he and the forester approached the loggers and chatted. Everything seemed to be in order: logs marked with the certification logo and numeric markings showing block and individual tree number. He was asking Mr Manapo something when a voice cut in.

'Those trees should still be growing. You shouldn't be endorsing it. Nothing should be felled. Period!'

He hadn't heard Linda's battered jeep arrive. Had she been following them? Checking what they were up to? Damn the woman!

'No trees to be harvested. Totally unrealistic!' Ben shouted to the eco-warrior who was striding towards him with a slight limp, looking like she was itching for a fight. 'Who's going to close down a global industry? The best we can do is to monitor it, keep it controlled and regulated, and make sure everyone benefits.'

'You really think the locals are benefiting from this?' A sneer spread across Linda's face. 'There's not one recent report showing the damned logging companies *aren't* taking local folk for a ride.'

A logger, who seemed to understand some English, knocked his knuckles on his safety hat, rolling his eyes before turning back to his job. Mr Manapo shot Ben an embarrassed smile and backed away.

Ben squared up to his adversary. 'Selective felling does work. I wouldn't be here if there wasn't evidence for that. Forests can still be here for coming generations.'

'Wanna bet? No, wait. You and I won't be round long enough to see who wins.'

He wasn't in the mood to engage in a battle of words in the middle of the forest. He turned towards their own jeep, where Mr Manapo was settling behind the wheel.

'Tell you what, Ben. Meet me at the Shack later. We can talk about what's realistic and what's not. I've some ideas to share with you.'

'Huh. I bet you have.'

A beer was an hour or more away, and he was ready for it, though not with Linda. He could feel her eyes following him. A duet of laughter emanated from the back seat of the jeep: Rick's rumbling baritone joining Ardhi's tenor. Perhaps another of Rick's corny jokes. He climbed in the front seat and fumed, rubbing the back of his neck where a mosquito had bitten him. Well into the drive back he was hatching plans of how to hasten Linda's departure from the village, from his life. The woman irritated him.

His first day's research documented, Ben was about to close his laptop and join his team at the Shack, when a grating voice rang out: 'Hey! Got something for you.' Linda's head appeared around the door and she thrust her phone in his face. 'Take a look.'

Ben scrolled through the photos: wasted trees, broken and left to rot; a logging skidder with a bulldozer scoop in the front and a cable behind dragging a log towards a pile of others. A short video… Ben's eyes widened seeing the AZTAR logo on the cab door.

'Yeah, Bambi. It's a nasty world out there.' Linda was gloating, enjoying what she seemed to consider a game of one-upmanship. 'I followed them along back tracks, further away.'

Ben could feel his face flushing. He waved the phone. 'Mind if I keep this?'

Linda smirked. 'All yours. Download them and give it back to me later. Oh, scroll down to the photos from last week. Nothing personal. You'll see an interesting log landing.' Ben looked at her sharply as she continued. 'Look, Rob's lovely, a real sweetie, but having a celeb along for the ride sort of cramped my style. Didn't get a chance to investigate further. Turned back before we'd even checked out the orangutans living there.'

'You've reported it to Mr Manapo?'

'Oh, sure. He's logged it. And, happy day, he's reported it to the local government guy. You met him, got his business card. How about you follow it up? He wouldn't give me the time of day when I tried to have a polite word when he was here to meet and greet you.'

Her eyes pierced his. 'Perhaps you'll join me for a drink after all?'

He watched her disappear down the stairs, then looked through the photos she had taken that day. Some irregularities were to be expected. But so soon? He scrolled back to the log landing taken a week before. He recalled she had mentioned something about being in a protected forest area. *Shit.* He put that aside for now. He needed to clear up something and get his own house in order.

Mr Manapo was leaving his office when Ben waylaid him. Drawing the forester back inside, Ben unrolled the forest map and jabbed his finger on the marked-off concession abutting *his* project.

'So it's AZTAR who are renting this concession? Is that right?'

'Yes,' Mr Manapo confirmed, looking ill at ease.

'OK. OK.' Ben took a breath. Better to know than not to know. It would be easy to share logging machinery on both concessions, but how could anyone be sure what was coming from the supposedly sustainable area and what from the other one? Was there sufficient oversight of the rented concession? Rick had been right when he'd asked Manapo about this. Ben's antennae were out, sniffing, feeling his way, sensing he needed to be extra vigilant as he questioned the forester further.

'How about recruiting Linda to our team, Fletch?' Rick cocked his head towards where Linda sat with Rob and Yulia, a bunch of noisy kids hanging around Rob. Ben sensed Rick's underlying respect for the American's tenacity.

Ardhi stubbed out a cigarette. 'Don't blame Manapo. He's unlikely to report something unpopular with his boss and it isn't illegal—'

Rick thumped the table. 'This damn culture of deference! But *you* can't ignore it.' His eyes drilled into Ben's.

'Strictly speaking, this adjoining concession has nothing to do with our project—'

'Hell, Fletch. Don't give me that—'

'And remember,' Ardhi moderated, 'we've got to balance encouraging good practice with—'

'Exactly!' Ben was relieved at Ardhi's common sense. 'And isn't that what we are trying to do? Support good practice where we find it?'

'Doctor Fletcher...' Yulia was at his side. 'I have some early observations to share with you.'

'Yeah, yeah. Thanks. Let's discuss that later. And call me Ben.'

Ardhi stood, offering her his chair. 'Please, join us.'

Ben sucked his teeth realising too late he had been ungracious. 'Sure, sure.' He gestured to the chair.

Yulia hesitated. 'I don't want to interrupt.'

'Please…' Rick half stood. 'It would be great to hear what you've been up to.'

'Yu-lia!' Rob's sing-song voice carried across to them. Yulia glanced at Ben and dipped her head. 'Excuse me.'

Watching her return to sit with Linda and Rob, Ben regretted his actions – or inactions – regretted he had missed the opportunity for some semblance of team bonding. And that was his job as team leader. He saw what the kids were clamouring for. It wasn't Rob's rock-star celebrity status – they wouldn't have a clue about that. The Australian had another attraction. He was entertaining them with a coin trick, deftly concealing it in the palm of his hand, then making it reappear behind a boy's ear. The kids were leaping about.

'OK.' Ben turned back to his colleagues, determined to nail the position they would take. 'We have a duty to emphasise that AZTAR's other logging activities compromise this project – ethically if not practically. We've got adjoining concessions being managed to different standards, and we'll highlight this in our report.'

Rick grunted, 'Right,' and Ardhi nodded.

The clamour of children around Rob grew louder as they urged him to do another trick. Ben turned to watch, happy to be distracted.

'OK! OK! Give me room.' Rob good-naturedly pushed the children away, produced a pack of playing cards and with great fanfare held up a card.

'Watch this. Watching? Watching…?'

He handed a boy the ace of hearts. 'Yulia, tell him not to take his eyes off it.'

The boy stared solemnly at the card while Rob did some sleight of hand tricks: discovering cards behind children's heads and pulling them out of pockets or from under T-shirts. He fumbled a little, clearly no professional, but the kids, along with Linda, and Yulia, shrieked in delight. All the while the boy clutched his precious ace of hearts, refusing to be distracted. Ben smiled, warming to this rock star on a mission to save the forests.

Rick laughed. 'Not bad…' He stiffened. 'Visitors!'

Ben followed Rick's gaze to see two police SUVs cruise into the compound. In the Shack, the raucous laughter came to a sudden stop, the pack of cards abandoned as children and cards scattered.

Four armed police officers got out of a first patrol car, their standard uniforms embellished by small accessories: reflective shades, crocodile skin belts, large wristwatches. Ben wasn't knowledgeable about brands but had an idea these might be costly. Glancing at his own old watch he saw it was 5.30pm. He'd been up for twelve hours; the sun hadn't set, and the day had more to offer. His eyes moved to the second vehicle.

A thick-set man, perhaps in his sixties, stepped out, his uniform crisp despite the stupefying heat. 'The boss, judging by his uniform,' Ardhi murmured. The man hitched his trousers, adjusted his belt from which a gun holster hung and surveyed the rapidly emptying compound.

Rick took the initiative, standing and leaning against the entrance.

The police chief approached, his face masked of any emotion. 'Mr Fletcher?'

'No, I'm not *Doctor* Fletcher.' Rick cocked his head.

Ben rose and stepped forward. The police chief looked him up and down.

'Good afternoon.' The officer smiled, offering his card. 'Are you well? Everything is going well?'

The Javanese man's English was good. But why was he here?

'Yes. Thank you, er...' He accepted the card.

'Inspector General Sartano. East and North Kalimantan are my patch.'

'Ah yes.' The local government official had passed him the police chief's card. Ben patted his pocket. 'I'm sorry, I haven't a card on me right now... Doctor Fletcher.'

'Never mind. I know who you are. So, everything is well?' Sartano held Ben's eyes as Ben nodded. 'Good... Very good.'

Ben gestured for Ardhi to come forward and introduced him and Rick, then Sartano's eyes moved to the remaining occupants of the bar: Linda and Rob still sitting, watchful, and Yulia, bending down with her back to them, gathering scattered playing cards.

'Any problems you'll let me know. Personally.' The police chief's piercing gaze skewered him. 'You have my details. We must look after our visitors.'

'Thank you for your concern.' Ben's eyes moved from the police chief to the four officers who were nonchalantly strolling around the compound. 'But we don't expect any problems.'

'Naturally.' Sartano nodded. 'We were in the district. A courtesy call.' They exchanged a few more stilted pleasantries before the police chief retreated to his vehicle.

'An honour,' Ardhi muttered.

'Nearby? Unlikely,' Rick whispered back.

As the four officers swaggered towards their vehicle Linda brushed past Ben.

'Hey! Thanks for dropping by, boys! Appreciate your concern. We're special visitors too!' She pointed to Rob.

'Linda!' Ben grabbed her arm, but she shook him off.

An officer, perhaps the senior of the four, turned and rested a hand on his holster. Linda walked towards him, eyeing him up and down.

'Cool shades. Must have cost a packet.'

'You and your boyfriend.' The officer's head jerked towards Rob. 'Go home.'

'So you knew we were here too!'

The police officer stared hard at her.

'See these.' Linda pointed to the welts on her arm. 'I wasn't afraid of poachers or the chainsaw gangs, and I'm sure as hell not afraid of you boys. Twenty-seven times arrested!'

'Linda! Shut up!'

Ben spun from her to direct his anger at Rob, who muttered, 'Didn't say anything, mate,' before walking casually towards Linda, drawing her away with a soft, 'Come on, leave it, hey?'

Linda! That damned woman. How long would she be hanging around, getting in the way? Ben was relieved to see the police officer she had goaded was laughing, returning to his car seemingly unperturbed. Sartano's vehicle was already moving out, tinted windows hiding their important visitor from view.

New sounds filled the early evening air: children's high-pitched voices clamouring for Rob; yammering adults whose anxious eyes followed the cars out of the village. In the Shack kerosene lamps glowed. Ben swatted away persistent bugs and retreated inside to sit near a smoking mosquito coil. Surely now he could get a meal without further drama.

'Yulia. You joining us?' He hoped his voice was inviting.

She handed Rob the pack of cards she had been slowly shuffling and Ben made space for her.

He longed for this project to shape up well, to prove the point he had made to Linda: selective felling does work, and forests can still be here for coming generations. And, he could admit, burnish his career prospects.

4

CONNOR'S EYEBROWS SHOT UP WHEN HE SAW THE businessman standing on his doorstep, wearing his favoured two-tone shirt, striped golf club tie and chunky gold cufflinks.

'Trevor!'

'Evening, Connor. I believe you're expecting me?'

Connor's mind raced. He recalled his secretary saying something about Mr Arnott wanting to drop by. He had assumed that meant making an appointment to meet at his office. He would much have preferred that. Christ. When had he and Trevor last met socially? It would have been a get-together that his father had initiated. Yonks back. A cloud of doubt passed over Trevor's eyes.

'Not a good time?'

'It's OK. Come in. Come on in.' Connor, still in his formal work shirt, top button undone, stood back and ushered in his unexpected guest. Trevor glanced around the sitting room.

'How's Tess? Is she home?'

'Hot yoga night, then on to a cocktail bar. She tells me some of the girls skip the sweat – the only exercise they get is raising their elbow. What're they like? But yeah, thanks, she's well.'

Tess wouldn't be unhappy to be missing Trevor's visit.

'Glad to hear it. Give her my regards. And the—?'

'The lads are fine too, but let's not talk about school, the less said about exam results the better... Well, that's not fair, they're doing OK.'

He barely saw their teenage boys; bedrooms were their domain. Glancing around his living room he recognised it was getting more formal and fashionable by the year as Tess redecorated. She was having what she called a retro chintz phase, reminding him of National Trust houses, or worse, granny-inspired furnishings. He didn't really care though. There was no comparison to the cramped living room of his childhood that Trevor would have remembered.

'Good. I hoped it might fit well here.' Connor followed Trevor's gaze to a recently arrived coffee table.

'Ah, this solves the mystery. Tess thought I'd ordered it, so she and the lads hefted it through.' Connor shifted documents he had been reading. He nodded to the table. 'You know I can't accept it.'

'A gesture, a sample product, that's all. I can sell it to you at discount if you want. We're testing the market in a few of our outlets. If all goes well, we'll roll it out. Should prove a nice little earner.' Trevor lightly ran his hand over the table. 'Lovely grain, don't you think? Guaranteed legal.'

Connor absorbed this as he fetched a bottle of whisky, one of his single malts. 'A small one?' He held up the bottle.

'Best not... Just a splash then. I'm driving.'

Connor poured, then raised his glass. 'Cheers.' He decided to let the businessman take the lead. Trevor's hand reached into his jacket pocket, retrieved a brochure and slid it across the table.

'Take a look.'

Connor glanced at the Green Line promotion. He swirled the whisky, both hands clasped around his glass, reluctant to pick up the brochure.

'A bit early to be trumpeting the green angle, I'd have thought. I see you're pushing it on your website too. Surely better to state it's an intention?'

'Customers want clarity. It's all pretty straightforward. All going fine.'

'Great stuff.'

'I want to assure you, and everyone else, I'm serious about this.'

'I should think so!' Connor caught Trevor's eye. 'I wish you every luck with your "Going Green" project. Good for the world in general and I've a lot riding on it. We need to show that it's not just niche, top-end companies who are taking a stand on properly sourced timber, but ordinary—'

'Oi, oi!' Trevor bridled.

'Come on now, you know what I mean. These things shouldn't only be for the chattering classes or whatever trope you want to give to liberal elites. They'll buy into this in any case. And let's face it, your products aren't likely to grace their homes and gardens.'

'Ordinary crap for ordinary folk, you want to say?'

'Did I say so?' Connor grinned, putting his guest at ease.

'I'm curious, Connor. Have you heard anything from our man in Kalimantan?'

'Early days…' Connor reached for his glass.

'But OK – so far?'

'I imagine so. You just said it was all going fine. Why shouldn't it be OK?'

'Yes, yes. In general. I don't know how these things work. Maybe your consultant chap updates you, daily reports, or you log on to something…' Trevor raised his shoulders.

'Ben will only report at the end.' Connor sipped his whisky, his eyes on the table. 'Tell you what, invoice me, full price. Then if anyone comes asking, I can declare it. You know what government scrutiny's like.'

Trevor blew his cheeks. 'Too much political correctness these days. Though, I get you. I understand.'

Trevor could not be unaware of stories of members of Parliament embarrassed by expenses scandals, and surely Trevor should know senior civil servants weren't above accountants' scrutiny? Connor placed a fingertip on the Green Line promotion brochure and slid it across the table to Trevor.

'So, yeah. Invoice me. Don't forget, now... How's business?' He smiled invitingly.

Connor crossed his legs and settled back, prepared to listen to Trevor's account of boardroom manoeuvres and profit and loss. He would steer the conversation away from his Green Line.

He knew he was pushing Trevor away; had done for years. When Trevor had offered to stand godfather to his oldest son, Tess had been alarmed. 'I think not, darling.' She didn't say "We can do better than that", but the inference had been clear. When the next boy was born, Trevor didn't offer.

Leaving Connor's house Trevor glanced up at the spacious Victorian terrace house. Not his style, though they cost a packet. He speculated they might go for near three million, and knew Connor had been lucky to buy in early enough before this part of London went through the roof. New build you could fit out to the spec you wanted was his own preference, and this neighbourhood was precisely the liberal elites Connor had referred to. Perhaps Connor, or more likely Tess, would give the coffee table away when she knew it was from his outlet. He walked the short distance to where he had found a parking spot and pressed his thumb to the door handle of his Tesla. The door glided open and he eased his body behind the wheel. There were too many cars clogging the streets these days, but he was doing his bit for the environment by going electric. At least *this* was something his children approved of, and there wasn't much of that.

And he was serious about this environmental business. He had been surprised at how many enquiries they had had via the website, or from customers visiting stores, asking if the stock was certified. And on occasion he had lost sales because his staff couldn't provide the potential buyers with the assurances they sought. Later the message changed from to "Sorry, no we don't" to "Sorry, not yet", and later still to "Sorry, but watch this space, we will be soon". He couldn't keep deferring, so he had been bold and gone ahead with the marketing. Customers wanted certainty; that was a fact. He was a businessman, he needed to stock what customers wanted, and if they wanted a green line, he would supply it. Simple as that.

It was this that had sent him searching for partners in Asia, and had led him to Agus Zumran, who was delighted to extend his connections and set up a new company with him. Agus's family had been logging for years so it was a small matter to get new permits and agree new rules and regulations. Trevor had been won over. That man could talk the hind leg off a donkey, had an answer for everything and had to be the best-networked man Trevor had met. He was confident their AZTAR project would be a market leader and was impatient for results. Impatient to get it out to customers. Impatient to show his family what he could do.

Family: that was the thing. His daughter worked for a charity and only allowed reclaimed furniture in her flat – junk with a "take me" sign stuck to it left in someone's driveway, or on a recycle website. And she was a vegan! His own bloody son was getting too up himself. At twenty-six Sean showed no inclination to join the family firm.

'Dad. It's great what you've done. But this isn't me. I can't see myself pushing this shit, with a sale every second week.'

Yes. His son who had had the benefit of his money actually said that! Trevor could feel his cheeks flushing remembering Sean, his hair flopping over his eyes, feet up on the settee, phone in hand. This is what a good education had done! Thinking on it, Sean was still studying. Was there no end to delaying becoming an adult? He himself had worked his way up, building on what his own father had achieved with his single outlet in Birmingham. It annoyed the hell out of him when people scoffed behind his back. Snobs, all of them. He could buy any of them three times over. Reaching the corner of Connor's tree-lined street, he smiled remembering the rest of that conversation with his son.

'But,' Sean had continued, taking his feet of the settee, 'if you can make this Green Line work, then you're talking. That's the future, Dad. I'd be proud of you. And you know, I could see myself getting involved.'

'You're on,' he'd told his son. 'I deliver. You're in.'

They had shaken on it.

5

WHILE BEN AND THE OTHERS WERE AT AN AUDIT SITE deep in the forest, Yulia was spending her day mingling with the local community. It was the second, and final, day of the market: an opportunity for exchanges, economic and social. This small village was a hub for a network of even more remote settlements. Some people had arrived by boat while others had managed to navigate the rough roads on prized motorcycles.

Earlier that morning Yulia had helped set out food stalls with eggs, chilli peppers, long beans, cassava root and branches of bananas while men stacked sacks of rice. All the while she was gently probing, building up a picture about what mattered.

Late in the afternoon, with remnants of leafy green cabbages wilting in the heat and the tangy smells of squished fruit abandoned on the ground, she threaded her way between mats and stalls to where a group of women, Asung among them, were selling produce. She held out an AZTAR promotional brochure written in the national language, Bahasa, showing a logging truck stacked with branded logs, a Javanese driver in the cab, elbow propped on the window, smiling cheerily.

'How are you getting on with them? Have they delivered what you hoped?' Yulia took out her notebook and pen.

The women's response was immediate as they passed the brochure between them.

'They promised Balan there'd be plenty of work for our men,' Asung scoffed. 'But they have their own people, and we're worse off now than we were before.'

'Balan's not firm enough.' A woman looked crossly at Asung. 'There's nothing to keep the young people here. They need jobs.'

'And where's the good road they promised?' another woman butted in. 'This mud road's impassable in the rainy season. Gets worse the more the trucks tear it up.'

'And let's not talk about the Health Centre!' A third woman raised her voice.

That provoked a roar of indignation.

'Slow... Speak slowly, please.' Yulia held up her hand.

Her understanding of the local language was limited. Back in Jakarta, arguing her case with government officials to be included in this team, she had breezily added, 'Besides, you can save money for an interpreter.' But it was hard to follow these women speaking over each other. It was more than a year since she had first been here, advising them informally; now she was in a stronger position as part of an official team. This was important. Again, she urged them to speak slowly.

'They're OK.' The woman who ran the Shack spoke in the loggers' favour. 'They buy beer and food. That's good—'

'And our girls. Not good!' Asung spoke firmly.

'Girls?' Yulia's voice was sharp.

Asung looked away, so Yulia let this pass. She would ask later, in private.

'And the environment? Changes?' Yulia probed.

'At my sister's village the timber trees are all gone, and their water's too muddy to drink now.'

'Or fish. We don't want that happening here.'

All the women affirmed.

'What do you want? What would make things better?' Yulia smiled at the gathered women.

'An easy life! That's what. The men leave us to do everything.' An older woman missing her front teeth cackled, and others joined in.

They turned to watch a group of local men, along with a handful of loggers, squatting around a cleared circle. In the makeshift ring two cocks were fighting to the death, sharp metal spurs attached just above one foot. Over and over they flew at each other – legs stretched, claws spread, feathers flying along with spurts of blood, their squawks almost drowned by cheering men. Gambling was not legal, but there were worse things, and Yulia knew the authorities were relaxed about it. She glanced at two police officers, men who had accompanied Sartano, casually standing back, looking like they wouldn't mind having a bet themselves. More feathers swirled upwards followed by a sharp squawk. The fight had lasted maybe thirty seconds. A man made his way out of the circle holding a rooster dangling by its legs, brilliant plumage specked with blood, neck floppy. Men's faces creased into laughter or hands gesticulated wildly in angry submission as money changed hands. More cocks were ready for their unwilling duel, either cradled in the arms of local men, or in wicker cages, belonging to men from further afield. Possibly the vanquished cocks would end up in the cooking pot at the Shack this evening. She must remember to ask. Still, they were having fun... the men, that is.

'You see! You see! They have an easy life!' The old woman

pointed an accusing finger, setting the others off cackling and laughing.

'What's the joke?' Rob ambled towards her, a grin on his face. He had made her so welcome, while others – OK, she could *think* it: Ben – had barely tried to get to know her. Tugging at his shorts, she drew him down to squat next to her.

'They're complaining about men.'

'Oh, come on, ladies, be fair! Us men aren't so bad.' Rob made a sad face and the women giggled. From his pocket Rob drew a postcard-sized photo of his band, Xcalibur. 'I promised one to Bai. Will you give it to her?' He offered it to Asung.

Yulia explained, and Asung shouted to Bai, who was perched on the back of a stationary motorcycle chatting to a teenage boy Yulia didn't recognise. At her mother's call, Bai came running.

'Here. I've signed it for you.' Rob grinned and passed the photo to Bai.

Yulia glimpsed the image: four men performing on stage, three with guitars – one of them Rob – and the other a drummer. Orange smoke swirled and a wall of lights glared behind them. She smiled looking at the leather outfits, bare chests on display, wild hair and kohl-rimmed eyes. This was Rob as she would never see him. She glanced from the photo to the man himself, faded T-shirt, sweaty hair pulled back in the sort of scrunchie women wore.

Seeing Bai blush and bite her lip, Yulia laughed. 'He doesn't give these to just anyone. I haven't got one. I'm jealous!'

The photo passed from hand to hand, the women curious. The old gap-toothed woman walked confidently to Rob, squatted beside him, lifted his shirt and patted his hairy chest. Rob raised his hands in mock surprise. 'Woah… one frisky lady.'

The women shrieked with laughter. Before Rob left to go back home, she would ask for a photo and get him to sign it, *to*

Yulia, with love. Something like that. Something she could brag about with her friends. Just for fun. She might post it on her social media account, the one for friends, where she could relax and post silly things. Her platform for her professional profile was a different matter; there her profile photo showed her in a city dress, presenting herself as a serious anthropologist, and her posts were designed to bring in work or increase her international contacts.

Bai had her hand in front of her mouth laughing as Rob played air guitar and sang, or rather shrieked, what she imagined to be one of Xcalibur's hits. Yulia joined in the laughter as Rob struck the same pose as in the publicity photo, chest pumped, giving Bai a sexy look. He was such good fun. She could feel the heat rise to her cheeks and rose to stand a little apart, away from the smell of this man who was enjoying teasing the women.

Asung was worried. It was late, the market long finished, but people, both young and old from further away, were enjoying fresh company and would be staying over. She had searched for her daughter in all the usual places, the friends' houses she might visit of an evening, and was making her way home.

'Mummy!'

When had Bai last used this babyish name? She peered into the dark. Her daughter was staggering towards her from the school yard. As she neared, Asung saw the dress she had bought for her daughter the day before was torn at the shoulder and Bai was clutching the fabric to cover a breast. Her hair, normally beautifully combed and held back in a clasp was loose and tangled; and her face... oh, the look on her face! Bai's legs buckled and Asung rushed to catch her. She soothed her, making shushing sounds, stroking her hair, not yet asking the questions she longed to. Who? Who would do this? Who would defile her daughter? Who would wish to bring shame on Balan! Was it a man from a neighbouring village? A logger unable to hold his booze? Who?

Wait… Asung's hands stilled on her daughter's head. Hadn't she seen Bai with that boy – his name would come to her – the one with the small putt-putt motorcycle he had part bought from Ngau and would pay off later? She remembered seeing Bai on the back of the bike tearing out of the village. It must be him. Though she wasn't sure she'd seen the boy around this evening. Perhaps he hadn't stayed. Perhaps he'd gone home…

'Bai.' Her voice was sharper than she meant. 'Were you with that scooter boy? Was it him?'

A shake of the head was all the reply she got. Was this the truth? Maybe Bai had *wanted* this to happen and it had somehow gone wrong, got out of control. No… No… She shook that thought away. Her daughter was not one of those fast ones.

Asung matched her steps to Bai's shuffling ones, reminded of when she had birthed her daughter more than fifteen years earlier. It had been the rainy season. She remembered the thunder and lightning that night, the rain pelting down on the roof. Drama outside and drama in her house. Drama inside her belly too. In her wildest nightmares she had not realised that birthing children would be so tough. Afterwards everything between her thighs had been so sore and she had walked just like Bai was walking now. She pressed her lips together as they continued back home, hoping they would not encounter anyone. This was private business.

Ah, Bai. Asung's heart was full for her daughter's pain. Perhaps they could hide this? If scooter boy was responsible, she would suck up her disappointment. Bai was not on her period, she knew that, so if her daughter were unlucky enough to be pregnant, would Balan accept this? Would he insist on a marriage? She sighed, taking Bai's weight as the girl leant on her for support. This was all wrong. She had hopes that her daughter would make something of her life. Move away. There was nothing for her, for any of the young people, here.

At the bottom of their steps, she paused and held her daughter at arm's length so she could look in her face.

'What happened?'

It seemed the bones in Bai's body had turned to cassava flour and Asung held her firmly.

'Mummy,' Bai whispered.

She helped her daughter up the steps, thinking what soothing herbs she had to hand. Then her mind turned to what plants she might need to gather if Bai was pregnant. She would urge her daughter to get rid of it, not grow a baby that had been seeded in her by force. She hoped Balan would agree to keep this thing private until they learnt more.

Closing the door, she crossed to where her husband slept.

'Balan. Wake up!'

Balan pushed aside the mosquito net rubbing his face. He took in Asung's expression as she bent over him, then his gaze moved beyond her. He observed how his daughter walked, legs apart, saw her flinch, a hand shooting out to touch her dress between her legs. He watched his wife help their daughter lie on her sleeping mat, sit next to her and stroke her hair. A hum expelled from his nostrils as his rapidly waking brain processed what was before him. Earlier he had drunk more than was usual. His fighting cocks had done well and with the extra cash he had enjoyed partying and gone to sleep a happy man, flopping down on his mat still wearing his shorts and T-shirt from the day without Asung around to tell him off.

'What happened?' he asked, but in his heart he knew.

'Shh.' Asung put her finger to her lips, gesturing towards the boys, although it would take a hurricane to wake those two. 'Do you think it's one of the men from upriver?' Asung whispered.

His eyes narrowed, thinking which of them might want to send him a message, get back at him for something. Nothing came to mind.

Loggers? They had been in town. Some of those men were troublemakers, getting into fights, though generally they got on with their job. In the past they had paid for sex with two teenage girls. He hadn't liked that, but when he'd complained, the logging boss had shrugged, saying, 'Yeah, it happens. But if they used condoms, no harm, right?'

Balan had lowered his eyes, not answering. How would he know if they had used condoms? He was not going to ask the girls – or the loggers. The boss gripped his shoulder. 'Right?' Balan had backed off.

He knew his community blamed him for not being tough enough, not demanding the company delivered what they had promised. Take the Health Centre… What a joke! It had been exciting seeing the new building go up. It had not taken long to construct the wooden sides and metal roof. Then he had beamed, bragging to his family and friends: 'See, we'll have a nurse here, one day a week!' Others had congratulated him, bought him a drink or two. Health Centre! He almost spat the words. The nurse had visited three times before disappearing for good. He was embarrassed by his failure. Everything he did was to make his community stronger and able to stand up in the world. Some people hinted he was hiding a wad of cash only he was benefiting from. Fat chance! That logging company! Their promises were as empty as his stomach had been when food was so scarce he hadn't eaten for two days. That company! Their promises were as useless as a dead man's tongue. Those loggers! They had done some bad things. But this? His eyes moved from Bai to Asung, who was busy mixing some drink for their daughter. She would know what was needed. The forest abounded in plants that were good – even orangutans knew a thing or two about medicine leaves to treat ailments. And about plants that were dangerous.

The musician's photo caught his eye. Bai had positioned it by her sleeping mat, and he had seen his daughter gazing longingly at the picture of that man and his Western music band; had caught her glancing shyly at Rob when he was showing off to the kids with his magic tricks. Balan's heartbeat quickened. Foreigners! He'd welcomed them to the village… *his* village. First AZTAR cutting their trees, now the government forest guys visiting to check up. He was sick to death of outsiders coming in and disturbing them all. This forestry business was not working out.

'I'll fix this.' He nodded brusquely to his wife then jerked his head to the photo.

'No! Wait and see what Bai tells us.'

He hesitated then nodded his assent. Asung turned her attention back to Bai, coaxing her into a half-sitting position and holding a cup to her mouth.

A kretek was what he needed. Balan knocked one from its packet, lit it and went out to the porch. Inhaling the tobacco and clove-flavoured cigarette, he wondered what he should do.

It wasn't just loggers they had to worry about. The other day Njau and Ule had returned from hunting and told him they had disturbed oil palm scouts. That too. Those bastards had thrust money in Njau's hand and told them to clear off. Clear off from their ancestral forest! What he would do if he ever came across those tree thieves.

He took a deep drag of his kretek.

No one disputed how much he knew about the old ways,

but all too often he felt himself flailing, his senses not fully alert to things he couldn't smell, taste or hear. Business things. Political things. He'd learnt the smells of a healthy forest, and one taste of flowing water would reveal much about that river and the fish in it. His knowledge of nature was the main reason he was elected headman – more an honorary role these days, but still, it was an honour. He was failing his people, failing his family.

He sucked on the remaining inch of his kretek, ground the stub under his heel and went back in. Bai lay on her side, turned away from Asung, whose hand rested on her head.

Again, Balan looked at the musician's photo, his pulse quickening. He *knew* it was this man. Had to be. Hadn't he watched him craftily slide a card or coin from hidden places? Now that man had craftily slid his cock where he had no right to.

'Enough of all this,' he told his wife. 'I'll round up some men.'

Balan could not have described what "all this" referred to, but it was everything. Everything. Asung had risen from Bai's side and was clutching at his arm.

'Wait, Balan. Please wait.'

He thrust her aside, picked up his hunting shotgun and headed out.

'What the fuck?' Rob was terrified.

It was the middle of the night and he was being bundled out of his hut wearing just his boxer shorts. The machete in front of his face could whack off a head, he was sure of it. And there were more: crazy men wielding machetes and shotguns. Were they high on something? 'What the fuck!'

A shotgun butt was thrust into his lower back, propelling him onwards. His eyes darted around about the compound. A whole bunch of village men and women had gathered. By the glow of kerosene lamps held aloft, he caught glints of metal: enough machetes to whack an army!

'What's happening, man? What've I done?' Nightmare images of sacrifices filled his head. *Heads! Shrunken heads. Shit, didn't they used to go in for that kind of thing?*

'Help! Linda! Anyone! Help!' He bellowed into the dark to be saved from the jigging, jittery demons set on killing him. Jutting an elbow, he warded off one man who was gibbering something, eyes wide, a knife blade close to his throat.

He took a deep breath, just as he might at the climax of an Xcalibur concert, and emitted an open-mouthed howl: 'Linda!'

'Hey! What the hell's going on?'

English! Someone was speaking English!

Rob twisted to see Ben, tugging on a shirt, the first on the scene. He'd never been so glad to see him. Moments later everyone he could take comfort from was there: Yulia, Rick, Ardhi… and – thank all the gods and goddesses that had ever been – Linda!

Linda's authoritative voice rose above everyone's. 'Get the fuck away from him!'

Rob was surprised how quickly she moved to yank the arm of the man nearest to her, despite his raised machete. Wasn't she even scared?

'What's got into you guys?' Her eyes looked as wild as the village men.

Rob's eyes darted right and left, fearful someone might sneak up behind.

Yulia was nodding rapidly talking with a group of women, then she rushed to Balan, who was shaking a clenched fist, the hand not holding his shotgun. Then Yulia was at his side, her eyes wide, her lips moving…

'What?' Rob tried to focus on what she was saying.

'I said, a girl's been raped – it's Bai – and they think it's you.'

'Shit, man! As if...' Instinctively he stepped back to distance himself from this fresh horror. Had Bai shafted him? Lied? He was aghast.

'I swore it wasn't you.' Yulia was all eyes. 'Said it was impossible. I told Balan—'

Ben had his arm now, shaking him. 'You need to leave. We've got serious research to do here and you're fucking things up. Both of you!'

Linda grabbed Ben, twisting him to face her. For all that she was much smaller than the Brit she wasn't taking any shit. 'Hey, Ben. You take that back. Surely you aren't implying—'

A fresh wave of distress swept over Rob. 'As if... Did Bai accuse me? I know that girl. Sweet as—'

Ben gave him a dirty stare. 'Just leave! A girl's been raped. The fewer foreigners here the better. We'll not be welcome, be sure of that, but some of us need to be here. You don't.'

OK, Rob thought. OK. Ben turned on his heel and stalked off towards Rick and Ardhi, who were trying to calm the local guys, machetes still in hand. *We've got serious research to do here and you're fucking things up!* Ben's words sunk in.

'Hey! Ben! At least I care enough to find out people's names. At least I take time to get to know them and make friends. More than you've bothered to do... Uptight Pommy twat!'

Ben spun around and was back in moments, clenched fists thumping his chest.

'Don't you dare presume to know what I care about! What the hell do you know? I've dedicated my career to this.' Ben, normally so bottled up, was letting loose. 'You've no idea...' His raised arm was drawn back.

'Woah!' Rob stepped back.

'You think you can charm people with your cheap tricks and celebrity?' Ben was almost spitting the words. 'Fuck off back to your recording studio or whatever—'

'No. You fuck off, Ben.' Linda kicked the Brit in the shins.

'Shit!' Ben thrust Linda away. She lost her footing and clutched about and found a bit of Rick to grab hold of.

'Cool it, guys.' The heft of Rick's voice and arms forced some distance between them, and Rob was grateful. Signing up for this gig with Linda he'd imagined being in the jungle fighting off tigers ('Not where we're going, Bud,' Linda had said) but he hadn't figured on fighting off locals – or the visiting forestry guys.

'OK... OK... I'm sorry, didn't mean to...' Ben blew out a deep breath and stepped back. 'Look, Rob, I know you'd not do anything vicious – that's too gross to imagine. Even so, you have no reason to stick around here.' Ben's eyes moved to Linda. 'Either of you. Especially you.'

'You don't have the authority to tell us—' Linda began.

'I *am* telling you.' Ben's hands were planted on his hips. 'You never had a good reason to be here, and now none whatsoever. Go!'

A hush had fallen; everyone quiet; everyone watching. Rob's eyes shifted. Some of the village men were frowning. What did they make of this argy-bargy between him and Ben? Shit! Maybe they thought that Ben thought that...

'Hey, Ben.' Rob grabbed Ben's arm. 'You tell Balan and the rest of them that you going bananas—'

'What?' Ben shook loose.

'—is nothing to do with Bai. Just in case any of them jump to conclusions. Let's set the record straight, hey?'

'Ask Yulia.' Ben turned on his heels. 'I'm going back to bed; we've a full day tomorrow. He turned around and shook a finger. 'And I meant what I said. You and Linda should leave.'

Watching Ben's back as he strode away, Rob conceded he might have a point. Yep, he might just be right on this. He would persuade Linda to move on out. Meanwhile, he was grateful to feel her arm around his waist and hear her caring, 'You OK, bud?' As they had spent more time together she had begun to mother him, and at this moment it was comforting.

'Yeah, I guess so.'

'I'm surprised I didn't wake when they came for you. Boy, they must have sneaked up.'

They sure did. Rob glanced at the local men, still looking far from calm, machetes dangling to their sides. 'You know, I might sit up for a bit. I'm not feeling very tired.'

As the foreigners disappeared back to their houses, Balan listened to the men and women he knew so well arguing back and forth, in no rush to disperse.

'If it wasn't him it might be one of the others.'

'Get rid of them all. Send them away.'

'What did Yulia tell you, Balan?'

He'd been surprised by what Yulia said. 'Rob and I were spending time together,' she'd told him, without saying exactly how. He didn't think she was *that* kind of a woman. He waved aside the question, but stated, 'It wasn't the Australian.'

'That big one then, it might be him.'

'No, no. Just because the Canadian's big, you can't…' Asung this time. 'Be patient. We must wait for Bai to tell us.'

He held up his hand, warding off further discussion. 'She's right.' He glanced at Asung, acknowledging the wisdom of her words. 'I was angry, too hasty. Go back home. We'll hold a meeting of the council when I find out what's happened. Go.'

He waved away the men, watching to see that none of them looked likely to head towards the visitors' accommodation.

On second thoughts... 'Ule... Njau.' He beckoned two men he trusted. 'Keep an eye out. Let the foreigners get some sleep. No more trouble.'

Back in his house Balan approached his daughter, huddled in the corner rocking back and forth.

'Tell me,' he coaxed. 'Tell me.'

Bai shook her head. He signalled to his wife to go to bed. Asung hesitated but he waved her away. A man had done a terrible thing to Bai, and another man – he, Balan, the headman – needed to take control. He had made a foolish mistake blaming the musician; that had been hot-headed when what was needed was a cool approach.

Balan squatted next to his daughter and lit a kretek. The tip flared and crackled as he inhaled, the smoke soothing his throat and calming him. He savoured it a moment before exhaling a stream of smoke through his nose. He was no longer in a hurry and would wait till Bai felt like talking.

6

Pain jagged Ben's brain each time the jeep juddered over a pothole. He pressed fingertips to his throbbing temples. For all that he had intended to sleep after last night's drama, he had found himself lying awake.

'That girl had better tell the full story otherwise it makes our being here difficult.' He had stated the obvious to Rick and Ardhi when they woke up; they'd mulled things over at breakfast and were now on the road.

'I've never known *this* to happen... not while I've been out in the field,' Ardhi said. 'I wonder if Balan will involve the police?' He swerved around a badly patched piece of road, then continued, 'The village might have some code of local justice. That would be interesting to find out. This could be a local thing.'

'Yeah, when we're back, you ask, Ardhi.' Rick was emphatic. 'I'd sure like to get to the bottom of it. All of us with dicks are suspect. I don't want any of the women afraid of me – or worse, any of their husbands thinking it was me. I don't fancy a midnight visit from Balan and his buddies.'

Ben was uneasy. It might be entirely coincidental that this

horror had occurred while he and his team were visiting. But until the matter was resolved it complicated relationships with the villagers – and with AZTAR. Every time he came across a forester at work an unspoken question would form in his brain: *Was it you?* Were those strong hands grasping a log the same hands that grappled with a teenage girl?

'This must be it.' Ardhi slowed down at the wide gates of a sawmill where an AZTAR logging truck stood ready to leave, driver at the wheel, engine idling.

They arrived to find the yard manager scurrying around to arrange a pickup for one of his men. A sawmill worker was sitting on a chair rocking back and forth nursing his hand wrapped in a grubby cloth. They soon learnt he'd just sawn off the tip of a thumb.

Ben flinched. 'Ardhi, how about you offer to drive him somewhere?' But the yard manager waved this suggestion aside, embarrassed by the fuss.

'Someone's on the way,' Ardhi told them. 'It's in hand.'

Ben shot Rick a "don't you dare" look in case he was tempted to pun.

He and Rick walked over to the open-sided sawmill where machinery rolled logs into place ready for sawing into planks.

'Jeez, look at this.' Rick nudged him, pointing to a huge unshielded saw blade. Ben grunted, his eyes moving from the machinery to the mill workers. None wore protective gear: eye masks, earmuffs, work boots.

'Think we'll be making some recommendations for health and safety.' Ben spoke quietly.

'Maybe one or two…' Rick's voice trailed off.

The rest of the timber mill was reasonably well-managed for all that it was messy. They found no inconsistency with the paperwork. An assessment of AZTAR's incoming logs showed them to be marked correctly, as was sawn timber ready to head out to the furniture manufacturer that was turning out products for Trevor Arnott. Staff safety notwithstanding, Ben could tick enough of the right boxes to show the flow of timber was controlled, thank God. He wanted to prove to nay-sayers – Linda among them – that schemes like this could work. What they could achieve on this scoping visit would just be the start. He would certainly recommend to Connor that a full audit was needed.

It was late afternoon when they arrived back at the village. Ben had thought that the Australian might have wanted to get the hell out, yet there he was at the Shack, notebook in hand, writing and humming still "inspired" by the bounties of the tropical forest. He clicked his tongue. *Good luck.*

At Rob's "Gidday" Ben nodded tersely, replied, 'Still here I see,' and made his way to where Yulia sat alone at a table, her back to him and laptop open in front of her. He could see she was catching up on social media.

'How're things going?'

'Sorry!' Yulia looked up startled, hastily closed the tab and brought up a document. He pulled up a chair.

'Everything OK today? Did you find out more?'

'It's been quiet,' Yulia said. 'Bai has talked, Asung told me, and they know it's not one of you.'

'Ah, thank goodness.' Any suspicion would have been enough to send them packing. 'And?'

Yulia shook her head. 'She didn't say, but told me they would deal with it. I didn't want to pry.'

'No. No. This might be local, something personal.'

'Maybe.' Yulia looked pensive.

'Let's look at what you've got for me.'

'Sure.' Yulia's face lit up.

He had an expectation of what her findings might be –

things he had already discovered about the village, or would have found out for himself without her being there – but she had a good rapport with the locals, and they might talk to her more willingly than to him via a translator. He found he was grateful for her presence.

Yulia turned her screen towards him. 'You know, Ben. I feel a little responsible. When I first visited, I saw how much they hoped to gain from this project, and now…' She sighed. 'Problems. A lot of problems.'

Ben scrolled through her findings and noted her recommendations to "meaningfully engage people at the local level" and urging "stakeholder involvement in decision-making procedures". He nodded these were totally in line with his own thinking. Projects such as this, with a network of threads from this tiny village deep in a rainforest all the way to Trevor Arnott's shops, had to work for everyone. Not easy. None of it was easy. He pushed back his chair.

'That's fine. Send it through to me. I'm going to draw everything together for a rough overview of where we've got to.'

'OK. See you later.' Yulia smiled.

Several days in the forest sites followed by the visit to the sawmill just about completed Ben's fieldwork. This, along with the earlier visit to the furniture manufacturer, had given them the data they needed.

Sitting at his desk working on the overview report, Ben was reminded that the non-functioning Health Centre he was staying in was one more issue to highlight. His fingers paused on the keyboard while he took a swig from a bottle of water before resuming typing: *Weaknesses have been identified in several key areas…* He paused again and stared into the middle distance then deleted the sentence. He would work on it some more before sharing the draft summary with Rick and Ardhi… and Yulia, of course.

Next day Ben headed to the Shack for a team meeting. The others were already there, laptops open. Seeing him arrive, Rick looked up.

'Oh yeah?' Rick pointed accusingly at the tablet screen resting on a table. '"Congratulations are offered for efforts—" What the hell's this, Fletch?' He sought support from Ardhi, who said nothing, then turned back to Ben. 'Well? What you gotta say?' The Canadian's face was flushed.

Ben had half expected this but hoped his team would agree on his approach. He kept his voice neutral: 'If we want to see change – and I know you do too – then we make damn sure this report is palatable, and—'

'What ya really mean is if it's not "palatable" you're not gonna see more work come your way!' Rick's face looked ugly.

'Don't give me that shit! You've known me long enough—'

'I thought I did—'

'And what about my work? I assumed there would be a separate section.' Yulia tugged Ben's arm. 'There are some observations and recommendations here and there, but…'

Yulia looked close to tears, Rick looked as if he'd like to slug him, and Ardhi was lighting a cigarette, not meeting his eye.

'Ardhi?'

His Indonesian colleague began cautiously: 'We need to show things are possible. Vital, yes. But we agreed we must be rigorous. I think—'

'Yes,' Ben interrupted, grateful for a morsel of encouragement. 'Remember, we were asked to report on this project's potential.'

'Yeah, right, Fletch. *Potential.* I'm with you there, but you don't need to brown-nose.'

'I'm not! This is a trade initiative. We need to be

encouraging. And you've seen one of the recommendations I've made is for the UK government to look at what the Dutch are doing in Indonesia – long-term investment.'

'Sure.' Ardhi looked approving. 'I've worked on one of those. They're worth noting.'

'But…' Yulia's eyes were pleading. 'Yesterday I thought you understood what I was saying, now I don't feel the rights of this community are being acknowledged nearly enough.'

The muscles in Rick's jaw continued to work. Ben hoped he could turn his team around to his way of thinking, or bedtime at the Health Centre with three men not on speaking terms would be like kids quarrelling at a sleepover. He glanced at Rick, who looked positively bellicose as he slammed his laptop shut. Ben tried again.

'Look, we know it takes years to develop and maintain careful management and planning. So let's show this has capacity to develop into something worthwhile. OK? You know I've highlighted failures and where procedures need—'

'Failures! Goddamn corruption!'

Linda! Ben turned to see her limping determinedly towards them waving a tablet in the air, his report on screen.

'How did you get hold of that?' Ben looked in turn at Yulia, Rick and Ardhi. Shoulders rose. Eyes shifted.

Ben was horrified anyone had allowed this to get into Direct Action for the Earth's hands.

Linda waved her hand. 'No one gave it to me. I found a laptop lying around and I'm not saying whose.' Linda was in his face again, poking him in the chest. 'I can't believe this, after what I showed you?'

'Everything's more or less under control in this concession and with the onward chain.'

'But out there? In the big beyond.'

Ben brushed aside Linda's jabbing finger. 'Right now, that's not our concern. We're trying to show that something can actually work. We've got to play the long game.'

'People's lives matter today.' Yulia's eyes beseeched him.

'And tomorrow will be too late, be sure of that,' Linda snorted. 'You tell orangutans to play the long game.'

'You think I ever stop thinking about it?' Ben stared at them in frustration. All of them wanted to make a difference – that was why they were here – just as all of them knew it was incredibly difficult and time was not on their side. He heard a collective sigh and watched bodies sag.

'Hey! I've a happy story for ya,' Rob's chirpy voice piped up. 'Our head honcho guy, Balan, is goin' to take me out tomorrow – show me the traditional way of hunting. His way of apologising. Apparently, Bai hasn't said who it was. Leastwise, Balan's keeping it to himself and hasn't told Yulia.' Rob's eyes shifted to Yulia. 'By the way, what did you tell him that night? Whatever it was, it saved my skin.'

'Oh, nothing.' Yulia blushed. 'You wouldn't have... so... Nothing...' She waved away curious looks.

'You trust him?' Rick asked Rob.

'Sure, why not.'

'I'd like to go too. I was invited,' Linda sounded regretful, 'but I'd never keep up. Hey, Ben.' She prodded him. 'Why not go along? You seem to have got your work wrapped up.'

He shot Linda an exasperated look. Didn't he have enough trouble keeping his team on the same page without her efforts to belittle him, driving a wedge between him and the others? He had dared to hope that Linda and Rob would be leaving the following day, but now Rob's forest excursion with Balan gave them another reason to stay.

'Yeah...' Rob looked welcoming. 'Come along, that'll be sweet. And, um, sorry for what I said the other night. You know. Things were a little crazy.'

'It's all right. Understood.' Ben had said some things he regretted too.

Rob beamed. 'If you come along, I can play some of my music.'

A groan escaped his throat before Ben could hold it back. The thought of thudding along rough forest tracks listening to Xcalibur's heavy metal music was almost enough to set his headache off again.

Rick caught Ben's eye. 'Redraft the damn thing.'

'Don't you see?' Ben's voice rose. 'It's about working *with* governments and businesses. It's the only way things will change.'

'Sure about that, Ben?' Linda pursed her lips.

'Come... Come!' Rob beckoned them away. 'Balan's invited us to watch him prepare darts. That'll take your mind off things.'

'All right! Sure will. Didn't know anyone still had the skill to do it.' Rick beamed.

Ben watched faces light up, problems put aside. He wanted to see this too; wouldn't miss it.

Ben squeezed in close to Ardhi, all of them huddled around the headman, squatting around a small fire outside his house. Only Balan was at home; the rest of the family was elsewhere. The boys would be at school, and Asung and Bai were probably out in the fields, Ben decided, or maybe Asung wanted to keep Bai away from them. He had hoped Yulia might find out more about Bai's attack, but following a cautious enquiry, Balan had held up his blowpipe: 'This is the business right now.'

This traditional hunting technique, handed down from male to male, had all but disappeared; the local men hunted with shotguns and dogs these days. Bullets were smuggled across the Malaysian border, from what Ben had gathered. Balan was full of pride to be sharing this ancient craft.

'Umm... He says a long time ago it used to take ages to drill by hand,' Yulia translated. 'But with metal drills they use ironwood now, not bamboo.' Balan nodded, holding up his long blowpipe for them to admire.

The darts were lined up ready to dip. Ben eyed the dark viscous substance that had been prepared: poisonous tajem tree sap mixed with other leaves he wasn't sure about. There was a hush as they craned necks watching Balan dip and twirl the tip of an arrow in the goo and carefully lay it out to dry by the fire. Ben reached for his camera. He would never get to see this again. Fascinating.

'About thirty minutes to heat,' Yulia told them, 'then leave them to dry so the poison hardens.'

Balan smiled proudly, marking on his fingers the animals they might hunt.

'Squirrels,' Yulia translated, 'hornbills... other birds.'

Ardhi asked about bigger prey: boar and deer. Balan shook his head. They might, if they were lucky, but larger animals were rare these days.

With a clean pointed twig, Balan pretended to prick the back of his hand and Ben understood this was all it took for the poison to take hold. The headman grinned, saying more, touching his hand to his chest. Yulia translated. 'He says our life is here, then it disappears. You fall over and die. That's it.'

Rick expelled a gentle whistle, and Ben leant in closer.

Yulia looked concerned. 'Perhaps I should go with them to translate.'

'That mightn't be a bad idea,' Ardhi agreed.

Ben glanced at an arrow Balan was dipping into the lethal concoction, knowing he wasn't the only one who might be thinking: could Balan *really* be trusted? He briefly flirted with the idea of asking to join them, but he had work to do before wrapping up the project and flying out.

Yulia asked Balan if she might accompany them, but the answer was an emphatic no from the headman. 'Nothing to do with being a woman,' Yulia told them. 'Balan wants to move quietly and they can communicate by sign. Two people are enough.'

'I'll just be following and doing what I'm told,' Rob said. 'I'll be on his heels. Don't fancy getting left behind in the jungle.'

DAE.org/Blogs/Linda

I'm an optimist. Gotta be in this line of business otherwise you may as well shut up shop. But boy, I feel like Job being sorely tested (reach for a Bible). Rob and I are about to leave, and I'd been hoping these sappy (forgive the pun) pen-pushers I'm spending time with would DO SOMETHING! But no. Happy to avoid conflict. Look at these **photos** of more devastation. But you know what? These trees fall outside the remit of the project my 'good guys' are reporting back to government about. They tell me they've reported their concerns to the forester and the local government official, but to say something is "outside a *remit*"? It does my head in. Moving on...

We were privileged to watch an elder of our village prepare poison darts for blowpipes, a tradition all but disappeared. Take a look at this **video**. A reminder of what else is being lost in our increasing globalisation. I'll store this in my "precious memory" file.

To find out what Direct Action for the Earth is doing to save our planet and how to get involved, go to our **Campaigns**. Check out our **Membership** schemes and don't log off till you've clicked through to **Donations**.

The following morning Yulia made her way to the Shack, book in hand. She paused to watch Linda waving off Rob and Balan, Rob in the driver's seat of the battered jeep, the headman at his side.

Linda patted the bonnet. 'Make sure you don't shoot yourself in the foot.'

'I'll do my best not to.' Rob waved to Linda and blew a kiss to Yulia. 'See ya later.'

As the jeep accelerated away, Rob honked a rhythmic rat-a-tat to his fanbase of waving children running after them.

'Breakfast?' Linda cocked her head, and the two of them walked towards the tempting cooking smells wafting from the open-sided hut.

'Have you really been arrested so many times?' Yulia had been longing to ask. Twenty-seven times, Linda had said.

'Yep. Some lock-ups were just a matter of days, others somewhat longer. I could write a book about the prisons I've been in.'

Yulia's eyes widened.

'I've packed a lot of experiences in these past ten years.' Linda looked thoughtful. 'For years I obsessed about all the wrongs in the world. But you know how it is: we've all got our lives. You make a donation to a favourite cause to coddle your conscience…' Her voice trailed off.

'What changed?'

'My husband died.'

'I'm sorry.' Yulia hadn't meant to pry, but Linda was happy to talk.

'Ted and I had so many plans for when we retired. Then

after he had passed, I figured I had to act; realised each day matters. We've only got one life.'

'Mmm. Maybe.'

'I've told my kids I'll be home for a while after this jaunt. Promised I'll make it for my granddaughter's birthday. She'll be five—'

'That's nice.'

'I've never managed to celebrate any of her birthdays. Always something more pressing to do. Funny thing is, for years and years I stressed over my kids, but now they stress about their crazy mom. Anyhow, I need to get back to my research.'

'Direct Action for the Earth?'

'Oh, that never goes away. It consumes me. But I don't need much sleep and I like to keep busy. I have a little side-line: company networks; who's in bed with who; where the pay-offs are. I'm linked up with some pretty savvy people. There're all sorts of ways to snoop, but it's real hard with so many bastards with complex offshore subsidiaries... Here.'

Linda reached into her wallet and pulled out a distinctive-looking business card titled Fat Cats with a cartoony cat wearing a massive hat.

Yulia chuckled. 'You think he's hiding something under that hat?'

'You can bet your bottom dollar!'

Yulia slipped the card into her book and followed Linda into the Shack. The friendly owner motioned them to a table where she had placed a large platter of fresh fruit. She knew Yulia's breakfast preference.

'Thank you! Delicious.' Yulia waved.

At another table, a group of loggers were tucking into steaming bowls of rice and fried egg. Yulia glanced away guiltily, knowing she had allowed a question to enter her head: *Was it one of you that hurt Bai?* Until they knew the answer every male was suspect and she was uncomfortable. Asung and Balan would not speak with her about Bai's rape and she hadn't dared ask to talk with Bai directly. This wasn't her business. She needed to tread lightly.

It was dusk when Ben and his team, with Mr Manapo, returned in the forester's vehicle. He was exhausted following their final day at one of the sites, and the heat rash under his dripping shirt made him irritable.

'Guys!'

Linda was hurrying towards them, her face taut. What now? He wanted to get back and shower. Couldn't whatever she wanted wait? He looked beyond her to Yulia and Asung, who were following, the village woman twisting the fabric of her dress in her fingers. Linda panted up to them.

'Rob and Balan aren't back. Don't know where they went, but they were due hours ago.'

'Phone?' Ben cocked an eye.

Linda shook her head. 'Tried loads. No signal.'

'It'll be dark soon—' Ardhi began.

'So, let's get out there.' Linda began pushing them back towards the jeep.

'No!' Mr Manapo resisted. 'It's too late. I'll arrange a second vehicle. We'll get organised for daybreak.'

'We can't leave them out overnight!'

'Hey!' Rick tried to placate her. 'Balan will know what he's about. They're probably waiting it out in the jeep. Flat tyre or something.'

Yulia was hurriedly translating and listening to Asung's reply.

'Asung says they mightn't be safe. He's not stayed out all night since he was a young man hunting with friends. He wouldn't do that with a guest anyway.'

'See!' Linda stepped towards Mr Manapo. 'You heard what she said. Let's go!' She began pushing him.

Mr Manapo backed away. 'Sorry. Please. Not now. We need to prepare. Really it will be best, you'll see. As soon as it's light we will start.'

Linda walked in a circle, pulling her hair. 'All right… All right.'

Ben wasn't unduly worried. Rob would be safe with Balan and this overnight adventure would add to the story he would take home. Ben reminded himself of his own travel plans now they had wrapped up their fieldwork. It wasn't just Mr Manapo who had transport arrangements to sort out. Ben turned to Ardhi, speaking quietly.

'Can you rearrange our pickup and the Cessna?'

Ardhi nodded. 'Yes, of course… Delay a day?'

'Yes… No… I don't know.' Ben frowned. 'Let's leave that open until we know more.

Rick laid a hand on his shoulder. 'Shit. I'll have to rearrange my connecting flights.'

'Yep, we all will.'

They exchanged worried looks. Relations had thawed during the day as they'd mulled over what would be, and what would not be, included in the final report. Ben's eyes shifted to the three women huddled together, faces strained. He would not allow himself to worry, but would be guided by Mr Manapo's pragmatic approach. He spoke to Linda.

'See you at the Shack later. OK?'

'Sure… OK… Sure.' Linda was barely registering his words, so he looked to Yulia, who nodded.

They had time to kill this evening so better to spend it together to take their mind off things before an early night. First a shower and change of clothes. Ben turned towards the Health Centre.

7

LINDA WAS BESIDE HERSELF WITH WORRY ABOUT ROB. There had been no point trying to sleep, so she had made a flask of coffee and attempted to read. That hadn't been too successful either. Since Ted died, she had been a lousy sleeper, rarely getting more than two hours at a stretch, and when sleep did come her dreams were far from serene. She always seemed to be chasing something, or something was chasing her in the weird logic of dreamtime. She would wake, heart palpitating, and reach out a leg only to find the far side of her bed cool to the touch, and a fresh wave of sadness would pass over her. No Ted.

Mr Manapo was as good as his word. Two jeeps were ready at daybreak and Linda was vaguely aware that Asung and other women were pressing packages of food, drinking water and flasks of hot drinks into their hands. She wasn't really concentrating as she climbed in next to Mr Manapo.

'Let's get going. C'mon!'

Ben and Rick hurried into the back, while another forester drove Ardhi and Yulia. Two village men, Ule and Njau, who

Mr Manapo assured them were familiar with the forest and knew Balan's favourite hunting areas, had crammed into the second jeep. Good thinking, Linda thought. The locals would have this sussed.

As the convoy bumped along rutted logging roads her unblinking eyes stared through the splattered windshield. Time after time they came across AZTAR loggers going about their work. One of the foresters would leap out and question the logging guys, and she would see shoulders shrug, hands raise, and heads shake. Linda listened as the two foresters stayed in touch with two-way radios; they would explore side-tracks only to retrace their route before continuing deeper and deeper. This was taking ages. Shit! She willed that damned jeep to appear, just ahead, and there would be Rob hurrying to meet them, waving his arms. Boy, she would give him the hug of his life!

Linda sipped sweet black tea from her flask. She had moved on from coffee, needing the clarity of a more refreshing liquid. She brushed aside Rick's offer of a biscuit, fearing its dryness might choke her.

Naturally she was worried sick about Rob, but then there was DAE. God forbid that anything had happened, but just suppose, just suppose something *had*, how would this reflect on DAE? Might fingers be pointed at her? At DAE? The organisation would not withstand too much scrutiny about health and safety. That had been going through her mind as well. She needed to ensure Rob returned in one piece – and brought the jeep back. She was mindful of that too, as she had borrowed it from a friendly sympathiser in a regional town.

When she and Rob had come across the log landing in the protected area she had been fired up and determined to plough on to get more evidence, but Rob had almost pissed himself. So she had turned back, but there had been no hiding her resentment. A lot of time and resources had gone into planning this trip. She had protected Rob, and now, when she was nowhere near the man, he might be in danger. The irony of it.

Through the side window she stared at the passing foliage. So dense, so impenetrable. Reaching for her flask she briefly wished it held something stronger than tea. Exhaustion and worry were making her hands shake. Damn. She needed to keep herself together to be any use on this rescue mission.

Ben had moved to the front, insisting Linda rest in the back. He twisted around and smiled to see Rick's arm encircling her, her head on his shoulder, jaw slack.

They bumped on minute after minute, mile after mile. Ben glanced at his watch and saw it was already after two o'clock. Mr Manapo was debating with his colleague via the radio whether to split up or stay together.

'There! There!' Ben reached across and blasted the horn alerting those behind. Along the track, Rob's jeep was pulled to the side, the driver's door ajar.

Mr Manapo speeded up then skidded to a halt, the other vehicle on its bumper. Moments later all of them were swarming around the abandoned jeep like flies on carrion.

Rick circled the stranded vehicle checking tyres: 'All good.'

Leaning into the driver's door Ben saw the key still in the ignition. He turned it, and the engine sparked into life. He twisted his head and raised his shoulders at Linda, who was pressing in over him.

'Shit!' Linda's single word and anxious face said it all. She reached for her phone. 'I'll try again.'

They fell silent, hoping to hear a distant ringtone, but the forest only offered the shrill cries of birds and insects.

'Three groups.' Mr Manapo took charge. 'Ben and Ardhi with me, Linda and Rick with Pak...' the second forester nodded, 'and Njau and Ule with Yulia... OK, Yulia?'

'Yes, yes, I'm fine about that. I trust these men,' Yulia assured him.

The head forester handed out remote control radios then opened the hatch of his vehicle to reveal a stack of machetes. Ben accepted a broad-bladed knife and tucked a simple whistle in a pocket. They waited for Pak to show Yulia how to use the radio.

'OK, I got it.' Yulia hung the radio strap around her neck and jammed a red peaked cap on her head.

'Ready?' The forester's normally placid face was etched with concern as he looked over the search teams. Search *and* rescue teams, Ben corrected himself.

With his left hand, Ben swiped at mosquitoes as his machete hand swiped back and forth at undergrowth threatening to trip him. Droplets of sweat dripped from his nose and his shirt clung to his back. Distant cries of 'Balan!' 'Rob!' mingled with the sounds of the forest.

Ahead, Mr Manapo inspected the foliage, looking for signs of recently broken branches, before beckoning him and Rick onward. This was impossible. It was like looking for a needle in a haystack. Questions filled his head: Balan had his blowpipe with poison darts, but what were they hunting? There was so little out here. Did Balan really believe Rob hadn't raped Bai? Did he mean to harm Rob?

They had been searching for nearly an hour when Yulia's urgent voice, 'Here! Here!' crackled through Mr Manapo's radio soon followed by shrill, distant whistles, trilling over and over.

Ben followed Mr Manapo and Ardhi, the summoning calls drawing closer. All of them pushing aside undergrowth, going as fast as the forest allowed: always roots, creepers, rotten logs, rocks. Soon his team of three converged with Pak, Rick and Linda.

'Go,' Linda urged, 'I'll catch up.'

Ben hurried after Rick, his broad back hunched, charging like a wild boar. Mr Manapo was somewhere in front, while Linda's voice gasped, 'Hurry. Hurry!' to his back.

Closer now, he could hear Yulia screaming something and Njau and Ule shouting back at her. Now he could see Yulia's bright cap; keeping that in sight, he pushed forward. Then he stopped. Stared. Took a steadying breath.

Balan's body lay curled in a foetal position. Yulia, Njau and Ule squatted by his side. He couldn't tell what they were saying. Balan's blowpipe lay on the ground and near it a machete. Ule picked it up, studying the bloodied blade. He saw all this. And flies. His eyes turned back to Balan. Hundreds of flies were feasting on his corpse. The sour taste of a partly digested meal rose in his throat and he fought the urge to puke.

Fearful English and Indonesian voices filled the air, his own joining a discordant chorus, shouting, swearing, questioning: 'What the fuck's going on?' 'A leopard, you think?' 'Where's Rob?' 'Oh, poor Asung!'

Ben's boots had become heavy, rooting him to the spot. Rick pushed past him, ripping off his own shirt and using it to swipe at the flies swarming over Balan. Ben's eyes went to Balan, back to Yulia, then to Rick's shirt whipping the air. The Canadian gently draped it over the dead man's head.

'Shut up! Shut the fuck up!' Linda arrived, waving her hands for silence.

Into the lull, above the chirruping birds and insects, a drone of flies. Heads swivelled towards a new sound.

Linda was the leader now, the first to move, pushing through undergrowth. Ben followed. Moments later her wail pierced the air and her arms flew skyward as if jolted by an electric shock.

Rob was sitting propped against a tree. Flies clustered on his eyes, in his nostrils and open mouth. And masses of flies, their shining black bodies a necklace of jet beads strung around his neck as they feasted on congealed blood. The gash across the Australian's throat was ear to ear. His arms flopped by his side. Hands that had previously held a guitar and coaxed music from strings had deep slices in the palms. Fingers had been sliced clean away as he tried to defend himself.

Linda clumsily knelt, fingertips touching Rob's hair, then softly brushed the back of her hand down his cheek. Her back heaved with silent sobs.

A shrill soprano wail filled Ben's ear and Yulia raced past. Rick's baritone and Ardhi's tenor next, voices that had laughed at a stupid joke now harmonising in a wretched cry of grief. It was a choir Ben couldn't find a voice to join. He was mute.

Flies that had been swarming around Rob had invaded Ben's head. They choked his brain, buzzing louder and louder till he could no longer hear what was going on around him. Mr Manapo was saying something, but he couldn't focus. He felt himself swaying. Steadying himself against a tree he retched and retched.

'Robert Gilmore, lead singer with Australian band Xcalibur and recent campaigner with Direct Action for the Earth, has been found murdered in an Indonesian forest. Police in Kalimantan province…'

Connor was in his office, his attention split between the TV news and the phone in his hand. The screen image moved from the newsreader to a prepared package: a testosterone-fuelled Xcalibur concert, all flying hair and spiralling sweat, and a Direct Action for the Earth protest with activists waving placards and banners. Editors had highlighted some of the front-line protesters, and Connor could see Linda Smith, jabbing her finger at a politician stupid enough to have turned up hoping to capitalise on the event and no doubt being turned into mincemeat.

'What do you make of it, Connor?'

The voice on the phone was his boss, Simone Bailey, minister for international trade. She was watching the same news bulletin in her own office.

'Give me a minute, Minister.'

Connor gave his full attention to the news. Fresh images now. There was Linda walking dejectedly towards a small plane following a coffin held aloft by a group of men. Connor squinted. Ben was one of them, along with another Westerner – perhaps Rick Wilson? – and several Indonesians, one of them possibly Ben's colleague Ardhi Durmali. It seemed that Linda intended to catch the flight – she had a backpack on – but he couldn't judge the intentions of the coffin-bearers.

'Police believe the murder was the result of a personal dispute and are not seeking anyone else. Gilmore's presence in the region was unconnected with the British and Indonesian government initiative in the same area. Government sources stress scientists involved are not at risk…'

Connor spoke into his phone. 'We've given the media this line, about them not being at risk. Still, it doesn't look good to have our team mixed up in any of this. Gilmore's a big name. There'll be a major hoo-ha—'

'Bound to be!'

'But his death won't impact on what we're doing.'

'It had better not! All the same, get them out of there. Tell the media we're taking steps to get our people out, in case more journalists take a line about scientists abandoned in the jungle. I've already fielded a question along those lines this morning.'

'Yes, Minister. I expect Ben will have arranged a plane to pick them up, but I'll check.'

'Do that. Remember, I took your advice on this. All of it. The whole "good news" project.' Simone's voice was tart.

'Of course, Minister. I'll update you on the way to the airport.'

The phone went dead, and Connor pressed his lips together. She was something, his boss. Simone had leaned on one of Connor's staff – bullied, more like – and Connor had had to defend his co-worker's action and request that Simone's queries were directed via him. His grateful colleague had half-jokingly told Connor: 'Glad you have to deal with her. You're more senior than me; paid more.' To which Connor had thought, *Not nearly enough*. His colleague had requested a transfer to a different department, which had been agreed. In Connor's view the civil service should be safe from ministerial interference, but Simone had made it clear she wanted her department to toe the line.

'When I set targets, I want them done in my way and met in my time, not yours.'

Yes ma'am, Connor had thought, resisting the urge to salute, instead producing his well-practised smile, maybe a little smarmy, before replying, 'Of course, Minister.'

Connor increasingly watched his back, not trusting Simone to stand up for him. In fact, he didn't trust her as far as he could spit. Aside from her ambitions, which she wore on her creased jacket sleeve as others wore their heart, he was mindful of the prime minister's threat of a root and branch review of the Civil Service. Now *that* was serious. He and his colleagues were closing ranks to ward off political reform. That would not do.

He had better check Ben was OK. Simone was right. The quicker they were out of there the better. In all honesty he hadn't given this Indonesian project much of his time. He was dealing with bigger, more important, trade negotiations on behalf of the minister.

8

DAE.org/Blogs/Linda

I haven't written for a few days, but no surprises.

Sometimes you meet people in your life's journey that shine, and Rob was one of those. I guess most people know his stage persona, all heavy metal and sexy posing, but that wasn't the real man. I got to know Rob, loved his good nature and his passion for music.

His parents are heartbroken, naturally, but I'm amazed at their strength, dealing with grief but thinking forward.

I met with Rob's band members. Nice guys. Meeting them would normally be awesome except that it was so darned sad. They want to make something positive come about from this terrible thing. I'll keep you posted.

Learn about what Direct Action for the Earth is doing to save our planet and how to get involved. Read about our **Campaigns**. We need your support and **Donations**. Don't just sit around and read my blog. DO SOMETHING!

It had taken Linda days to muster the energy to write this. Her posts were usually spontaneous ramblings, thoughts flowing seamlessly from brain to fingers. Now what she had written was flat and inadequate – and not fully truthful. Rob's parents *were* heartbroken, and she *was* amazed at their strength and forward-looking attitude. Mom and Dad Gilmore had driven from a small town to meet with her and they talked about Rob's death over coffee and tea at a café. So surreal.

'Mrs Smith…'

'Linda, please.'

Mom Gilmore nodded and said to call her Rae. Her gaze was direct, reminding Linda of Rob's eyes, and if Rob had lived, the dark hair he often wore in a top-knot would surely have become a thick greying thatch like "call me Stu" Gilmore's. Linda told them nice things: about looking for orangutans; Rob making friends everywhere; that this was a hunting trip gone wrong and the police were investigating. She didn't say she had little faith in the local police, and she didn't describe the murder. No need to go over all of that.

Rae put down her cup, shaking fingers making the liquid slosh.

'Linda, could you have done anything to stop it happening?'

'I don't know. I ask myself the same thing.'

Boy, was *that* true. Night after night she went through "what ifs?" If only she'd gone with them, or Ben or one of his team, or some village men. Might that have changed things?

'Rob had been hanging out in the village, there was nothing to suggest this might happen. We weren't doing anything risky.'

Rae's gaze dropped. 'Your poor arm. What happened?'

Linda flinched. She should have worn a long-sleeved shirt. Today wasn't the day to expose her welts like badges of honour. They shrieked *this woman takes risks!*

She had been in the Bwindi National Park at the time, hoping to see mountain gorillas when she and her guide brushed up against poachers. It had been her fate to avoid the gun but not the machete. It was the dedicated conservationist who took the bullet. One more cut-out cardboard star added to the wall on the visitor centre – each with the name of a dead ranger killed in the call of duty. She tried to skate over the story but on hearing the words "machete", "poachers" and "gun" the tremble in Rae's hands increased, and she could see the muscles at the edges of Stu's eyes twitch behind his glasses. She hurriedly asked about funeral arrangements.

'A family affair next week,' Stu said. 'There'll be a memorial service down the line. A big affair for his fans, I'm guessing. We're not sorting that.'

'I'd love to attend his funeral—'

'Just family.' Stu ducked his head.

'Well, if you change your mind, you've got my details. It would be an honour to be with you.'

They had chit-chatted for a while, then shaken hands and separated. That evening her heart leapt seeing their name appear on a newly arrived email, but the message wasn't inviting her to the funeral, instead asking, 'Would you mind making time for us again tomorrow?'

So Linda found herself back at the same café. Stu and Rae did have more questions: ones formulated by a lawyer on an email printed out on the table.

'What were the terms of Rob's involvement with Direct Action for the Earth? Was there a contract or anything similar?'

Linda was caught off guard. 'Rob was a guest.'

'But there must be some kinds of *terms of reference*?' Rae's voice rose at the end of the sentence as her finger followed the words.

Linda's mind whirled. She hoped Jade, DAE's Australian co-ordinator, had kept an email trail of Rob's enquiry to them. Jade was a very reluctant office and membership manager doing a few hours' paid work a week for a pittance. What Jade enjoyed was organising – and participating in – direct actions. Jade had no more love for dull management duties than she had herself.

Linda put on her teacher's face, the firm look she had used for students whining why their assignment would be late.

'Rob *asked* to come with me. He was doing his own thing. It was a delight to have his company, but I need to be clear with you, Direct Action for the Earth has no legal obligation to Rob.'

There would be no invitation to the family funeral.

The guys from Xcalibur were nice, just as she had said, no fibs needed there. When she had told Rob's tale yet again they'd wept openly, exclaiming, 'Oh man!' 'Bastards!' 'A walkabout gone wrong, hey?' They'd parted with hugs and handshakes promising they'd think how they might commemorate Rob, but right now this was far too raw. Fans had lost a celebrity they thought they knew, but these guys had lost a mate who was dear to them.

In her blog she missed telling about the police interview. Interview! Two dunderhead cops came to her hotel and asked pitiful questions until she screamed, 'For fuck's sake! The man's dead and you're asking me what time it was when we found him? Who the hell cares? You know how quickly a body deteriorates in the tropics?'

'Yeah, I do actually,' one of them said. 'Worked in the Northern Territories… came across loads of bloated—'

'Who's leading on this anyway?'

Both men shrugged, saying it had been "passed up". Meaning this was a political thing. They were just filling in some gaps since she was in town.

The Australian government, she noted from interviews, took a dim view of one of their nationals being killed abroad. They were putting pressure on their Indonesian counterparts, but so far, judging from the TV news, they had no answers. She wondered if any channel other than CNN would give her five minutes' coverage should she die in a similarly sticky way. But then she was old, not sexy, and patently not a rock star.

Rob was a big fish. She hadn't truly appreciated just how big until, arriving at Sydney airport, she was overwhelmed by a tsunami of journalists and TV cameras, all there to record Rob arriving home. The flow continued: thousands of grieving metalheads determined to witness this, to snatch photos and videos of the coffin. She was almost crushed by the surge, her ego squashed when she realised no one was interested in *her*.

She was exhausted. Having discharged any obligations she, or DAE, had by accompanying Rob's body to his home soil, she wanted to get home too. But before that, she was meeting with Jade. When she'd seen Rob's fans at the airport and all those grieving young people blubbing on the TV, she'd clocked that their profile was a perfect fit for DAE. They could be harnessed. Why waste a good crisis?

9

INSIDE HER HOUSE, ASUNG DREW BAI TO HER SIDE and peered through a gap between loose planks. She had allowed the boys out, but not Bai. *Oh, Balan. I need you now. How could you leave us?* The ache in her heart was like the monsoons: it had washed her out, leaving her limp when she needed to stay strong. Balan was her husband, the father of her children and the only man she had slept with. Yes, they had bickered, and she had been angry with him for not demanding more from the logging company. 'I'm trying,' he had said. 'Try harder,' she and elders of the council had urged. So Balan would have another meeting asking for this or that or reminding them about this or that – things that should have been done. He would come back and not meet her eyes. 'You're the headman,' she would remind him, then felt bad because he looked so crushed.

Soon his body would be dust.

Asung, her eye to the gap, watched police officers talk with men she knew. One officer leaned against the open door of the police vehicle; two stood together by the eating place the foreigners called the Shack; another was knocking on a door. She would not reply if he came knocking here. Those men in uniform were putting the blame on them for the Australian's death, saying it was Balan, saying he was a bad man. As if!

'Which ones?' she asked, as matter-of-factly as if she were asking Bai whether she wanted to buy purple or yellow flip-flops. She moved aside so Bai could see.

Her daughter was trembling. Asung had to stay strong for Bai now. 'Any of these, or were they different?' It had been dark after all. Perhaps Bai couldn't be sure?

'Him. The one talking with Ule.' A dry whisper. A pause, then Bai's head moved slightly. 'And the one talking with Mr Manapo.'

So they were here. Asung expelled a breath she hadn't realised she was holding, and she gently pushed Bai aside to see for herself. She stared and stared at the men in their smart uniforms talking to Ule in his shabby old clothes. Every feature of those men's faces became ingrained in her brain. She tried to shut out the image of what it must have been like for her lovely girl, as first one then the other took a turn hurting her. Didn't they have wives or daughters? But then they were Javanese, they didn't care about her people.

Oh, Balan, I need you. Her plea was silent. She wasn't sure what to do with this new information. The village council knew it was the police – Balan had told them – and now she could identify them. What to do, then? Who to tell? Not Sartano, that was for sure. Not him!

She smoothed her daughter's hair from her face. 'Bai. It won't happen again.' But of course, it might.

Might Yulia help? The council had been meaning to have a long talk with Yulia, *really* talk about how badly things were going. Should she talk or stay silent? Asung's fingers twisted the fabric of her skirt. *Oh, Balan, I miss you. What should I do?*

Yulia stood on the porch of Asung's house and knocked. Already the cars had arrived to take her and the men to the airstrip, so this would have to be quick. Asung opened the door.

'I'm so pleased you asked to see me, Asung. I didn't get a chance to talk with you at Balan's funeral and I wanted to say goodbye.'

Yulia put her backpack down and stepped inside. Asung stood, shuffling from foot to foot.

'Asung?'

'It's about Bai.'

'Ah.'

Yulia's eye swept the room and beyond to the outside kitchen. They were alone. She drew Asung to a chair. Ben would just have to wait. She couldn't rush this.

'I know which two—'

'Two?' Yulia's eyes widened.

'Sartano's men. They were here yesterday.'

Yulia found her heart was thudding. Had she understood Asung correctly? She was mindful her grasp of this language was slender. She needed to be sure.

'*Police* officers?'

Asung nodded, and Yulia tried to recall the faces of the officers who had been around, wondering which of them had done it while the other held Bai down; tried to imagine the brutal scene.

'"Tell that father of yours to stop bothering the logging boss. Leave things alone. Things are fine as they are"... That's what they told Bai.'

'Oh, Asung. Why didn't you tell me earlier? None of you have been open about how bad things are!'

Yulia was shocked. This is why she had come, to make an honest assessment of this community's needs, and they had not been honest with her. Now she was leaving.

'Don't tell Ben and the others. It's not their business.'

'Ben must know. This impacts on the project!'

'No!' Asung drew back. 'It will make things worse, but I wanted you to know.'

'Ah, Asung. Thank you for telling me. I hadn't wanted to pry. I thought it was something personal. This is different. Quite different.' Yulia reached for Asung's hand. 'When I'm back in Jakarta I'll think how best to respond. They can't get away with this. Poor Bai.'

Deep lines etched Asung's face. Yulia squeezed her hand.

'And Balan? Rob? Do you suspect the police for that too?'

'Not them. It wouldn't be them... You should go.'

Yulia nodded. She could not ignore the staccato horn honks summoning her. The vehicles were ready to leave; the pilot's time was valuable.

'I have to think. I promise I'll contact you when I'm back.'

After a hasty hug, she hoisted her bulging backpack onto her shoulders and her day pack on her chest, and made her way towards the waiting SUVs. As she tried to jog with all the added weight on her shoulders, her heart was heavy with all this new knowledge. What could she do?

Ben shook Mr Manapo's hand, thanking him one more time. He slung his camera around his neck and watched Yulia, who had finally arrived but was now engulfed by people keen to bid her farewell. He willed her to hurry up. Rick and Ardhi had already loaded baggage into one vehicle and their driver sat at the wheel, the engine idling.

'Any news from Linda yet?' Rick paused, his hand on the door.

'No. Nothing.' He hadn't given Linda a thought. In truth, the past days had been a blur, his emotions numbed, and he had not wept for Rob or Balan. He imagined Linda would be back in the States... or maybe she was still in Australia. The last he had seen of her was looking ashen-faced, a hand placed on Rob's coffin in the small plane before the door closed and he had just seen her eyes through the window: sad; old.

Rick raised a hand. 'See you there.' He and Ardhi set off for the airstrip. Ben flung his backpack into the rear of the other SUV and settled in the front seat next to the driver.

Among the chaos of the past days, Sarah had contacted him – as of course she would. Although their breakup had been painful, they had stayed – or rather she had stayed – in touch, determined to remain friends. Following news of Rob's murder, Sarah had sent an urgent message, all exclamation marks and question marks: *OMG, Ben. Just heard! Are you all right? We're worried sick!!* Followed by a sad face emoji. This was unlike her, or at least the Sarah he had known, or believed he knew. She was not one to overdo the "Oh my God!"s or overuse emojis – so girlish – and he flinched at the *We*, reluctant to be embraced by her new coupledom. He had contacted her immediately assuring her he was fine and about to leave, and she made him promise he would "check in" when he arrived home.

Pocketing his phone after the thread of messages, he found himself inexplicably angry. Clearly he had not forgiven her for the way she had left. He could feel his pulse racing. He glanced at his watch. Yulia was endlessly hugging and saying her goodbyes, her smile warm, her laugh easy. There was no time for this. He leant over and honked the horn.

'Sorry... sorry.' Yulia extricated herself.

Someone stowed Yulia's backpack in the rear, and she threw her day pack into the back seat and hopped in after it. The driver set off, avoiding a bitch lying in the road nursing a clutch of puppies, all disinclined, or unable, to move.

Ben remained wrapped in his own thoughts, moving from his irritation with Sarah to the horror of Rob's unresolved murder, and on to his report he needed to finish and file with Connor. Yulia chatted a little with the driver, then fell silent. Ben took up his camera and looked for interesting images to capture. Anything to distract himself from the images of Rob that kept invading his head. He had been jerking awake at night, sweating with horror, starting at the slightest noise, his imagination running riot. Returning to London would never be so welcome.

Yulia tapped him on the shoulder and he lowered his camera.

'Ben. What do you really think happened to Rob and Balan?'

'I've said as much as I want to these past days.'

'Not much. At least not to me.'

'I've said enough, to the police—'

'Police!'

'I want to put it behind me.'

At the sight of a family group hoeing a field he took up his camera, always keen to record ordinary life.

'What does it take, Ben?' Yulia spoke quietly.

'Huh?'

'Doesn't what happened change anything?'

'How? What happened to Rob was terrible. Unreal—'

'Oh, it was real. Very real!' Yulia's voice rose a tone.

'Maybe Rob was wrong about things being sweet with Balan—'

'You can even *think* it was Balan?'

Ben twisted around to face Yulia. 'We're done. There's nothing more we can do.'

'So that's it? That's all you have to say?' Yulia glared at him.

'What do you want me to say? We've got to leave things to the police.'

'That's not good enough.' Yulia's face screwed into a look he couldn't figure. She seemed to be grappling with something. 'The police… No. Not nearly enough!'

They had gone over and over things, so why Yulia was having a go at him now he had no idea. Ben turned away and took up his camera again. He wasn't in the mood for an argument.

'This isn't right,' Yulia said. 'It's all wrong. All of it.'

'I've told you. We're done here.'

'No!' Yulia's fists pummelled the back of his seat. Then she grabbed a fistful of his hair.

'Shit!' His hand reached to his head. 'Yulia! For God's sake. What's got into you?'

'I've just decided. You might be done, but I'm not… Stop, driver!' She repeated her command in Bahasa before continuing to berate Ben. 'I know you're stubborn, and cynical and so… so…' She threw up her hands, searching for the right word. 'But I didn't think you were a coward.'

'What?' Ben flinched. This woman who was always so polite was losing it, and he was bereft of words. What on earth did she expect of him? Again, she commanded the driver to stop. The vehicle drew to a halt and she leapt out, dragging her day pack after her. He was out of the car immediately.

'Yulia! What're you doing?'

'I can't leave. Something. Something – for Rob's sake! And Balan's. And Bai's. And, and, all of them!' She threw up her hands then went to the back of the vehicle and hauled out her big backpack.

Ben put a restraining hand on her arm. 'Yulia…'

Shrugging his arm away she grabbed the strap of his camera. 'You've got to see things, Ben. Really *want* to see things, with your own eyes, not through a lens.'

'What are you on about?'

'Don't turn away from what's before you. I was stupid. Didn't probe enough. I have to go back.'

'Yulia! What on earth can you hope to achieve? We've answered every question the police put to us, and all those bloody journalists—'

'Yes, I know.'

'So? What else?' he urged.

'People, Ben. People!'

She levered her heavy backpack on and slung her day pack over her chest. He watched her retreating back as she set off the way they had come, walking past an old woman stooped under a large bundle of firewood strapped to her back. Beyond in the paddy fields, people were hard at work. Ben frowned. What more could he do? Slowly he got back in the car and motioned for the driver to continue.

At the airstrip a small plane was waiting, and Rick and Ardhi were standing by their luggage.

Rick peered past him into the vehicle. 'Where the hell's Yulia?'

He jumped out, shoulders hunched, face set in a scowl. Yanking his backpack from the rear of the vehicle he flung it to the ground. 'She totally lost it. Went nuts. Started pounding me.' Hands on his hips he glared from Rick to Ardhi, who stared at him blankly.

'What happened? Did you do something?' Rick sounded wary.

'Course I bloody didn't do anything! She's decided she's not flying out. She's staying.'

'Why?' Ardhi asked.

Ben raised his shoulders. 'It's about Rob and Balan. Haven't the faintest idea what she wants to do. Nothing to do with me, though, well… Do *you* think I'm a coward?'

'Fletch, are you OK?'

He turned from the surprised men, cursed and kicked his backpack.

10

'THANK YOU.' YULIA ACCEPTED THE CHIPPED enamelled plate, inhaling the delicious aroma of rice and chicken. She had arrived back in the village without the slightest idea of what to do next, acting on her instincts that this was unfinished business. Soon she must get in touch with her work colleagues in Jakarta to explain she had been delayed. She wasn't sure what to tell them, what feasible excuse to give.

While eating her meal she again thanked the couple, expressing her gratitude for their offer of accommodation. She chatted, asking after their children, grandchildren, inconsequential things. Playing with her food she smiled at the old man and woman before casually asking, 'What do you think really happened to Balan and Rob?'

Yulia smiled encouragingly. The local couple averted their eyes and stopped eating. Yulia took a mouthful and chewed, waiting to make eye contact. The meal progressed in silence and she noted the glances the husband and wife shared. She made her meal stretch. Gradually the old couple opened up to her. She listened carefully, nodding and offering encouraging "umms" to keep them talking without interrupting, allowing pauses to settle as they ate before sharing something new.

Later, Yulia walked slowly towards the Shack, the interior illuminated by kerosene lamps, the night having closed in on another day. It would be lonely drinking by herself, and she didn't fancy joining the noisy group of out-of-town loggers thirstily downing beer after a hard day in the forest. They were rough-looking men, and she was beginning to regret her hot-headed behaviour. It was stupid not to have caught a flight out. It would take fresh organisation to arrange transport, and she didn't have much money. Perhaps she might hitch a lift on a logging truck? She eyed the logging men at a table, weighing them up, wondering if she dared request this. Ben was right: her work was done here. Back in Jakarta she could add more to her report for Ben, and she might be able to raise concerns about the police. Particularly Sartano. Oh, yes, most particularly that man. What had she been thinking, storming back?

As she approached the Shack her mouth went slack. A man sat alone at a table hunched over a beer.

'Ben?'

His head jerked up and he gave a tight smile before pushing back his chair and coming out to meet her. 'You weren't the only one to give the plane a miss.'

They stood facing each other, an awkwardness between them. Had he come back because of her? Following him back to his table, she mumbled a hasty, 'Sorry for what I said.'

Ben brushed her apology aside. 'I know you were upset.' He bought her a beer and they sat drinking, saying little. He hadn't yet asked what she hoped to achieve, and she was grateful for that, because, well, what could she say? But first she had to tell him, whispering, not wanting the loggers to hear.

'Ben. About Bai. Two of Sartano's cops raped her.'

He looked stunned. 'She's sure?'

'Ben!'

'Sorry…' His eyes silently asked, *Why?*

'To put pressure on Balan. To make him stop pestering the logging guys.'

A sound like air escaping from a tyre came from Ben's throat. 'Including AZTAR's enterprise?'

'Maybe?' Yulia wasn't exactly sure. Her conversation with Asung had been short and there was a lot she didn't understand.

'What more can you tell me?' Ben was all eyes, all ears, leaning forward ready to listen.

'Well, this morning, when the police were questioning—'

'Yulia!' She looked up to see Ule, keeping his distance, the old couple she was staying with hovering beyond. Ule turned and walked away, glancing over his shoulder, so she and Ben pushed back their chairs, left their unfinished drinks, and followed. The old couple disappeared, but at the edge of the village, near the vegetable plots, Njau and Asung emerged from the shadows.

Ben shifted from foot to foot, watching Yulia huddled close to the three villagers, hearing her "mmms" and occasional prompts and their agitated responses. What the hell were they saying? He scuffed the soft dark earth with the toe of his shoe, paced a few steps in one direction, then back again. Asung's head darted up as he brushed against a tall corn stalk, setting off an unexpected rustling noise. 'Sorry,' he whispered. Njau was gesticulating wildly with Ule hushing him.

Ben tapped Yulia's shoulder. 'Well?'

Yulia raised her hand to stop the flow of words and turned to him.

'In the past, guys have been hired to beat up some of their men. Keep them from asking questions. Now the police really want to get the message through. Really want to keep them in check.'

'Ah.' None of this surprised him.

Yulia turned back, listening carefully to Ule and Njau. She held up her hand again and switched to English.

'Where we found Balan and Rob... wasn't it somewhere within that concession AZTAR have rented?'

'Could be.' Ben frowned. 'These are massive areas, and I don't know... Why? Do they think so?'

'They reckon Balan came across guys scouting. Looking for new places to chop down trees before anyone notices, then when it's cleared, they'd go ahead and plant palm oil trees.'

Yes, the heavy gang waving documents they had paid a hefty price to have stamped and signed. He could just imagine it, and who was going to challenge them? Who would care if someone got hurt? Ben watched the village men talk animatedly, faces earnest, hands gesticulating, then Yulia continued.

'It's happened before, they say. The guys sent from Mr Zumran, or palm oil companies, waving fake permits saying they're allowed to clear fell. All the village men had been telling Balan he needed to stand up to the tree thieves and he was being too soft – so they think that's what happened. "A pity Balan didn't dart them with his poison",' Yulia translated for Ule. The village men had their theories. Balan's body had showed no signs of injury. They thought it probable his attackers had known enough about poison darts to use one against the headman. It looked like they'd tried to set him up.

'But how does Rob fit into this picture?' Ben asked.

'Their guess is that those guys wouldn't have a clue who Rob was. Didn't know he was famous. Probably thought he was a hippy no one would care about.'

'OK. It's plausible. I can buy that. But the police… Bai… This doesn't make sense.'

'Pressure. More and more pressure.'

Asung could not control her tears and reached for Yulia's hand, appealing, and Yulia's eyes filled as she explained.

'She says without Balan it is so hard… and it's their ancestral forest.'

Ben gazed at Asung, Ule and Njau: three people representing a community they were both desperate to see thrive, with the odds, and history, against them. He felt he might explode with the injustice of it. 'It's the same story across the world – thugs brought in to do the dirty work – and for sure Sartano and his goons will be top slicing profits from logging.'

A sound like a hiss escaped Yulia as she repeated Sartano's name.

'But Yulia, not from the concession we've reported on – even they wouldn't have the nerve for that – but the other, rented, concession… And the march of the damned oil palm plantations goes on and on. They'll probably get a top slice from those too.'

'My country is being destroyed in my own lifetime and I can't bear it.'

Ben felt for her, felt for all of them. Indonesia was a mess of flouted laws and backhanded bribes.

'Look, I know the brutal intimidation that tends to—'

'Not *tends to*; *is* happening. Right *here*.' Yulia stamped her foot.

'And don't I know it!' He didn't need reminders. 'Let me tell you something.' He swung her around to face him. 'A forester friend of mine found the price on his head was a hundred dollars. One hundred fucking dollars! And he's a Westerner. If his life was that cheap, what do you think the life of anyone in this community will be?' He gestured to the three villagers, who were watching them with no understanding of what this argument was about.

Yulia lowered her eyes.

'Yulia…' His voice was softer now. 'We have to be careful. It's inviting more trouble – on *them*. Is that what you want? Well?'

Somewhere dogs started barking, and he found himself alone with Yulia; the others had withdrawn, a slight rustling of crops indicating their trail. He shivered.

'I want to do something to help.' Yulia spoke slowly.

'I know. We both do. I'd like to see if there's light at the end of the tunnel with our forest project. Some grains of hope for the way forward. And you can best help back in Jakarta. Get a land rights lawyer on to this. That would be a start.'

Yulia nodded. 'Maybe. They trust us now we've come back. You know, not just dipping in for a professional visit then heading home. There's something they want to show us. Something they know is happening upriver, where Linda was investigating.'

He wanted to put a limit on things. He had come back, stung by Yulia's words, and he was pleased to hear the villagers were finally trusting them, willing to be honest. Now he could do a better job of reporting back on their true situation, but he didn't expect to stay long, didn't want to be sucked in deeper.

'Where Linda was has nothing to do with our project, not even anything to do with the abutting concession that's giving us grief.'

'I know. But, Ben, they think we should take a look.'

'Linda's already reported it.'

'They're asking for our help.' Yulia gripped his arm. 'Please.'

His instincts told him to leave, to rebook flights. This was well beyond his brief, beyond his experience and well outside his comfort zone. What could they hope to achieve?

Speeded-up satellite images came into his head, images from space showing how rapidly the earth's forests are disappearing, nibbled away day by day.

'Please,' she urged him again.

11

TREVOR WAS IN MAINLAND CHINA AT AN INDUSTRIAL town within easy reach of Zhangjiagang Port. After this he was heading to Jakarta. Then home. He longed to call out to his wife to put the kettle on. That would have to wait, but he would phone her when he was five minutes from his driveway. This was the ritual when arriving home each day or from a trip abroad. They both enjoyed that shared cuppa: Yorkshire tea, strong and milky, no sugar. 'Shaken not stirred, Miss Moneypenny,' he liked to say, and his wife would give him a saucy look. 'Just as you like it, Mr Arnott.' Innocent fun. Yes, he was a simple man, he supposed.

But first, Mr Li. He chuckled recalling that when he had first seen the man's name written in a furniture catalogue, he had assumed it would be pronounced *lie*. He'd learnt a lot since that first visit when he had grasped the Chinese man's hand saying, 'Pleased to meet you, Mr Lie,' and had been courteously corrected. He checked his watch. He was five minutes late and he had meant to be punctual. Every so often he arranged face-to-face meetings with his suppliers to keep relations sweet, but at the same time it was an opportunity to turn the screw. If one supplier wouldn't bring their price down, there were plenty of others he could go to. He would make that clear today.

The car Sung Woods had sent to pick him up barrelled along the highway and he tried not to think about how vulnerable he was sitting on the plastic-covered seat without a functioning seatbelt. He gripped the door handle trusting that fate would deliver him this time just as it had in the past. He was a valued customer after all.

It was Agus who had pointed Trevor here. When the Indonesian businessman learnt that he was looking for new suppliers, Agus had been quick to get the ball rolling. The Zumran family had connections everywhere throughout Asia, and particularly in China. Trevor was grateful for his advice, and even more grateful to be partnering Agus with their AZTAR initiative, allowing Trevor to get a foot in the door in Asia.

They turned into a road lined with timber yards and factories. A kilometre along, the car slowed at Sung Woods and swung into the compound, easily four acres, the lot stacked with machined timber stored in open warehouses. Through the car window Trevor watched workers unload timber from a kiln-dryer. Behind the factory door he heard a whir of machines, and at the front a pallet of wrapped timber flooring was being forklifted into a waiting truck.

The courtesy car drew up in front of the office.

'Mr Arnott. Please, come in.' Mr Li, a middle-aged Chinese man wearing a polyester business suit, ushered him into a small office reeking of cigarettes, an ashtray overflowing. Ugh! Smoking had been part of his youth until a girl he was keen on drew his attention to the lingering smell on his clothes and didn't fancy kissing his tobacco-tasting mouth. That was enough to make him see the errors of his ways. If you want to attract the best girls in town, you smarten up, give them what they want.

He resisted the temptation to dust the seat of the battered fake leather chair he was directed to, and accepted a small cup of green, or perhaps white, tea. Either way he despised it, but he would drink it all the same.

When Trevor had first visited, he had been relieved to find the sales manager's English was passable. It needed to be; the Chinese company did a lot of business with the outside world, and he had no intention of trying to learn Mandarin, or any other language. Life was too short.

Trevor got straight down to business. 'I thought you'd like to know our flooring lines are selling well, and indoor furniture's not doing too badly either.'

'Very good.' Mr Li beamed. 'Happy to supply more.'

'I hope so. If I increase our order, I'd expect a more competitive price.'

'You have good price, Mr Arnott. You a very special customer.'

'But let's see if you can sharpen your pencil a little.'

Mr Li looked confused.

Trevor rubbed the fingers and thumb of his right hand together and Mr Li smiled and nodded. The salesman told him of new sources of tropical timber opening in Africa. 'Congo. Lots of forest there. And Russia. Pine. Plenty... Plenty!' Mr Li rubbed his hands and Trevor nodded. Hadn't he read something recently about percentages of what was authorised to leave Siberia somehow jumping by multiples of ten by the time it was received at Chinese ports? Best not to enquire too closely. Mr Li began telling him about new finger-jointed products they were developing... At least Trevor thought so – Mr Li wasn't always easy to understand.

'Mr Zumran is well?' Mr Li asked.

'I hope so. I'll be meeting him in a few days actually.'

'Good. Good. Sung Woods is always grateful for his kind introduction... More tea?' Mr Li stood, bowing, ready to pour.

'Oh, no, no... Thank you, thank you.' Trevor's large-knuckled fingers covered the tiny porcelain cup. 'Let's look around the showroom.'

He always perused the catalogue Sung Woods posted twice a year, but he liked to see and touch the products, use his judgement about quality – or not – and what might sell back home. Others might not appreciate it, but there was an art to this.

'Please. This way,' Mr Li said.

As Mr Li guided him through the showroom Trevor was mulling over what tack he might take to get the salesman to cut him a better deal.

Simone stood next to her Indonesian counterpart, the minister for trade, a man in his forties wearing a traditional Indonesian *blangkon* and a high-collared shirt under a formal jacket. The trade talks in Jakarta had gone smoothly, Simone reflected. In fact, the entire visit had been without incident, and now their hosts had arranged this outdoor cultural display to wind things up; TV cameras and press photographers captured the carefully orchestrated ceremony. Teenage girls performing a traditional dance were quite something: stately and controlled, elbows elegantly jutted, wrists perfectly angled, heads tilted, faces serene. They looked beautiful in their carefully arranged batik sarongs with long golden silky scarves draped over one shoulder which they gracefully flicked and manipulated as the

Gamelan orchestra played and sang. The message was one of continuity. Tradition.

At a gust of wind, she patted her carefully coiffed hair back into place and folded her hands on her thighs, the manicured magenta nails contrasting with her outfit. She had chosen a tailored linen dress designed by an up-and-coming UK fashion house, the mint green – a *light* minty colour – complementing her dark complexion. Earlier, when she was already in an official car on her way to this function, someone had mentioned in an off-hand way, 'I thought that green was reserved for the Prophet Mohammed,' and had looked at her sideways. Simone had gone ballistic – not at the messenger – but had snatched up her phone and railed at her new advisor back in London. Her *ex*-advisor. It was advice like this she paid the blasted woman for. She glanced down. In a certain light the colour was almost duck egg blue. No one could take offence. No one *had* taken offence, to her knowledge, but then these Javanese politicians were the politest people you would ever hope to meet.

Glancing at the Indonesian dancers, she thought her own appearance gave them a run for their money. They all veiled whatever insecurities they were feeling, or bad day moments they were experiencing, with perfectly composed faces and costumes, worn like upholstery. She identified with that. Hadn't she been doing the same for years?

Her grandparents had been of the Windrush generation – but she considered herself nothing other than British, a Londoner, a girl from Peckham. After a management degree she had set her sights on industry, only later thinking of politics. She hadn't been tempted to stand for the local council, but instead weighed up her chances of election to Parliament. Her first results were dismal, but second time she turned the left-voting constituency her way. She learnt the importance of clear, simple messages; studied how to project the winning image. She was local, a girl from an estate, understood her patch, knew the multiple problems. Her brother had been stabbed, a victim of local gangs. Her family's history had toughened them – or more precisely, toughened her. She rode the tide of dissatisfaction and beat her white liberal opponent with a slim majority. Now here she was, representing Her Majesty's government. A smile played around Simone's lips. With any luck her parents would watch the news. And her husband surely would, possibly with their older children, or he might record it "for the album", as he liked to say.

Towards the back of the UK trade delegation Connor stood with other government officials and representatives from British industry, Trevor Arnott among them. Connor would not normally accompany a minister on such a trip, but Simone had been feeling edgy and a little isolated after her special advisor had quit – the one before the advisor who had just been sacked.

'You had best come with me,' she had told him. 'Brief me on the Indonesian forest PPI. It's got far too newsworthy for my liking – all for the wrong reasons.'

'Yes, Minister.' He had dipped his head, thinking he had too much to do in the office with the trade summit just around the corner. But there you go, his job was to support her, and she was right, this PPI was something he had advised on. At home, seeing him packing his bag, Tess had raised her eyebrows.

'Again? Another junket at tax-payers' expense.'

'If you only knew how wrong you are,' he had countered.

He shared some workplace gossip with Tess, that was natural, but even at home, even post-coital, when such talk is supposedly shared between man and wife, he never bad-mouthed Simone. If his true feelings were to be leaked – he imagined Tess and her friends chattering at après-yoga cocktails – that would be curtains for his career.

'So, Connor,' Trevor edged towards him. 'Going well, don't you think?'

The businessman loosened his tie and mopped his brow.

'Yes, for sure, and Simone's happy.'

'She should be! That lady's presided over a string of failures – car industries pulling out of South Wales and the North East. She needs something to cheer her up, bless her. The PM's given her more chances than she deserves.'

'Don't be patronising. He rates her highly.'

Trevor guffawed. 'Right sex; right colour; three kiddies back home.' He looked directly at Connor. 'What's she like to work for?'

Connor smiled noncommittally. He glanced further along the road where a group of protesters were being kept far away by armed police wearing helmets and carrying shields. He could just make out banners written in English advocating human rights and environmental issues. Their shouted protests were too distant to be caught by the TV cameras focusing on the official ceremony, though he spotted one freelance cameraman jogging towards them.

Connor turned back to Trevor. 'You staying on?'

'A few face-to-faces. I like to do that every so often. Just been in China. Touching base with my manufacturer there who do our regular lines.' Trevor glanced as his watch. 'I'm meeting with Agus Zumran soon. He's in Jakarta at the moment.'

'Are you both heading out to the project? The forest?'

'No, no, neither of us has time for that – we've others doing the leg work. This will be more about the big picture, how we can expand. He's got some ideas he wants to share.'

'You're keeping your eye on the ball, right?'

Connor knew a thing or two about the Zumrans. The only reason the PPI project had his backing was because no other members of the clan were dipping their sticky fingers in. Agus's profile was clean as a whistle. Too good to be true? He sucked his teeth, suddenly concerned, and looked directly at Trevor. 'Right?'

'Yes, yes. Don't worry, everything's going well out there. You might like to know I'm flying out tomorrow to swing by the furniture factory in Samarinda to check on our Green Line.'

'Great stuff.' Connor was relieved.

'You know…' Connor hesitated, then said what was on his mind. 'I was a little sceptical about this PPI business. Things are often more complex than you business people expect. Not so much a straight line of rules to follow as a mesh that can get tangled.'

'No way! You set up the right systems, and they'll work. I'm confident Agus has it sorted out at this end. Your man Ben will see that.'

'Pleased to hear it. None of us can afford cock-ups and this is shaping up very well to form a show piece for the summit – along with everything else we're achieving here. Simone's happy, so I'm happy.'

'Good.' Trevor slapped him on the back. 'Strange as it may seem, I hate travelling, particularly in Asia. Chaotic, and they do things differently. Food, for instance.' Connor followed Trevor's gaze towards a far-off street vendor doing a brisk trade. Trevor pulled a face. 'Don't trust it. Never know where the food's come from, or if they're washing their hands.'

'Really? It bothers you?' Connor was surprised. So far, touch wood, he had never succumbed to illness when travelling. Trevor was missing a trick spurning the delights of local cuisine. The man's outlook was limited.

Trevor was still gazing at the street vendor. 'I'll be back home on Friday: steak and chips night. You can't beat it!'

Connor glanced at the satisfied businessman but said nothing.

Connor matched Simone's stride, departmental colleagues trailing in their wake, as his boss headed towards the VIP lounge at Jakarta's Soekarno-Hatta airport. Once Simone had settled into a chair in the blessedly cool room, Connor flipped open his phone to check on UK news websites. The BBC was on the ball and had posted a video of a smiling Simone shaking hands with her Indonesian counterpart, the Gamelan and dance display in the background. The visuals looked good, and the headline "NEW TRADE AGREEMENT WITH INDONESIA" was followed by a few paragraphs of reportage which he skim-read. He checked out *The Guardian* and *Times* before smiling at Simone and holding up his phone for her to see.

'Good coverage for a change. It seems your messages are getting through.'

'Thank the Lord. No mention of that rock star's death?' Simone slumped back in the seat, fanning her face, accepting a glass of chilled water from an aide.

'There is, but different news coverage. It's got the Indonesian government on the back foot and the Australians are piling on pressure to get answers. Nasty way to go, poor guy: going in search of songs and ending up in a wooden box. Thing is, Minister, no one in the media is stringing the two stories together. It's seen as a coincidence – happening in the same patch of forest.'

'That's a relief.' Simone began to heel one of her shoes off then caught herself. 'I know that project is a small matter considering what else was on the table, but the PPIs are the prime minister's baby. It's crucial the report, *my* report, is positive, and demonstrates successful business partnerships. That's what the whole initiative is about after all.'

'I'm sure it'll be going well. However...' Connor sucked his teeth, but she needed to know. 'There might be a slight delay getting the report to you. Ben's withholding it. Hasn't said why.'

Simone sat up. 'I'd expected to read your brief on the flight. I need to provide an update when I'm back.'

'I know... Sorry, Minister.'

'Push him along. You know our schedule.'

'I've been trying to get hold of him these past days. One of my staff checked with the airline he was booked on. Apparently he cancelled.'

'Well, where is he?'

'We're working on it, Minister. Can't say *exactly*.' He waved a hand, indicating the back of beyond. 'But you know phone and internet connections can be a little unreliable out there.'

That sounded feeble, even to his own ears, given how well practised he was at smooth responses with just the hint of lilt in his voice, thanks to all those summer holidays visiting grandparents in Ireland.

Simone's laser glare could have cut granite.

12

THE BOAT WAS MAKING PROGRESS AGAINST THE sluggish flow of the river, outboard motor throbbing, bow creating a wake through the brown water. On one side dense forest pressed in. At intervals on the other bank, upright logs with notched steps rested against muddy slopes leading to wooden dwellings.

Yulia sat next to Ben, almost identically clad, she noticed, in beige sunhats, cotton trousers and shirts, and canvas-sided boots. At the stern Njau steered; Ule squatted at the bow smoking a cigarette, every so often indicating submerged rocks to avoid. They wore what they always wore: shorts, T-shirts, sun caps and flip-flops – no fancy jungle gear for them.

They had set off in the pre-dawn murky light along the tributary bounding the village. Now the sky was piercing blue, and they were on a wide river journeying deeper into the interior. She was confident it looked like a leisurely tourist outing. Ule raised his hand in greeting to passengers in boats travelling downriver, and they passed fishermen in dugout canoes in quieter spots away from midstream.

'Sorry?' She realised Ule was talking to her.

'Njau and I were the best at fishing. We'd always bring the most home.'

'You grew up together?'

'Known that bastard all my life.' Ule laughed, gesturing to his friend. 'Hey!' Njau met his eyes. 'You've been pestering me since you could walk. Right?' Njau waved a hand dismissively. 'Then he pestered my sister too. She married him, so now we're related.' Njau grinned.

'How far have you travelled from home?'

Ule named a town she didn't know; it can't have been very big. 'A shit hole,' he called it and laughed.

These men belonged here: belonged to a world that was rapidly changing, and it was her dearest wish to help them retain their way of life.

She turned to Ben. 'They're like highways, aren't they, these rivers?'

'The rivers are arteries. The forests are lungs.'

'The lungs of the world.' She pressed her lips together, thinking of all the harm forest destruction was causing. 'You know, last year a friend of mine who has really bad asthma had to stay home, the air was so bad from the fires. And we were far away in Jakarta.'

'I was reading the other day that the World Health Organization is linking deforestation to the spread of coronaviruses.'

'Really?' She frowned and was silent. Was there no end to the damage?

Now they were deeper into the interior there were fewer crafts on the river. Ben felt the boat swing and noticed they were turning off the main river into another tributary, where trees pressed in close. The village men had swapped places; Njau now squatted at the bow and Ule steered.

'How much further?' he asked Yulia, and Ule, guessing his question, gestured forward. Still some way to go obviously, so Yulia rummaged in her bag for a book and he took up his binoculars again. The birds were magnificent when he could spot them.

A while later he glanced at her book, which was in English.

'What're you reading?'

Yulia held it up for him. 'A romantic thing – an easy read – to practise my English.'

'I never got beyond one language.'

'I like languages. My mother's family is Javanese with some Dutch on one side, and my father's family is Cantonese.' Using a business card as a marker, Yulia closed her book, the smile on her face inviting him to talk. 'And your family?'

Ben shrugged. 'Nothing interesting. English for generations, as far as I know.'

'Parents alive?'

'Yup. Old hippies. Used to campaign about nuclear disarmament in the past, now it's keeping public footpaths open, that sort of thing. Mind you, recent politics is getting them hot under the collar and they've taken to joining demos, making placards—'

'How wonderful!' Yulia clapped her hands.

'Embarrassing for a kid.'

'Brothers? Sisters?' Yulia pressed.

'Two older brothers—'

'Ah!' Yulia laughed. 'Third sons have it tough, don't they? That's what fairy tales say.'

'I don't know.'

But he did know really. As a third son he had a sense of not being up to scratch with his older brothers, who were always ahead of him: bigger, stronger and knowing more about, well, everything. One was a scholar, and the other had been captain of the first fifteen at school. He fell short on both the academic and sporting front. 'A plodder,' one of his teachers had said to his mother at a parent-teacher evening, not meaning to be unkind, but when his mother repeated the words back home his brothers' teasing was ruthless. He had plodded through his first degree, economics, before surprising everyone by announcing he was going to undertake research at the Oxford Forestry Institute, which led to his doctorate. Both parents and brothers had been impressed by that. He and his brothers got on well enough these days, though Ben didn't see much of his family. Irregular phone calls were bolstered by an inevitable seasonal gathering, though in recent years Christmases had been divided between his family and Sarah's. He grimaced, imagining years of Christmases in Gloucester stretching before him.

Ahead a flock of hornbills rose raucously into the air, splaying black wing feathers and flashing coloured beaks against the brilliant blue of the sky. Ule shouted a warning, and swerved to the left bank and cut the engine. He ducked as overhanging branches threatened to tear his shirt. Njau clambered out, hurrying Ben and Yulia along. Ben clawed his way up the slippery bank, reaching back for Yulia's hand as the two local men hacked at branches, tossing them over the boat. It was barely camouflaged but would have to do.

He could hear it now: a low rumble of an approaching engine. Rounding a bend, the blue bow of a tugboat came into view. Standing on the tug were a couple of armed police officers. Yulia's fingernails dug into his arm. Did she recognise these men? He was about to ask when a barge piled with logs followed, as of course he had known it would. Instinctively he drew back, allowing foliage to shield him, and raised his binoculars. Linked to the first barge was another stacked high with logs. And another. And another. Lowering his binoculars, he lifted his camera and began videoing and taking photos of the massive raft. The letter Z was painted on the butt end of each log, but other than that there was no identifying tag.

'Wow.' The word escaped his mouth, almost a sigh, almost in awe. It was like a freight train chugging along its waterway rails. On and on. This constant assault on precious natural resources was too much; his heart tugged with the hurt of it all. He didn't take Linda's line, but he sometimes doubted his own way, working through government channels, was enough. He lowered his camera, and spoke softly: 'Where the hell's this going to?'

Yulia whispered, 'It's a protected area: orangutan habitat.'

'They'll have stamped documents for sure, but which timber mill would take this?'

The final raft rounded the bend carrying a frontend log loader, the bold logo of AZTAR clearly visible.

'And what's AZTAR's machinery doing up here?' His voice was barely audible. 'This is way beyond their bloody rented concession.'

He zoomed in and clicked and clicked. Through the camera's lens he spied another officer keeping guard, a semi-automatic rifle held across his chest. Yulia nudged him. Ben had recognised him too – the one with the cool shades Linda had goaded.

The chug of the tugboat diminished as the wash of disturbed water settled at the river's edge. He saw the urgency on Ule's face as he conferred with Njau before whispering to Yulia, then their guides hurried them into the boat.

'Not far to go,' Yulia told him.

Ule and Njau propelled the craft onwards, not daring to risk the motor, the only sounds dipping paddles, cricket chirrups and bird calls. Egrets fished in the shallows and Ben saw a flash of coloured wings as a kingfisher skimmed the surface. It looked idyllic...

The water had become brown and muddy where bare earth slipways had eroded the soil and tree cover close to the river had been thinned. By one slipway stacks of logs awaited transport. It triggered a memory.

'Linda got this far. I've seen this log landing.'

In the distance a chainsaw whirled into action.

This was the point where Linda had wanted to explore further, the point where Rob had become afraid, the point where it made sense to turn back. He had evidence – all those stolen logs on the barge. Surely that was enough.

'Yulia. You want to go on? You sure?'

'Yes, yes, we must.'

Njau manoeuvred the boat to a side stream, then he stepped out carefully and beckoned them. Ule secured the boat, his face tense, and Ben understood he would wait there. Stepping on to dry land, still by the boat, he could call a halt, could say this was far enough. He could see the village men were nervous, and Yulia was scared. He could even admit he was afraid. But they had come so far, and he heard Linda's voice in his head, goading him, calling him Bambi.

He gestured forward. 'Let's go.' He hung his camera and binoculars around his neck.

Njau led the way through roughly hacked tracks. Yulia and Ben followed. Some minutes later Njau stopped, holding up a hand. In a small clearing ahead a makeshift logging camp had been established. Ben raised his camera and recorded the scene: tarpaulin-roofed open-sided huts with hammocks slung inside; tatty clothes slung across branches to dry; charred wood in the clay cooking fire with a windshield.

A nudge to his elbow drew him away. He and Yulia continued to follow their nervous guide. Njau drew to a halt and pointed upwards. High in the canopy Ben could just make out an adult orangutan's head peering over the edge of its nest.

'Oh.' Yulia expelled a breath. 'How precious.'

Quickly he focused his camera and grabbed a couple of shots before Njau's insistent whisper moved them on. The sound of a chainsaw was closer, then a new engine started up. Njau picked his way forward, Yulia almost walking in his footsteps and Ben right behind. Through the tree cover he saw a tractor moving. Njau tugged at Yulia's shirt and spoke softly. She turned to Ben. 'He says we must go back. It's too dangerous.'

'Not now. We can't now.'

He had committed to this thing, and it was foolish to turn back before he had gathered all the evidence they could.

Again, Yulia and Njau conferred.

Yulia whispered, 'He really doesn't want to. Shall I offer them more money?'

'OK... Whatever...'

Ben picked his way through the undergrowth and squatted, looking out at a narrow rough track with deep tyre treads imprinted on freshly cut earth. To one side was the stump of a large tree, top and branches discarded, its main trunk gone – possibly one of those rafted away. He edged forward for a better view. A logging skidder with the AZTAR logo dragged a large tree by means of a cable around the trunk. One more log to be stacked by the waiting piles at the river's edge. Did the Z painted on the butt end of logs relate to Agus Zumran? *Fucking Zumran and Trevor Arnott!* While he could allow for the inconvenience of AZTAR's renting of the adjoining concession to "his" project, and small-time chipping away at legalities here and there, he could not turn away from out-and-out illegal trade. Not on this scale. Not ever.

Ben froze, waiting for the skidder to pass, then motioned to Yulia. He set off, picking his way through the undergrowth keeping parallel to the skid trail, the chainsaws much louder now. Drawing behind a tree he motioned to Yulia to stay where she was. Njau hung back, jiggling from foot to foot, rapid hand signals beckoning him back. But he would never get such a chance again. He felt emboldened by his mission and held up a hand, mouthing, 'One minute.'

This had been pristine rainforest. Had been. Trees and plants allowed to seed, grow, mature, die. Animals allowed to be born, grow, die. Mycelium allowed to colonise. Just as arteries and veins conducted blood, and bronchi allowed air to reach deep into his own lungs, so these forests – these green lungs – relied on a network of underground tendrils to nourish and sustain them. He didn't fully understand the complexity of it all; this was not his field of expertise. But he had other expertise, and he was networked with governments. And he had a camera.

Hiding behind a tree he peered into the clearing at the gang at work. A man, Ben could not tell what ethnicity but he looked local, wielded a large chainsaw. Tree-cutting kit normally includes a safety helmet with a visor, Kevlar gloves and trousers and steel-capped boots; this man was wearing a ripped dirty T-shirt, shorts, old trainers and no protective eye shield. It wasn't just forests that were being exploited. People too. He allowed himself a slither of sympathy for these guys. They would be poorly paid, and should there be an accident, they might not make it out alive. Second only to active armed service, forestry recorded the highest number of casualties. He'd been surprised to learn that.

Chips flew up around the logger as he sawed deeper, cutting a wedge into the base of a massive straight-trunked tree. On the opposite side of the trunk a deep wedge had already been cut.

Ben turned his lens to two men sitting on a log, rifles propped by their sides, a smaller chainsaw at their feet. Two other men, both in faded old shorts and flip-flops, completed the gang. Five, he counted. To the edge of the clearing a pile of trimmed roundwood logs waited for the skidder to return. He lowered his camera and realised his hands were shaking. Taking a steadying breath, he blew slowly through his mouth.

A yell of warning as the chainsaw man retreated. The huge tree quivered, failing to maintain its balance. Wood strained and cracked then it toppled, crashing to the ground, bringing down smaller trees around it. The earth vibrated, and in the canopy birds reacted, taking to the wing. He edged forward, watching the loggers move to the fallen tree with machetes. A second chainsaw started up, beginning to crosscut the tree just below where the branches started. God, he hated to witness this. As a forestry consultant he was used to seeing trees felled, but when it was *managed*. Not like this. There was no respect here, just as there had been no respect for Bai from the men who had defiled her. Here nature was being defiled. He clicked and clicked. He would get every bit of evidence he could.

From her hiding place Yulia watched a lean-faced logger casually circling the clearing, a rifle across his shoulder. She glanced at Ben, who was holding his camera to his eye. Had he noticed this one? She edged forward, then froze. The gunman stopped, put down his rifle and lowered his shorts. A stream of pee arced out. He glanced up sharply. Something had caught the man's eye. She squinted, following his gaze. What was it? She gasped; a glint of light reflected off Ben's camera.

Oh, she was regretting this! She was the one who had pushed for Ben to make this trip, not realising, not thinking clearly. What had she done? She was a bad woman. Perhaps the gunman hadn't spotted anything, perhaps it was OK. She relaxed a little. Perhaps...

The gunman shouted, his voice drowned by the chainsaws, then he snatched up his rifle.

She filled her lungs. 'Ben!'

13

'Ben!'

Ben jerked back, loosening his grip on his camera, which dangled and thumped against his chest. Instantly he saw the gunman. His eyes swivelled to see Yulia's retreating back, and Njau just visible beyond her, weaving in and out of tree cover. This was the direction he needed to go.

Creepers and coiling vines twisted in front of him, so unlike the broadleaf forests of Europe. This was jungle. Stumbling through the undergrowth he willed his legs to pump faster, reminded of ghastly school cross-country runs when it always seemed to be raining and he was one of the last in the race. 'Go!' he willed himself on.

A shot cracked through the air and Yulia screamed. Ben flinched, waiting for the pain. Nothing… yet. He had heard of adrenaline kicking in, making badly injured people initially unaware. His heart thudded. Was it Yulia? Had he fired at her? His anxious eyes raked her back as she ran on, unharmed. Only the gunman's furious voice had reached them, not his bullet.

The chainsaws had fallen silent. The rest of the gang would join the chase now.

The only word that formed in his head was, *Fuck!* Nothing about this made sense. He lifted his feet higher over fallen branches and dodged twisting creepers, hoping the mass of trees would shield them from more bullets.

Not knowing what was happening behind him was unbearable; his imagination played havoc. Was the gunman aiming his rifle again? Ben glanced back to see that the gunman had momentarily snagged a flip-flop. *There is a god!* He stumbled on before risking another glance. The gunman was running, clutching his rifle, yelling and yelling. In the distance Ben could hear the loggers yelling back.

Ben pounded on, keeping Yulia in sight.

It was a battle to suck in enough air to fill his lungs, to pump his heart, to drive his legs. 'Uhh!' He was jerked backwards, his neck whiplashed. Damned straps had snagged. Stupid to carry his binocs and camera around his neck. Should he leave them? No, no, too valuable and his Nikon held evidence. His fingers fumbled. It was taking ages. Suddenly free, he set off again.

Another shot cracked the air and he stumbled. 'Fuck!' As if in slow motion he felt the tip of his right boot snag in a tangle of roots; saw his arms outstretched; felt his trapped foot slip deeper within the clasp of strong roots and his ankle twist. He landed heavily.

Pulling himself free, he jumped to his feet. Jagged pain shot through his ankle and he could only stagger. His brain went into overdrive imagining what lay ahead. Yulia had seen him and was coming back. Shit. He didn't want her getting caught but didn't want to be left either. He saw Njau hesitate before dashing away. For fuck's sake! Was he leaving Yulia and him to the gang? Glancing back, he saw the gunman was in easy range, and the others wouldn't be far behind. They were stuffed.

Ben raised his arms as the gunman cautiously advanced.

'*Jangan tembak!* Don't shoot,' Yulia pleaded.

The man edged forward, speaking rapidly.

'What's he saying…' Ben's eyes swivelled from the man to Yulia.

'Government business… *Kami menjalankan bisnis Pemerintah,'* Yulia appealed.

The gunman spat contemptuously and yelled back to his colleagues. He looked Ben in the eye and casually raised his rifle. Ben froze, his eye on the barrel aiming at his chest where he imagined his thudding heart made an easy target. Then the gunman swung the barrel to point at Yulia, and back to Ben. He was toying with them.

Behind the gunman Ben caught sight of another figure and his heart sank. The others had arrived! No. No, it was Njau hiding behind a tree, Njau who had circled back clutching a stout stick in his hand.

'Take it easy… I can't go anywhere. See? See?' Ben groaned and limped dramatically: a mother bird pretending to be injured, limping, drawing a fox away from her nest of hatchings.

Njau was an experienced hunter. Out of the corner of his eye Ben watched him place his feet delicately, like a dancer. *Hurry, Njau, hurry.* Ben's eyes locked on the gunman's, who was levelling his rifle at Yulia again. 'Don't shoot!'

Hurry, Njau!

Just as the gunman's cheek snuggled closer to the stock and his trigger finger looked like it would squeeze any moment, Njau made a sound in his throat. The gunman turned, grinning, assuming his mates had arrived, was opening his mouth to say something.

Njau's makeshift club caught the side of his head with a resounding crack.

'Ooph.' The man spun around, arms flung wide, and dropped to the ground.

Njau snatched up the rifle and ran, Yulia on his heels.

When Njau twisted around to urge him to be quicker the fear on the guide's face was obvious. Njau would be regretting his decision to lead them here, now more than ever. Yulia had told him that Njau and Ule had argued deep into the night. The money helped, but it was Asung's insistence that some men from the village had to help the outsiders, show them what was really going on, that convinced them.

They hadn't been keen on Yulia coming. 'No place for a woman,' they'd said, but of course she had insisted.

Hurrying as fast as he could, a fresh anxiety filled Ben Because he and Yulia had been spotted they could easily be identified and traced to the work they had been doing monitoring AZTAR's project. There would be no question where the guides had come from. Might there be retribution?

'Please hurry,' Yulia urged.

Ben glanced back, fearful he might see men darting between trees, but no, only their voices carried.

Nearing the boat, Njau dared raise his voice: 'Ule!'

The outboard motor whirred into action.

Ben dived headlong into the boat, dragging Yulia with him. Njau leaped in as Ule set off at full throttle. Raising his head Ben saw two loggers had reached the river's edge, both with machetes dangling from hands, then a third and fourth man emerged from trees. One raised a rifle.

'Watch out!' Ben pulled Yulia down.

A crack of a rifle shot reverberated. He flinched and glanced at the others: Ule hunched over the tiller, steering his course; Njau faced back, feet wedged, raising a rifle; Yulia lay towards the bow, face on the floor, his arm around her. He shared a look of relief with her.

'It's going to be OK. We'll be—'

A second shot rang out, and moments later Ule's piercing scream filled the air. His hands flew away from the tiller and the boat veered towards the bank. His body twisted, and Ben saw a bloom of scarlet spread across the back of his shirt.

Ben caught the rifle Njau tossed him and the village man grabbed the tiller and pushed it hard to swing them around. With his free hand Ben gripped the gunwale as the craft tilted crazily, threatening to spill them out.

Yulia was scrambling back, hurling herself to support the slumped helmsman, her voice shrill: 'Ule. Ule!'

Crouching low, Ben tentatively drew the rifle to his shoulder. He lined up the figures on the bank. His index finger hooked around the trigger. Those figures – those flesh and blood men – were getting further and further away. His brain would not give his finger the command to squeeze. He laid the rifle down. He had no idea what Njau, Ule and Yulia were yelling, but right now words didn't matter.

Ben ripped off his shirt, bunched it into a ball and pressed it onto Ule's back, where blood seeped in a steady stream from under his right shoulder. Ule was juddering, his body going into shock. It had been traumatic helping to carry Balan and Rob's bodies out of the forest and back to the jeeps, but those men were dead; Ule was alive and must be saved. With shaking hands, Ben pressed down firmly over the wound.

He glanced back at the loggers, now a blur of tiny figures at the river edge.

Njau steered the boat around a bend and Ben expelled a breath. He had escaped with his life, but an innocent man was clinging to his own. He gazed with compassion at Ule. He imagined the hard metal resting snugly in soft lung tissue, imagined airways flooding with blood. He looked into Ule's frightened eyes, placed his hand on his cheek and tried to reassure him with a smile.

They had reached the main river now, and Ben was counting the hours, willing them to make haste. Yulia was at the tiller, maintaining a brisk pace, her face set. She had not spoken for some time, and had ignored his offer to take over from her. Did she blame him for what had happened?

Ule lay on his side, his head cradled in Njau's lap. Njau used his own balled-up T-shirt, drenched a deep scarlet, to staunch the flow of blood, all the while talking softly to his badly injured friend. All Ben had to offer were off-the-shelf painkillers from his first-aid kit, but trying to get a few of those pills down Ule's throat had only added to his distress and he doubted they would do a damn thing. And the neatly folded scrap of clean bandage in his kit had been pathetically inadequate. Everything, including the three of them, was inadequate, he most of all. He loosened the laces on his right boot to ease the pain in his swelling ankle. Gingerly he lifted the rifle, doubting he would use the thing even if some fresh danger awaited them. He tried his phone, but still had no signal. In any case it would be hours before any medic could reach them. He was out of his depth, utterly and completely.

Small bubbles of blood dribbled from the corners of Ule's mouth as he struggled to breathe. Ben breathed deeply, as if to compensate for Ule's inability to do so. He caught Njau's accusing stare. *Yes, I don't blame you. You're entitled to hate me, and right now I hate myself. Couldn't run, couldn't shoot. Damned useless!*

Death of someone you love. How terrible this is. Yulia watched as Ule tried, yet failed, to suck in air, watched as he died cradled in Njau's arms. She steered the boat onward, refusing to give up the tiller to Ben. She wanted something practical to do and steering was the easiest thing right now. If she were a magician, she would turn back time, would not urge Ben to make this trip, would not agree to Ule and Njau guiding them. Foolish! So pointless! So selfish!

It was getting dark and they would need to camp overnight. Yulia drew the boat to the river edge, and with difficulty, they lifted the dead man ashore. This was unbearable. Tears streamed down her face as she watched Njau kneel and rock back and forth, keening his goodbye to his childhood friend, his brother-in-law. She imagined Njau would be taking responsibility for Ule's children. She choked and gulped and reached out to squeeze Njau's shoulder. Njau brushed her hand away.

'As soon as we're back,' Njau said, 'you two go far away. No more trouble.'

'Leave him for a while.' Ben took her arm and, limping, led her away.

Yulia's heart thumped against her ribs. *This is all my fault.* It had to be said, so she summoned her courage and whispered: 'It's my fault.'

'Yulia, you're not to blame.'

'Ah, but I am—'

'Don't be silly—'

'Yes, yes, I am.' She pulled away. 'I dragged you into this—'

'No… well, yes—'

'…and now I've made it worse. I'm responsible for this wonderful man's death. A man I wanted to protect, and make life better for. Now look! Look! One more woman who'll be without a husband and children without their father.' Her clenched fists beat her chest, sobs racking her body, grief and guilt engulfing her.

'Stop! You couldn't know this would happen.' Ben gripped her wrists. She twisted away from his grasp. *It had to be said.*

'But I knew Sartano had to be involved and I wanted to nail that man!'

Ben looked confused, and why wouldn't he? She took deep, steadying breaths waiting for her sobs to ease, then wiped her cheeks and nose with the back of her arm.

'I grew up in Pontianak. Lots of Chinese immigrants there.'

'I don't understand...'

'My father...' Yulia turned away, annoyed to find she was nervously picking the skin on the back of her hand – something she had started to do as a child but hadn't done for many years. She clasped her hands together.

'Most of the killings happened before I was born, but it didn't stop. Not altogether.'

Yulia lowered her head, silent for a moment, grateful Ben didn't interrupt. 'I was four years old, and I was with my dad. He took my hand, shouting, "Run!" But I was too little. He picked me up. I can still feel his arms clutching me to his chest; I remember feeling his heart bumping through his shirt, and seeing the fear in his eyes. I remember everything...'

'What?' Ben wasn't keeping up. How could he? She continued steadily, letting her story unspool.

'He put me down and told me to run home. Fast. He pushed me away. But I didn't know the way. I saw them chase him – that man: Sartano and his thugs. Watched them catch him and crack his head, over and over...'

'Police chief Sartano?'

'He was a young man then. Just starting out. Maybe it was good for his career...'

'Yulia, you aren't making sense.'

'Sorry. Sorry.' Yulia tried again. 'Yes, Sartano was behind it. My father was Chinese. Good enough reason, and his real estate business was doing well... so my mum told me later.'

'Oh, Yulia.'

'Of course I care. Ule... Balan... Rob.' She took a breath. 'Of course I care about my work and everything to do with community rights! What happened to my father was what made me want to study anthropology. We have to preserve cultural diversity. It's my passion, it's what drives me. All the things we're putting in your report...' She flung her arms wide. 'Then when I found out about Bai...'

A fresh wave of sobs racked her, and again Ben waited. She coughed to dislodge a lump in her throat. It felt very real, this lump trying to stop her talking. But she had to tell Ben. 'Deep down I want to get him! That animal, Sartano.' She swung around to face Ben. 'I thought because you're from London – a government-backed project—'

'What!' Ben looked aghast. 'That it was OK to risk my life...' he gestured back to Njau, 'and the lives of people you're trying to help, all for some personal vendetta? Are you crazy?'

It was as if one of Balan's poison darts had pierced her heart. She dropped to the ground, wrapping her arms around herself, sobs rising from her belly, feeling that at any moment her heart might stop. She deserved to die and in her next life she would pay dearly for her mistakes.

'You're nuts. Fucking crazy.'

She shrank from Ben's condemnation. Through a blur of tears she could see him shaking his head, trying to make sense of what she had said; trying to put together the puzzle of why a woman he had believed to be rational could endanger them all. Her head dropped to her chest and she groaned.

'Look, Yulia.' Ben's voice was harsh. 'We know forestry can be as dirty as the arms trade. First Rob and Balan, now we've got to take Ule back to his wife. Well, I'm not about to risk my life again and I don't care what you think of me.'

She winced. Ben had been stung when she had called him a coward, but now he wouldn't care. Why should he? Perhaps she was crazy. Nuts. But that word sounded too funny to be serious and she deserved a harsher word. Unbalanced? Demented? She squeezed her eyes tight. This had turned into something beyond what any of them had imagined.

'I'm sorry… so sorry.' She rose to her feet and bowed her head.

'Shit, Yulia. I'm not the crusading type. I leave that to people like my parents… and Linda.'

'It's not you. I'm to blame.' Tears trickled down her face.

Ben ran his hand through his hair: an inadequate gesture of an inadequate man. One dead man and two distraught people. Yulia's revelation had shocked him, and he wondered if she was unhinged. How could anyone who was sane put others at risk for some personal vendetta? And was she telling the truth? This was a truly gruesome story. He had some idea of racial tensions in Indonesia, particularly between indigenous groups and the authorities who wanted some sort of bland homogenous blend, but he didn't know anything about the history of Chinese migrants.

He stared at the slender woman standing with her head bowed, arms hanging to her side. Tentatively he placed an arm around Yulia's shoulder. She did not shrug off his gesture of comfort. He allowed his hand to slide down her back and slowly began to stroke her as if she were a child, becoming aware of the sharp edges of her shoulder blades. Gradually he felt her muscles soften. He kept his hand on her back until she quietened, then his fingers explored the small bumps of her vertebrae at the nape of her neck, so slender, so vulnerable.

A stirring of compassion rose in him for this woman he had pushed aside, not wanting to engage on any level, work or friendship. No, she wouldn't make up a story like this.

'Come.' He led her back to where Njau sat by Ule.

Yulia knelt by Njau's side, placed her palms together and began what Ben supposed to be a Buddhist chant. He had no spiritual belief, let alone any god to acknowledge, but he bowed his head, closed his eyes and offered his own reflections on this departed life. What a waste, what a goddamn waste. Guilt at his own part in the guide's death sat heavily on his conscience. He helped arrange Ule's body, laying his cool arms to his side. Njau kissed his friend's forehead in farewell, then covered his face with a soft scarf before drawing the coarser tarp over his head. They bound his wrapped body with ropes and would keep watch through the night, then at first light they would set off.

He had been part of the procession which brought Balan's body home, and now here he was, about to carry a second murdered man back to be buried. He would steel himself to witness their grief – and their wrath. What would they think of him? Might they suppose he had brought some curse on them?

14

THE HOMECOMING WAS EVERY BIT AS BAD AS BEN HAD envisaged. Worse. The community was distraught all over again, and he took the brunt of their anger. He wouldn't allow Yulia to share the story about her father; that would have complicated matters and done nothing to further anyone's cause. Yulia agreed gratefully.

He could barely look Ule's wife in the face. This was what raw grief looked like, when a brain tried to absorb that a loved one was gone. Had they argued before Ule set off? What had she planned to cook for him tonight? All those small precious things that were to do with living… This was going through *his* mind, as she yelled and clawed at him. He could feel his face set hard, allowing her grief to bounce off him. Then her face crumpled and folded in on itself, and he watched helplessly as her tears flowed. It was a blessing he didn't understand what anyone was saying. Yulia translated some of it, but he suspected far worse insults and threats were being levelled at him and he didn't blame them.

After the outpouring of grief and incriminations he asked a simple question. 'What can I do?'

He and Yulia were with Asung, Njau and others, in the council room. He listened without comprehending to what Asung was saying, only understanding the passion in her eyes. Then Yulia translated.

'Don't stop,' Asung was urging. 'Don't let the lives of our men be wasted. Don't let us down. We want better lives for our children. If we don't stand up now, our community will be crushed; our spirit will be crushed. It's so hard...'

'Yulia, please tell Asung I will do my best not to let them down.'

'Oh, I've already told them we won't.'

'We?'

'Yes, we.' She crossed her arms. 'You'll have to put up with me a little longer.'

The feeling he had was of mild surprise, no more than that.

'Come.' She beckoned him and he followed her into the small office Mr Manapo had based himself in. She unrolled the forest map and weighed the corners down. His finger traced the boundaries of the forest concessions, their Positive Partnership Initiative abutting the concession rented by AZTAR. That much he knew.

'Look.' Yulia pointed to a small river creating a boundary between the rented concession and the protected forest area they had returned from. These areas were vast. While it had taken many hours to journey by boat, there were other possibilities. Yulia's finger traced the river.

'Not difficult for AZTAR to get heavy equipment across the river, right?'

'A barge would do it. Could haul it upriver to where it was needed.'

'Hello.' Mr Manapo's voice made them both jump back.

'Excuse us,' Ben said. 'We were just…'

Mr Manapo waved his apology away. 'They said you were in here. As soon as I heard I hurried back.'

The forester joined them at the table. He looked at them both then lowered his eyes. 'I'm so sorry, so ashamed.'

Ben shared a glance with Yulia and waited for him to continue.

'Over the years I have raised concerns with the regional government official – you met him. His answer is to leave. But I have a family. I love my work.'

Ben was embarrassed and angered by his fumbling excuse and at a loss to know how to respond. Mr Manapo saved him from the decision. He looked Ben directly in the eye.

'May I assist?'

'Truly? Yulia ventured, perhaps as unsure as he was whether the forester was to be trusted. But no, he felt he had the measure of this man. There was a hierarchy and Manapo understood his place.

'Thank you.' Ben kept his gaze on Mr Manapo. 'I'm not sure how you might help, but let's trace the river system.' He reached into his bag and retrieved his laptop. 'Let's see where that barge ends up.'

As Google Earth opened up and magically revealed the world, he zoomed in to the Malinau region, revealing a spiderweb of meandering riverlets and rivers. The small river within the protected area led to the Sesayap river which meandered through forest and farmland to reach a broad delta on the east coast.

'Those logs mightn't get that far,' Mr Manapo advised. 'There are sawmills en route, here and here.' He pointed.

'Well?' Ben looked at Yulia.

'Yes.' She nodded, her head snapping decisively.

'Please take care,' Mr Manapo cautioned.

Ben felt calm. There was an inevitability about the flow of things, taking him God knew where.

Simone had summoned Connor to her office and left him standing like a naughty schoolboy.

'What do I have to do? Hire a private detective to track him down? This is ridiculous, Connor. The man is on our pay, yet we are running after him. No more contracts for him after this. Understood?'

'Quite, Minister. We've spoken with one of Ben's team, the one in Vancouver. He's sure he can shed light on the matter. They're good friends.'

Simone looked relieved, but what Rick had actually said was, 'I haven't a clue. I've not been in touch since I flew out. And just so you know, I'd like his report filed as much as you do. I don't get paid till it's in.'

'Good,' Simone said. 'Let's see if he has more luck than you. Really, Connor, you are his point of contact. This is unacceptable, from Doctor Fletcher and from you.'

'I understand. Anything else, Minister?'

'The press. Our comms people are briefing me. The Australian media have descended, wanting any fresh angle they can get on Rob and any connections with our team. They want to get to the bottom of what happened to their pop idol. I had them doorstepping me the other day.'

Connor nodded. He had heard.

'So, if you've got any angle, *any*, then speak to comms.'

She waved him away and Connor ducked out. He was running out of excuses about dodgy internet and phone so had resorted to ensuring he had a full appointment schedule, making it tricky for Simone to skewer him.

The following morning, as he was leaving his house, Connor found himself doorstepped too.

'Mr Ahearn! From ABC, Australia.'

He was taken aback by a cameraman who trained his lens on him, and a female journalist thrusting out a microphone. And… was that someone from the BBC? This had never happened before. No one should want the views of a civil servant. What the hell was he supposed to know about bloody Rob Gilmore? He took one look at them and ducked back inside to gather his thoughts.

Tess was quick with a response. 'Darling, I'm lost here. Have I got a new job taking out cups of tea? It's one thing for you to bring *work* home, but this lot aren't welcome. I don't like this.'

And not only Tess. At his second attempt to leave for work, he spotted his opposite neighbour peering through the window as Connor tried, politely, to steer the journalists away.

'I'm sure we'll have an update for you later. You're welcome to check back with the minister's communications team. You've got their contact details? Good, good. They'll be delighted to help you. Good morning.' He hurried off, feeling the back of his neck sticking to his freshly laundered shirt.

His whole career was predicated on being faceless, blending into the background, quietly shaping government policy without anyone being any the wiser. His job was all about keeping the wheels of government well oiled. He was good at that and wanted to keep it that way. He had bigger fish to fry than this forest project in Indonesia. It was getting in the way.

Damn Ben, where the hell was the man? He was not responding. He would email him an even stronger message as soon as he was at his desk.

15

TARAKAN, IN NORTH KALIMANTAN, IS ON AN ISLAND at the heart of a maze of many such low-lying islands and inlets in the conjoining deltas of the broad Sesayap and Kayan rivers. The mid-size eastern seaport a hub for ferries and commercial shipping. To either side, the modern port facilities give way to old-style wooden wharves and pole huts, with salt-tolerant trees half submerged. A range of ship suppliers and chandlers line the quayside and a depot of stacked containers await collection or onward journeys. That day a bulk carrier with a South Korean flag and an Indonesian container ship lay offshore, while dozens of smaller craft – fishing boats, tourist boats and luxury yachts – were berthed, or cruised far from shore.

Ben and Yulia had spent the afternoon observing and checking things out. Friendly uniformed officials in a meticulously clean customs office looked equally meticulous, and from Yulia's casual conversation with the staff, Ben couldn't imagine them letting anything go by undetected.

That said, this was *exactly* the place where palms would be greased, where official export forms and government stamps and signatures would be arranged. But how would he know? Soon after dark they watched a car ferry depart, then they turned away from the seafront.

They found a restaurant – a place favoured by locals – and, yet again, Ben voiced the question: 'So how are they doing it? How are they getting those damned logs out? What aren't we seeing?'

'Could bribe the port authorities.' Yulia was pensive. 'Wouldn't be the first time.'

'Yes, but that would be a big ask considering only cut timber and finished products are allowed out these days. Everything's on the port authority's website: what vessels are here, what's expected in the coming days – it's all straight up.'

'But Sartano will have shipping connections, for sure.'

Ben agreed, but couldn't see where there might be a chink; yet this was the closest port, and the loaded barge could only make its way along the Sesayap river. There was no other route from where they had been in the interior.

They finished their meal and headed out.

'Let's walk. It's not far to the guest house,' Yulia said.

Cars and motorbikes streamed past on the busy street. Riders were helmeted here, Ben noted, men and women both, bright headscarves billowing from beneath some of the women's helmets.

'This way.' Yulia let him down a side street then tapped his arm to draw his attention to a seedy-looking karaoke bar with neon strip lights.

'This one?' Ben was surprised. Yulia had been telling him about Sartano's other business interests. She had mentioned real estate – but a karaoke bar? Two well-muscled bouncers guarded the entrance, and nearby among the parked cars and motorbikes he spotted a top-range Mercedes Benz, a minder leaning against the bonnet smoking a cigarette.

'Sartano sometimes comes here to let his hair down. Isn't that the expression? Anyway, it makes sense he's in town now we know the logs are heading from the interior.'

Ben stared. This was unexpected.

Yulia drew him away. 'You know, we should ask Linda for help. We're out of ideas.'

Ben snorted. 'Linda! She and I aren't best buddies.' He glanced again at the bar, then matched his steps with Yulia's, who was walking more quickly. The idea that Sartano was most likely in this joint fascinated him. If the man was so close…

'Why don't you go—?'

'Ben!' Yulia looked horrified. 'The idea of being anywhere near that man.'

'Sorry… of course.' *Thoughtless idiot!* 'Then how about if you stay here? I'll go in.'

'You can't! He'll see you! There won't be many Europeans there. What can you do? Who would you talk to? Stupid idea. Stupid!'

'Just thinking aloud.'

'We don't even know what we hope to find out. We can't just go and ask politely, "Excuse me, what have you done with all those trees you've stolen?"' She tugged him away and they said little until they reached their guest house.

'I'll go.' Yulia spoke softly. Ben looked at her face setting into the determined expression he had come to recognise: a crease between her eyes and her lips pressed together.

'You can't. You were right, it was a stupid idea, we haven't got a plan.'

'I've made up my mind. I can do it. But first I have to find a mall.'

'What?'

'Wait here.'

Ben allowed himself to be pushed through the guest house door, then Yulia set off without further explanation.

Later, hearing a knock at his bedroom door, he opened it to find a transformed Yulia. His eyes widened, barely recognising the woman wearing a short tight-fitting dress – a "sheath dress", she crossly told him – and strappy high-heeled shoes. And her face? He was startled. She had applied thick eye make-up and glossy red lipstick, and had managed some sort of updo hairstyle. Ben couldn't stop staring.

'You think I look OK?' Yulia bit her lip.

'Sure…Yes… Different.'

'Mmm.' Yulia frowned but seemed satisfied with his answer.

Despite her lacquered shell, she looked vulnerable. 'Yulia, you don't have to do this.' He reached out to stay her, but she shrugged him off and walked self-consciously down the corridor. 'See you later. Don't wait up.'

Yulia clutched her purse, took a steadying breath, greeted the security guys and walked into the nightclub. She had never set foot in such a place before. Lurid lights lit up a stage at the far end where a DJ played popular music, and the room was packed with dancers: Indonesian women – many of them surely prostitutes? – and men of different nationalities, surely off the ships? Self-consciously she tugged the hem of her dress and inched forward, her eyes darting left and right.

An arm slid around her waist, startling her. A sandy-haired man was leaning in, breath stinking of liquor. 'Dance?' He spoke the single word with a thick Eastern European accent. Yulia shook her head and shrank from his touch. 'C'mon!' He pressed her, and again she stood her ground, not offering any explanation. He looked annoyed, cursed in what sounded like Russian and moved away. She needed to be careful, not draw attention to herself. Why else would a single woman dressed as she was be here?

'Wait!' She darted forward. 'Sure!'

The sandy-haired man tugged her deeper into the sweaty mass of heaving dancers. She was relieved he didn't try to get close. Not yet. He wiggled his hips, eyeing her with what she supposed was his best sexy look. *Stupid man!* Feeling foolish she did her best to imitate the women dancers around her. Each time she swivelled or spun her body to present her rump to her partner her eyes raked the room, searching between the wildly gyrating bodies.

There! Yes, he was here! Her heart jumped. Sartano was at the bar.

A hand was on her elbow, the man leaning in just inches from her face.

'You wanna drink? A beer or something?'

'No. Let's dance.'

Yulia's body was getting sweatier by the minute. This would not do. The sandy-haired seaman was talking to her, speaking loudly above the music, making his intentions clear. 'Wanna good time. You give me a good time?'

'Sorry. Sorry...' *Why apologise?* She cringed and backed away. The man said something under his breath then went in search of fresh prey.

Yes, all of them in this room were either raptors or prey, and she was a raptor. She moved with purpose to the bar.

Sartano, looking relaxed and at ease out of uniform, was wearing a brightly patterned open-neck shirt with a sort of gaudy Hawaiian pattern. A woman sat to his right, her vivid pink nail extensions toying with the stem of her glass. Yulia glanced at her own hands. She hadn't thought to visit a nail bar and the nail polish she had hastily applied to fingernails and toenails looked like a five-year-old had done it. Insecurities piled up. She had no plan. What could she ask him, even if she got up the nerve to get close? She eyed two men, backs to the bar, keeping a sharp eye out, guarding the police chief.

Avoiding eye contact with anyone, she stood watching. Thinking.

With a fanfare the DJ announced: 'Hey everyone. Favourite time of the night – karaoke time!' This was met by a rousing cheer, and two giggling young women staggered to the microphone. They argued about what to sing, came to an agreement, and the DJ made the selection. The tipsy women launched into a popular song while the clubbers raucously sang along, following the lyrics displayed behind the two singers, who were having trouble keeping to their feet. Everyone was enjoying themselves, including the foreigners, who clapped and waved their arms above their heads.

Yulia sidled closer to the bar, her eyes glued on Sartano. In her head she rehearsed a chat-up line. Nearer now, she could reach out and touch the man responsible for murdering her father.

Memories flooded back – her small child's perspective, low to the ground looking up. The uniformed men had looked terrifying, and her father who had always seemed big was being battered and making sounds she had never heard from him before. He had yelled, 'Run!' but she had dared not leave him. Everything had been blurry through her tears. She had screamed, 'Ayah! Ayah!' as warm pee trickled down her thigh. She had worried for a moment that her mother would be cross with her for wetting her pants, but instinctively understood this new badness would overtake everything else. As it had. Her mother had never got over it.

Sartano's eyes were on her, she knew it without checking. Now. She must act now. Yulia inhaled sharply, a glued-on smile stuck to her teeth, as she forced her face into a shape resembling what was required. Casually he flicked a hand, brushing away one of his minders to make room at the bar stool on his left. Here she perched, forming a sandwich – Sartano their meat filling – with the talon-fingered woman, who eyed her warily. At a click of his fingers the hovering barman was instantly attentive.

'Take her order.' Sartano spoke casually, not even asking if she wanted something.

Yulia pointed to the cocktail the talon-fingered woman was drinking. 'That looks good.'

Sartano nodded then turned slightly away to speak to talon-woman. What was she supposed to do? Sit and wait for his attention? She drummed her fingers. When the cocktail glass was placed before her, grateful for something to occupy her, she took an incautious sip. The tequila-based concoction scoured her throat and she choked, spraying liquid on the bar.

That got Sartano's attention. He chuckled. 'Strong drink for strong ladies.' He peered closely at her. 'I've not seen you before.'

Through her burning throat, Yulia managed to whisper, 'I'm new, working at the mall. Clothes retail.' She fingered her dress and hoped he didn't ask more. 'And you? What do you do?' She smiled innocently. Sartano looked surprised. He turned to talon-fingered woman. 'What *do* I do, *Sayang*?'

Talon-woman leaned forward, her eyes meeting Yulia's. 'Big man. *My* big man.'

Sartano chuckled and cocked his head to Yulia. 'Maybe two lucky ladies tonight.'

Yulia bowed her head over her glass and risked another sip. Her heart pounded and she tried to still her trembling hands. Gripping the stem of her glass she pressed on. 'I had a sugar daddy in Jakarta. He looked after me. What makes you a big man?'

Sartano turned fully towards her and she sensed a slight reluctance to be drawn in.

'General! General Inspector! Hey, boss!' one of the tipsy women who had been singing screeched through the microphone.

Sartano looked at Yulia and grinned. 'There's your answer.'

'Oh!' Yulia's eyes went round in admiration. 'So many things to tell me about.'

'Come. Come, nice Mr Policeman. Sing. Sing.' The tipsy woman beckoned the police chief, and talon-woman jumped off her stool, coaxing him to his feet. He made a token protest as others took up the chant of, 'Sing! Sing!' Before allowing himself to be led away Sartano placed a hand on the back of her neck, squeezing slightly, saying, 'Talk later.' Her entire skin puckered in revulsion at his touch.

Sartano swaggered to the microphone and in a swirl of changing coloured lights launched into a sentimental song. She watched, fascinated yet repelled. A lounge lizard. A lizard. A reptile...

Yulia gagged and pushed her way through the sweaty thong of clubbers towards the door. She could not take this further. She had achieved nothing, worse than nothing, and spent money on clothes she could ill afford and would never wear again. Outside the club she yanked off her new shoes, tossed them away and ran.

Back at the guest house she pounded on Ben's door with the heel of her hand. Moments later he opened it, eagerly asking, 'How did it—' before taking in her dishevelled appearance and her make-up smudged by tears.

'Take it!' She thrust Linda's Fat Cats business card towards him.

'How about you come in and tell me…' He opened the door wide. She shook her head, unable to talk to him right now and waved Linda's card, insisting, 'Take it!'

Ben leaned against the doorframe, arms folded, not accepting it. 'Investigating the shadowy world of global corporations?'

'You need to make peace with her.' Yulia thrust the card out again. 'Have you got a better idea?'

Ben accepted the card without looking at it, and his eyes held hers. 'Never mind that right now. You're back early. Want to come in? Tell me how it went?' He stepped back, inviting her into his room.

She hesitated. Maybe it would be nice to talk, tell him what a shitty evening she had had, but instead she backed off. 'Didn't work out.'

'You sure?' Ben coaxed. 'We could go downstairs to the bar if you'd rather.'

She fisted her palms and turned away. 'I'll tell you tomorrow, over breakfast.'

As she unlocked her door she glanced back at Ben, still watching from across the corridor. She appealed: 'Contact Linda. Please.'

Once inside her room, she struggled out of the dress, stamping it under her feet, needing to get to the bathroom to shower and scrub the back of her neck. The imprint of that man's hand was almost tangible. She shuddered. *Some raptor! I couldn't pick a field mouse from the ground, never mind a snake in the grass.*

16

LINDA'S LIVING ROOM WAS A MESS. DUSTING SURFACES and vacuuming the threadbare carpet was getting progressively difficult with so much clutter. Even her own kids were reluctant to stay over these days, so she should do something about it. Eventually. She liked to pretend her arthritic knee meant housework was troublesome, but no one fell for that. Her computer desk was heaving under a pile of printouts, letters and things to be done. She was getting the hang of the state-of-the-art laptop her son had insisted she buy when he last visited.

'There's nothing wrong with the one I've got,' she had told him.

'Look at it, Mom.' He'd stared in disgust at her ten-year-old model. 'It's just taken ten minutes to reboot. Get a new one.'

'Nah. Too much money.'

'Don't be so tight. If you've got enough to gad around as you do, you've got enough money for an update. Shit, Mom, the damn internet keeps cutting out when we're talking.'

'It's the internet connection.'

'No, it's your computer. It's on the way out.'

Seeing her family on screen was great with this new high-definition camera – though, my Lord, didn't her neck look like a turkey's? – but mainly this new purchase allowed her to work more efficiently. Too often in the past she would storm off to get a coffee when the old beast crashed and she waited for the darned thing to reboot. Who had time for that?

Her shabby couch and ill-matching lounge chairs were stacked with books and documents. She bent to pick up a bound file that must have tumbled off with a pile of others. Ah! She'd just been wondering where to lay her hands on this one, as there was something she wanted to reference. Serendipity! She glanced at the others on the floor, deciding they could stay there for now.

Bookcases overflowed with academic publications: psychology, her field of interest, and Ted's anthropological ones. She couldn't bear to get rid of any of them, though more and more student resources were online and the world of academia was behind her. Ah, Ted. Her eyes were drawn to a volume he had contributed to. She would never part with that.

Storage boxes crammed with files were stacked against a wall and on the floor, cardboard boxes overflowed with Direct Action for the Earth T-shirts, sun caps and other paraphernalia. These obstacles all required she detour around them when walking between the kitchen and her computer desk. Long ago Fat Cats and Direct Action for the Earth had taken over her life, or rather she had poured herself into these roles: bottomless pits demanding more and more of her energies. In her opinion, every right-thinking person on the planet who had resources – time or money – should do the same. They were all going to hell in a handcart, the rate the environment was being trashed.

When Ben reached out to her with an email starting, *Yulia insists I contact you* – no *Dear Linda* – she knew he must have swallowed his pride to take this step and resisted the desire to send a catty return message. Reading on she found herself saying, 'Oh, boy... Oh, boy...' as he outlined where the two of them had been. Damn it. That was what she'd wanted to see for herself, before Rob had a hissy fit. Ben had evidence she wanted to get her hands on, so best keep on his good side. She sucked up his slight, told him to keep those photos safe, begged him to share them with her, then delved into the online corporate documents and company information he was after and got others in her network to do some digging. You never knew what fresh shit might emerge.

She leant back in her computer chair, spooning yoghurt from a small carton, the time on her laptop showing 20.11, her phone on loudspeaker. Internet messaging and phoning were a boon she had embraced years ago.

'So... T A Holdings is UK-registered. AZTAR was set up in Hong Kong—'

'Yeah, yeah, I know all that...' Ben's impatient voice cut in and Linda pulled a face.

'But Panama registered, as of last week...'

'Ah!'

'How about I tell ya they're expanding their Asian operation? Big time. Loads more places to get hold of trees in South East Asia if you have connections and deep pockets. But I guess you know that too. Vietnam, Papua—'

'OK... OK...' Ben's voice was placatory. 'Do you know anything about shipping? If Sartano has—'

'Nope. Not my area. Do your own digging.' The words were out of Linda's mouth before she considered them. What the hell did she know about shipping? Shipping wasn't a Fat

Cats specialty. Then she remembered those photos Ben had hold of and her tone turned conciliatory: 'So, what're you guys up to today?'

'Hiring a boat. Seeing what ships are heading in – if they square with the port authority's info. Unmilled timber can't be sent from the port – restrictions and so on – but those logs won't have disappeared. We're planning to head north then back up the main river, scout around the delta—'

'If you're going to snoop around, make sure you know what you're doing. How's Yulia, by the way?'

'Fine.'

Linda put down her yoghurt. 'Listen, Ben. You weren't responsible for Rob – I wish to God I'd gone with him – but as sure as hell I hold you responsible for Yulia. You could all have been killed up that river, not just that poor guy Ule. Remember, you and I get to leave, go back to our nice safe homes. Yulia doesn't. It's not just hit jobs on environmentalists in the Amazon Basin, Latin America or the Philippines—'

'Yeah, yeah! Don't preach.'

'And you remember the Indonesian activist who was poisoned? And what about Bruno Manser—'

'OK! Enough! I get you.'

Manser, the Swiss activist, had lived among the Penan in Sarawak for some years, rallying them against the loggers until the Malaysian government "allegedly" (she would make quotation signs with her fingers when telling the story) put a price on his head and he simply disappeared in the forest one day. Foul play or bad luck? The jury was out. Over the past decade well over a thousand environmental activists had been murdered. She knew that. And he knew that.

'You take care, then. And stay in touch.' She ended the call.

As he pocketed his phone Ben's body sagged. He was irritated by the American's hectoring but knew Linda was right about the risk to Yulia. He watched her coming out of a tourist boat hire office at the wharves, looking cheerful again after last night's aborted attempt to befriend Sartano. That had been a stupid idea and he shouldn't have agreed to it. And was what they were about to do a good idea? Should he – or she – be setting out on some cat-and-mouse mission?

'Well?' he asked.

'He's checking which skipper is free to take us out. He was kind of surprised we wanted it for a day and didn't want to go fishing.'

On cue, the boat hire man walked to the open office door, phone to his ear, and waved casually.

The small speedboat bounced through the swell, surging past the anchored container vessel, and headed north following the coast. On a bench seat behind the skipper, Ben sat next to Yulia, binoculars and camera at the ready. Earlier that morning he had agreed with Yulia this was the last roll of the dice. They would be flying out tomorrow to go their separate ways, she to Jakarta, he to London.

'I wanted to be a hawk eagle,' she said. 'You know them?'

'Remind me.'

'So colourful, kind of cute with tufty feathers on their head, but deadly. I tried to be one of those at the nightclub but instead I was a pitta bird. You know them?' He shook his head. 'Small. Also cute with lots of bright colours. Very pretty. More likely to be eaten by the eagle.' Yulia looked so serious and he resisted the temptation to smile.

On his phone map app they had followed the logical route from the forest waterway towards the coast, agreeing this had to be the only way out for that barge.

'Maybe they've been offloaded near this delta?' Yulia pointed to the map. 'Maybe there's a timber mill here.'

They researched and found a couple of possibilities: locations near the river to offload and transport to a yard.

'If they do that,' Ben considered, 'the milled timber could be given fake documents and sent through the port in the normal way.'

'Let's find out.' Yulia pushed aside her unfinished breakfast. 'Let's go.'

Against the background drone of the speedboat engine, he looked around him as Yulia leaned forward, conducting a raised-voice conversation in Bahasa with the skipper, a sinewy local man who, judging by his wrinkled skin and the stowed fishing tackle, had spent years at sea.

'Just telling me about his family and his work,' Yulia told him. 'And he's asking about us: what we're doing? Why aren't we fishing? Maybe he gets more money that way. I told him you are a vegetarian, interested in preserving nature, not eating it.'

'Smart!' He smiled.

The skipper was pointing, calling out. Flying fish broke the surface of the water. Ben grabbed his binoculars for a closer look, watching the flash of light on fins, before shifting the focus of his lens upwards to sea birds circling and diving.

It was good to be out on the clear blue sea, the mid-morning sun scorching the back of his arms, salt spray settling on his lips. Almost a real tourist. On the coastal side, brown water hugged the land, the monsoons and rivers having washed away thin soil from previously forested areas to make way for farms and plantations. They had spotted several fishing boats, and in the distance some sort of container vessel which must be one of those expected at Tarakan. The port authority website listed everything, day by day. Ben raised his binoculars for a view of the forested coast further north and focused on the vessel. It was lying off the coast… and its mobile crane… Was it in action? It was too far away, and from the bouncing speedboat he couldn't be sure.

'Yulia, tell the skipper to change course, further out to sea. I want a different angle.'

Soon Ben could make out the name, *Pacific Dawn*, with a clear view of the arms of its crane rising into the air. Clamped in its claws, a clutch of crosscut logs rose into sight from the far side of the vessel. He watched the harvested timber swing across before being lowered into the open hold. The crane driver dexterously positioned the logs before swinging the empty arm back out and reaching over the side again.

'Yulia…' The speedboat's position was revealing what lay the far side of the open-hold vessel: 'Our barge. Got to be the ones we saw. Not going to any sawmill. No port control. Straight out. Straight to Malaysia, I bet!'

He passed the binoculars to Yulia.

'Illegal, but efficient, heh?' The frustration in her voice was tinged with admiration.

'And if rules are expendable, so are people. Tell the skipper to get closer, but to be careful.' Ben took up his camera and steadied his arm.

Yulia was peering through the binoculars. She gasped, 'Guns! Look out.' She clutched at him, pulling him down, then screamed to the skipper, gesturing at him to turn the vessel. '*Mereka punya senjata! Cepat. Kembali!*'

The skipper ignored her and again Yulia yelled.

'What the hell're you doing?' Ben screamed at the skipper, who continued to steer towards the huge vessel with a fixed expression. Ben shook the man's shoulder. 'Hey!'

The man shrugged off his hand. 'Yulia, tell him to turn away!'

But instead Yulia threw herself at the skipper's back. She tugged at him and he jabbed his elbow, warding her off. The speedboat swerved and rocked. All Ben could hear was yelling in a language he didn't understand.

'Yulia! What's going on?'

'Says we're spying… should mind our own business.' She jumped on to the rear bench seat and it looked to Ben as if she intended to leap on the skipper's back. He made a grab for her just as the skipper spun the wheel and the boat tilted crazily. Ben had a fistful of her shirt in his hand as she stumbled, swayed, tried to retain her balance. The fabric of her shirt was stretching, slipping from his grasp.

With a cry she pitched overboard.

'Yulia!' He lunged to the side, but she was already far from his reach, flailing in the sea, her bobbing head becoming more distant by the second. 'Bastard! Turn back!'

The skipper hesitated and looked to Ben as if he was about to turn the boat, but he jabbed a finger at him, said something indistinguishable and motored on.

'Stop this! Turn back!'

What did he need to do to get this guy to save Yulia? Did he mean her to drown? Did he mean to deposit him with the loggers then pick her up? The skipper pointed ahead, and Ben had a feeling that was *exactly* what he had in mind. But Yulia? He glanced back to see her thrashing in the water. Could she even swim?

Panic surged through him as surely as vomit had risen in his throat seeing Rob's mutilated corpse.

Swinging the binoculars by their strap, he slammed them down on the skipper's skull. He heard the crunch and saw the skipper's face react with the pain of it. He had never deliberately hurt anyone in his life but what could he do? The man shrieked something. What? Ben had no idea. The skipper reached for a fishing rod and jammed one end through the wheel, securing the other end under the seat.

Ben glanced away, looking back. Fuck! Yulia wasn't there!

He swung back to face the skipper to see he had armed himself with a fishing knife. Ben's eyes were on the serrated blade glinting in the sun.

The skipper jabbed, unknown words streaming from his mouth. Was this just a threat, or might the man kill him? Ben shrieked, 'Bastard! You bastard!' What did he have to fend off his attacker with? Nothing, just his fucking binocs. He swung them from their strap in a pathetic attempt to defend himself. He was trapped with a lunatic set on killing him, struggling to keep to his feet as the boat circled, churning water in its wake.

The blade flashed towards his belly. He instinctively swiped his left arm outwards, making contact with his attacker's forearm. The blade ripped through his shirt, and he felt it slice into the softness of his skin and meet hard resistance of a bone. With his right arm, Ben smashed his binoculars into his assailant's face. The man's head jerked back. He brought his hand to his nose, which streamed blood. He staggered, releasing his knife. It skittered on to the floor between the seats. Ben's eyes flickered away. From the crazily circling speedboat he glimpsed a rigid inflatable dinghy – large enough for an outboard motor – being lowered from the *Pacific Dawn*.

Pain was kicking in, blood seeping through his shirt. He had never been in any kind of a fight, apart from wrestling tussles with his brothers or kids at school. He figured he had the weight advantage, but the seaman was strong; sinewy muscles thrust Ben aside, and he bent to grope for his knife. With his right hand, Ben yanked him back. He had no weapon, and even if he had the knife, he doubted he would have the courage to use it. Instead he dived back for the only loose thing in the boat: a fishing net.

Snatching the pile of nylon, Ben loosened enough of it to throw forward as the skipper's hand clasped the knife. Momentarily strands of netting encumbered him and Ben pounced, pushing his attacker off balance before leaning his weight onto his chest. He punched and punched, horrified at what he was doing but terrified of doing nothing. The man didn't struggle, brought a hand to his head, went limp. Ben shuddered. Had the clout with binoculars to his skull done real damage? Surely it took more than this to kill a man. Surely his future wasn't in an Indonesian jail.

He turned away from this problem to the more urgent one: Yulia. Nothing. Just an expanse of sea.

The launched dinghy was in the water now, and the three men on board were bound to be armed. Ben scrambled to the front seat and yanked the fishing rod from the wheel. The boat shot forward straight for the *Pacific Dawn's* dinghy as he fought to control the wheel with one arm. He pushed the throttle, not quite in control, and the boat spurted forward. Spinning the wheel to the right, he veered sharply, sending a massive wake towards the dinghy. The small boat rocked dangerously. He doubted it would be swamped but its progress had been slowed and he had the faster vessel. His shoulder throbbed and shakes convulsed his body.

Yulia. Where? Where?

Sun glinted on tips of waves, but her dark hair was nowhere in sight. He wasn't sure how far they'd gone and had no idea about currents. Or sharks. His mind went into overdrive. He scoured the sea searching for her, trusting she could swim well enough to stay afloat. Glancing over his shoulder he saw the dinghy had turned back. One thing less to worry about, though the skipper was unresponsive. Shit.

But Yulia… He needed binoculars to scan the water, but his hands were needed on the wheel. Was this the right direction? Did he need to alter course…

There! In the distance, two stick arms waved frantically. Momentarily he closed his eyes in relief then directed the boat towards her. Closer and closer, his heart racing.

With the engine idling Ben reached over, and with his good arm hauled Yulia aboard. They clung to each other, shivering, repeating each other's name, talking over each other:

'Yulia! You all right?'

'Yeah, yeah. You? Oh!'

'Thank God!'

'You're hurt!'

'Thought you'd drown. Didn't know if you could swim.'

'Ben!' Yulia drew back and touched his shoulder. 'What happened?'

'He came at me with a knife. I don't know how bad…'

She opened his shirt and flinched. 'Uhh. You'll need stitching up.'

He twisted his neck. Seeing his opened flesh, he reached to steady himself, suddenly feeling faint.

'Sit down. Sit down.' Yulia pushed him and he sank gratefully onto the bench seat.

She scurried to open his backpack, dragged out a first-aid kit and, with shaking hands, wrapped a makeshift bandage around his shoulder. 'That will have to do for now.' She ripped off some adhesive tape with her teeth and fixed the bandage in place.

Wearily he looked back at the *Pacific Dawn*, its dinghy nowhere in sight. It had been sent out to scare them and he doubted they'd really have shot at him – more likely they want to warn him off. Perhaps…

He jerked his head towards the prone skipper. 'Check him, will you. I don't know… hope I've not…' He could not finish the sentence; could not conceive of having killed a man, even in self-defence.

Yulia felt for a pulse at the skipper's throat. 'He'll live.' She touched his head. The man grimaced and opened his eyes. She spoke to him gently and the man answered. 'He's OK. One more small fish caught up with the gangs. Hoped they'd pay him. What's for sure is that he didn't like you spying: a privileged white man interfering in another country's business Well, not exactly those words... more... umm... a fucking whitey sticking his nose in.'

'And that's about the gist of it.'

Ben was spent. It would be hours before he could get to a hospital, and his shoulder ached like nothing he had experienced before. He nudged the skipper out of his way and lay down.

'Yulia...'

'Mmm? You OK?'

'I was thinking. We'll throw everything we can at them. Everything. They'll have to listen to us.'

'Maybe. Let's hope.'

Yulia had described herself as a pitta bird, small and inoffensive, but there was more than a touch of a sea eagle as she used fishing cord to bind the skipper's wrists before settling behind the boat's wheel.

As Ben lay on the bench seat, trying to take his mind off his throbbing shoulder, he watched a plane high above, speculating on its destination. He had changed his return air ticket to London once, now he would be doing so again. Next stop Jakarta.

17

'No police! We sort this between us. OK? Here... Here!'

The boat hire guy thrust a wad of money into her hand and Yulia accepted it. Why not? A refund for the hire and more besides, looking at the pile of notes. The hire guy hadn't seemed too worried about the skipper when he staggered in. 'A sore head. That's all.' She glanced at the skipper slumped in a chair. He deserved his sore head, and by the look of the purplish swollen lump, a broken nose. No one wanted the police involved. The boat company did not want bad publicity to put off tourists and she didn't want to stay longer than necessary making claims against them. Besides, the thought of meeting up with Sartano or any of his department made her shiver. Not all of them would be corrupt, most would be decent guys, but she didn't want to find out. She took the money and ran to Ben, who was waiting in a taxi.

'Hospital... Let's go!'

Later, arriving back at the guest house, Yulia settled Ben as she had promised his doctor she would. She looked down at him sprawled on his bed wearing bloodstained shorts. Hmm. She wondered if he could manage to change out of these easily. How might she ask? Seeing him grey-faced and woozy with painkillers, bare-chested except for a large dressing on his shoulder and his arm in a sling, she had tender feelings for this man.

'I'll look in later, OK?' She lightly touched his good arm.

In her own room she stripped off her clothes and dropped them to the floor. Her skin had scaly white salty patches, and running her fingers through her hair, she could feel it crusty with seawater. She was so tired… A shower. Oh, a shower.

Suds gave way to fresh water as she tried to wash away the horror of the day. Deep sea terrified her. While treading water she had imagined her life ending in a sudden snatch of an open jaw from below. Sharks were common here. She had drawn up her legs, making herself small, then floated on her back, keeping as still as possible. In her effort to stay calm she recited a Buddhist prayer of non-attachment, which hadn't helped at all out there in the deep. The image of big teeth in an open jaw would not go away. She remained as still as she could, every so often risking gentle paddles with her hands, even trying to keep her heartbeat quiet in an effort to blend with the sea. When she heard the speedboat's engine getting closer and closer with Ben at the wheel, she had erupted in a frenzy of waving arms and thrashing legs.

She lifted her face to the spraying water, grateful it had not been her time to die. She forced herself out of the shower, towelled her hair dry, glanced longingly at her bed, before changing into a light dress and crossing the corridor to Ben's room.

More than an hour later she was still sitting on the floor

across from Ben's bed, her back against a chair, not yet ready to leave, though her head kept dropping.

'Tell me more,' Ben said. 'I'd love to know more about your childhood.'

'Mmm?' Yulia jerked awake.

'What happened after your dad was killed? If you don't mind talking about it.'

Did she want to tell him more about herself? She'd told him some: the worst bits about her father; things that related to Sartano.

Ben prompted: 'You said your mother never got over it.'

Yulia hesitated, reluctant to be drawn back to this painful time, yet a crack had opened between life and death for both of them today, demanding more intimacy, making it inevitable.

'There was just me and her. I remember I always had a sore tummy, started wetting my bed and I wouldn't leave her side.'

'You were traumatised.'

'I guess.' She shrugged. 'I'm not sure that people – you know, professional people like doctors and teachers – took much notice of that back then. I was too young to really make sense of things... We didn't stay in Pontianak. We moved to a small town in East Java. Somewhere my mum felt safe.'

'You haven't talked about her.'

'Umm.' Yulia bit her lip. She had a difficult relationship with her mother. 'She's a teacher. She's used to kids doing what they're told to do. Teachers here are a big deal, you know, kids defer to them. You have to. There's a... umm...' Yulia frowned, 'emotional distance encouraged. Teachers don't get too involved with students' problems.'

'I guess your own teachers didn't ask about you either?'

'Not really. And I think my mother wasn't well for some time: depressed, I suppose. I understand better now.'

'Bound to be.'

'She never married again. Got clingy, didn't want me to leave to study in Jakarta. Wanted me to marry and settle near her... Huh! It made me pull away.'

Ben grunted. 'I had you down as a dutiful daughter. You've completely ruined my idea of you.'

'No, no!' Yulia was suddenly worried. She didn't want him to think more badly of her than he already did, nor of her mother. 'We get on OK now, but she worries about me. I haven't told her where I am right now. She uses social media, but I send her cute pictures of a cat or something, or a meal I'm eating and a short message—'

'Crafty!' Ben laughed.

'She would be here in a flash. Fussing. And fussing over you too.'

'Oh. That might be nice.'

Ben was teasing, but she became conscious of her duty and went to his bedside. 'Can I get you something?'

'I'm OK, thanks. I can reach what I need.' He gestured to the bottle of water and painkillers on the bedside table.

'Can you, you know, mmm, get to the bathroom OK?' She could feel herself blushing.

'I'll manage. I'll get a shower soon. I just have to avoid getting water on this.' He indicated the dressing.

'You sure?'

'I'm sure.' Ben smiled.

'In that case, I'm going to bed.'

'Goodnight, Yulia. Sleep well.'

He reached for her hand and squeezed it. She met his eyes. He had nice eyes, sort of a greeny-blue – she hadn't noticed till now – but he looked so tired, dark rings under his eyes. Ben brought her hand to his lips and lightly kissed her fingers. Then he drew her forward and kissed her lightly on the lips. Just a brush of a kiss. Nothing to read into it. Just a "thank you" sort of a kiss. Drawing back, she smiled down at him.

'I'll leave your door ajar. Mine too. You know, I think this guest house is safe. If you need me, please shout. I hope I hear you.'

Despite her exhaustion, she noticed a spring in her step. It was odd. On the one hand they had shared dramatic, brutal, life-changing experiences – things most people never go through in a lifetime. On the other, there had been basic things, moments when one or other of them had discreetly disappeared behind a tree in the forest to pee. There was a huge gap in between, and she wanted to fill in some of this. They were heading to Jakarta next day. Ben wanted to arrange a meeting with politicians, and she needed to get back to work. She smiled, happy they wouldn't be separating just yet.

Ben adjusted his position, angling himself into the aircraft seat, trying to keep his strapped shoulder from being bumped. His knees constantly knocked Yulia's; she was trying to keep her body compact, her left shoulder wedged against his right one. The flight from Tarakan to Jakarta was full. Every few minutes the back of his seat was kicked by an energetic toddler on his mother's lap, and he was learning more than he wished to about the relationship of loud American tourists sitting in front. They were two hours into the three-hour flight, and he wanted to make the most of this journey. It was time to tell Yulia about Sarah.

He had not seen it coming. Sarah was a desk-bound solicitor who enjoyed letting off energy at her women's football club. What started as a Monday evening out became two then three evenings, and Saturday matches with other clubs. Then one evening stretched to an overnight. Initially he thought he must have forgotten an away match, but he became anxious, and texted, 'Where are you?' Eventually a reply came: 'With Mandy.' Even then he didn't explore further, but he felt uneasy. The next day Sarah arrived home and perched on the sofa while he sat across from her in a chair.

'You must have suspected,' she ventured.

His mouth was dry, heart racing, even then not willing to make the leap. He waited for her to spell it out.

'I mean, about me and Mandy...' She looked at him candidly, not shrinking.

He had been totally blindsided. Mandy was team captain, the kind of woman who bounded everywhere, strong-bodied and proud to be gay. He had met her on several occasions, after matches, with the other women in Sarah's team, when the footballers had invited their partners to join them at the pub. It was a kind of role-reversal scenario he imagined playing out at pubs across the country.

Sarah reached across to take his hand. 'I'm sorry.'

He jerked away, unable to bear her touch, her sympathy. Suddenly his wife was a stranger. 'Are you leaving?' His mouth was dry, but he found the words that needed to be spoken.

She nodded. 'I know this will be a shock. It was for me too. But, oh, Ben, I'm so relieved to tell you. I want to stay friends. You mean a lot to me. Truly. I mean it. We've shared so much...' Her words trailed off, but her gaze remained steady and compassionate.

People talk about rugs being pulled from under them, falling apart, being gutted – all manner of ways to describe emotional shock and betrayal of trust. Trust. That was the biggest thing. He had trusted Sarah and she had hurt him to his core. At that moment Ben had no anchor. It was as if the certainties he believed in no longer applied. He hadn't known how to deal with it, didn't like to talk with people he worked with and said little to his parents or brothers. Sarah had left him for a woman she had grown to love, and ten months later he was still raw, stripped of his manhood, reluctant to trust another woman.

Ben turned his head slightly to look at Yulia, his heart beating uncomfortably.

'I'd like to tell you about Sarah. My ex.' He kept his voice low, not wanting to share *his* private life with all and sundry.

'Sure... OK.' A frown creased Yulia's brow. She didn't look too keen. 'Rick mentioned you had split. I wasn't sure what that meant exactly. If it was a temporary thing.'

Ben shook his head.

'OK.' Yulia looked more encouraging.

By the time he had stumbled through his story, the frown had disappeared and she looked intrigued. 'I know about women who love other women, but not personally, or at least no one has told me. So you two won't be getting back together again?'

'We're divorcing. Amicably.'

'Oh!' A smile stretched across Yulia's face. 'Oh,' she repeated.

18

Ben squinted at the reflective glass in the cluster of high-rise buildings in downtown Jakarta. This city was far from his favourite place: there was congestion, noise, pollution and, yes, the place was sinking – the land on which it was built no longer sustained the sheer bulk of it. Plans to move the capital to a new location in eastern Kalimantan filled him with dismay. Foul a nest; abandon it; start afresh and create another ecological disaster. People! At times he did not like the species he belonged to.

The conversation he had had with Linda earlier that day added to his gloomy mood.

'About that ship—' Linda had begun.

'We checked it,' Ben cut in. 'Chartered. Malaysian-registered.'

'Not now. It changed its flag mid-ocean. Chinese.'

Ben had grimaced at the news. He had supposed the vessel to be heading to Malaysia, where there were plenty of places to offload illegal timber, but the *Pacific Dawn*'s journey would take a little longer.

'I can guess what's coming,' he sighed. 'Straight to China.'

'Yep, I reckon. We've got people tracking it and to do undercover stuff at whichever port it arrives at.'

'You have people in China?'

'Get real.'

Ben shouldn't have been surprised. Although there were no official environmental groups in China working on the illegal timber trade, there were always individuals ready to risk their liberty. Even their lives.

Ben adjusted his left arm in its sling. His shoulder would take a while to mend: the muscle and tendon were cut, the clavicle chipped. He was sore and pissed off with everything and everyone. Connor had been trying to reach him: calls, voicemails, emails and text messages, the tone moving between threatening, cajoling and pleading. He meant to reply, but first he wanted to speak to those in charge at this end.

With his small backpack slung over his right shoulder, Ben walked through the doors of the Department of International Trade, where he found Ardhi waiting.

'Ben!' Ardhi leaped to his feet and hurried to hug him. 'Sorry.' He drew back as Ben flinched. 'I couldn't believe what happened. You two going after those guys.'

'We wouldn't have if we'd known what we were in for. Shit. Yulia almost drowned.'

Ardhi shook his head. 'I want to know everything. Tell me later.'

'Thanks for arranging this.'

'No problem. I'm as interested as you to hear what they have to say.'

Ardhi had tried, but failed, to make an appointment with the minister for trade – he couldn't access that level – but he had arranged a meeting with a senior civil servant. Mr

Marpuah was Connor's equivalent, one of those who had initially briefed them. They were expected.

Ben sat with Ardhi across the desk from Mr Marpuah in the air-conditioned office. The large man, overflowing his business suit, was shuffling printouts of photos Ben had sent through – the illegal logging camp, the barge, the *Pacific Dawn*, all of it – along with his accompanying notes and recommendations. At least some effort had been made to give this attention, rather than a cursory glance at information on screen. And judging by the numerous highlights and handwritten comments, the evidence had been given due consideration. A promising start.

They danced around the social niceties: refreshments, enquiries about Ben's injury. Then, impatient to get on with things, Ben cut short Mr Marpuah's enquiry about Yulia.

'She's fine, fine… Please, what are your thoughts on this?' He gestured to the incriminating documents spread out on the desk.

'I have shared it with my colleagues – we are working with other departments, as you know. Indonesia is vast. Central and regional interests need… negotiating.' Mr Marpuah was picking his words carefully.

'You mean Sartano?'

'He is part of a complex chain.' Mr Marpuah paused. 'If he were removed – which is totally beyond the power of our department, I must add – another would take his place.' He paused again. 'And if my minister tried to influence, or others suspected he was trying to influence… well, he would be replaced. As would I.' He smiled. 'You are an economist, Doctor Fletcher. You understand what drives these elaborate plans to bypass systems; this cycle of corruption we understand so well.'

'Western-led markets. I know.' Ben met his gaze.

'Consumerism. And we all want a piece.'

The government official picked up a printout of the AZTAR logging skidder. 'One of the directors – Mr Arnott – English, I believe.' He flicked through the notes Ben had sent.

'Yes. And Agus Zumran is, as you know, from here.'

'This, er, report and photos aren't related to the project you were assessing—'

'For heaven's sake!' Ben felt Ardhi's foot nudge his leg. He took a deep breath, attempting a polite smile. 'Sorry. I consider this urgent and I hope you do too.'

'Doctor Fletcher. We look forward to receiving your *actual* report. In the circumstances it may be a little premature to consider these recommendations.' Mr Marpuah picked up a paper reading the bullet points: 'Confiscate stolen timber; end AZTAR's contract; confiscate equipment and trucks…' His voice trailed off.

'And excuse me, sir. The sawmills,' Ardhi reminded him. 'Please don't forget the part the sawmills play.'

'We aren't forgetting anything, Doctor Durmali. I assure you we do take this seriously. Please believe that. And this is not how we expect visitors to be treated.' His gaze moved to Ben. 'I wanted to meet with you personally to let you know this. What happened to you is truly shameful. Once again, I apologise for everything you have been through.'

'Sir. Are you able to say what you might *do* with Ben's evidence?' Ardhi leaned forward in his chair.

The government official met Ardhi's gaze then he rose and extended his hand. 'I appreciate you have both taken time to come to see me. Particularly Doctor Fletcher, coming back here specially. I know you will be wanting to get home and put all this behind you. So thank you, again.'

'And thank you for your time, sir.' Ardhi was all politeness as he shook hands.

'Thank you.' Ben spoke reluctantly, quickly lowered his gaze and picked up his bag.

Outside the building Ardhi lit a cigarette. 'Don't hold your breath, Ben.'

'I'm not. Sadly.'

'What are you doing tonight? How about a meal? I'd like you to meet my wife. And there's a lot to fill me in on.'

'Thanks. That would have been nice, but I've arranged to meet Yulia.'

'Of course! Please, both come.'

Ben looked at Ardhi's welcoming face. He didn't want to spend his last evening in a group, knowing the three Indonesians would politely speak English for his benefit. More to the point, he had seen so little of Yulia.

'She's arranged something with her housemate.' The lie came out seamlessly. 'But if you've got time now, let's grab a beer… and give my apologies to your wife.'

'I know just the place. I want to hear everything.' Ardhi hailed a taxi.

In his office Connor hunched over his laptop screen. He scrolled through image after image Ben had forwarded: photos of a barge stacked high with felled timber – he assumed illegal – and there was Trevor's damned logging machine with his company name blazed across the fucking door. *Trevor! The idiot! What the hell does he think he's playing at?*

Connor's hand reached for his phone. No. That could wait. He needed to think carefully about Trevor, and focus on what was immediately needed. His eyes returned to the screen.

More images: a cargo ship anchored offshore… and… he

began reading Ben's recommendations. Christ! A whole raft of things he was recommending the Indonesian government take action on. Damn the stubborn mule of a man. This was not Ben's role. What on earth would Mr Marpuah make of this? Perhaps he thought the UK government were behind Ben's none-too-subtle exposé? None of this was any use to Connor right now. This Indonesian PPI was meant to be a sweet little project. He really didn't have time to untangle any diplomatic fallout. His staff needed to focus on the upcoming summit and give their attention to other countries. OK, country singular: China.

With furious fingers he typed an email to Ben demanding he send through his commissioned report. The official report. The only report that mattered. He stopped short of saying he would cut off Ben's balls – an empty threat with the man so far away – and, of course, civil service professionalism excluded such language. He instinctively crossed his legs, protective of his own balls: Simone's office was too close for comfort. The prime minister had severely criticised her at a recent Cabinet meeting and she hadn't enjoyed the roasting. After, she had stalked back to the office and turned the heat on him. Par for the course. Connor checked his watch and reached for his jacket. His boss was expecting him.

Simone's heels clattered on the Whitehall corridor. Connor, as always, struggled to keep up with her brisk pace, astonished how she managed such a stride with the high heels she favoured. She was off to a Cabinet meeting and was grabbing a chance to walk and talk.

Connor had shared Ben's "unofficial" report with Simone – there had been no point in holding it back. He'd sent a bullet-point précis by email, telling her: 'Ben's finally sent us some information. Not his report, sadly, but other material. Attached you will find a summary. If you would care to see everything (photos, videos, report) I will get it straight to you.' He was pleased he had sent it through promptly when he found Simone had already received a cautious email from her counterpart in Indonesia. Judging by the bulging folder tucked under her arm, Simone had received more than a message.

'Connor, you swore to me this project was beyond reproach.'

'I said it showed potential.'

'Potential? With links to all this?' She shook the folder in his face. 'Even if it's shown there is an innocent explanation, mud sticks – to the project and to me. And my entire department.' Simone shot him a look. 'What am I supposed to tell the PM? That this is our idea of good news?'

Her heels struck the floor forcefully with each step. Two staffers walking towards them stepped aside as they made their way out into the street.

'You said this man Ben was a safe bet. This seems more Indiana Jones to me.'

Connor grunted. He had made the same comparison himself but the idea of Ben swinging into action didn't fit the man he knew. And yet, from Ben's terse message he understood he had narrowly escaped with his life.

'Links to China!' Simone hadn't finished her dressing down. 'Just what we need right now.'

'The timing could be better,' Connor conceded.

'You think he'll pass all of this to those radical investigative agencies and the media and so on?'

'Of course not, Minister. That would be well outside the terms of our contract with him. I know Ben. That's not his way.'

'Ha! Your professional instincts have been blunted recently. Must everyone in my department be so useless? Can't

I depend on any of my staff to deliver? I get more organised in one hour myself than any of you do in a week. I'd be better off without you, or at least bringing in my own people. And Connor...' She shot him a look. 'It goes without saying that this stops with us.'

He had not imagined it otherwise. It would be buried, and they would focus on the PPI. He trusted Ben would behave professionally and focus tightly on his project. 'Yes, of course, Minister.'

And with that Simone swept past the police officers securing the gate into Downing Street and strode towards Number Ten. Connor allowed her some seconds by herself, not so much to gather her thoughts, but to enable the waiting press to film her arriving looking crisp in her tailored outfit and totally on top of things. He trailed at a safe distance. He had his own meeting with Number Ten staff.

But it was worth having another go reaching Ben before then. He reached into his pocket.

Ben was dozing in his Jakarta hotel room when his phone woke him. He had ignored Connor's previous calls, but he couldn't keep doing so. He wasn't due to meet Yulia for a while, and besides, he needed to know where Connor stood. Swiping the incoming call icon to the right he swung his legs over the edge of the bed and sat up. 'Hi, Connor.'

'You've finally answered. Where are you?'

'Jakarta. And how are you? Wait... First you'll want to know how I am. Let me—'

'What you've been up to has nothing to do with—'

'I hear Simone's voice loud and clear.'

'Your job's done.'

'You're backing off. Every bloody government: spineless.' He had dared hope Connor might back him on this one.

'Ben.' Connor sounded a touch appeasing. 'You can't do more than you've done: your own job and much more besides. Come on now. Book a flight back—'

'I'm leaving tomorrow.'

'Great! That's great. But before you do anything else, email your report through – the official one. Promise me you'll do it as soon as we end this call. I need you to formally hand it over.'

'Why the rush? All the quicker to bury the truth?'

'Your contract is with me! You'll do as I say if you want to be paid… You want your team to be paid, don't you? Think of them, if not yourself. We need—'

Ben pressed the end call icon. He glanced at the time, calculating how long it would take to get to the restaurant where he was meeting Yulia, when the ringtone jangled again. He was not in the mood to find out what else Connor needed, and prepared to dismiss the call, but Linda's name flashed up on the screen. This call he would take.

'Linda… OK?'

'That trade summit in London – it's going to be focused almost totally on China. That's where your people are heading, about now actually, to do some glad-handing.'

'You sure?' Ben frowned. 'I've just been talking with Connor…' Well, in all fairness the conversation had been brief. Maybe Connor would have got on to that.

'Yeah, I'm sure. Indonesia, Japan and Korea are pretty pissed off. Their delegations will still attend, but China's where the big bucks are. Trouble is, the summit's hobbled by the environmental clauses they were pressured to include. Hah! Gonna be loads of fun.'

'That's why they need our Positive Partnership Initiative forest project to provide a rosy glow. I knew that much. But thanks for the heads-up about China.'

'I'm sure as hell not doing any of this for you – not sure I even like you that much – but you owe me...' Ben closed his eyes. Linda's voice was becoming more abrasive, more insistent. Sure enough: 'Listen, Ben. Send me evidence. We can do serious damage with those images and videos!'

'You know I can't. Not yet. I need to go through the proper channels.'

Proper channels! Linda wanted to thump Ben. Thump someone. She snorted. 'Mother of God, Ben, you sound like a Sunday school teacher!'

Her computer screen was open to the Direct Action for the Earth website news tab. She could *imagine* those images up there: the barge piled high with logs wending its way through a dark forest river; the rusty container ship skulking offshore; some crisp reportage – the death of that poor sod from the village and Ben's heroics (injured but not dead) would make a fantastic story with some dry stats to back it up. She leant into the screen, closer to her phone that was propped up on loudspeaker.

'If you give everything to us, we can make a difference. Not those stuffed shirts you still put faith in.'

'Linda, I can't—'

'Damn you! Show me you've got the balls to use what you've got! Do it!'

'Linda, listen! You know—'

She ended the call and tossed the phone down. Her resolve to stay calm had lasted for all of two seconds. Her fingers drummed the desk. She didn't give a fig for the smug Indonesian forest project that was keeping its nose clean. If Ben wouldn't play ball... Yulia then. She might talk some sense into that man. She picked up her phone, scrolled through her contacts and touched Yulia's phone icon. Yulia's sweet-voiced answerphone message kicked in and Linda hung up. Again she tossed the phone aside.

She wanted to scrabble in the mud and dish up the dirt. She didn't have Ben's evidence, not directly, not yet, but there were things no one could stop her saying. She opened the portal to her blog and furiously began typing:

> DAE.org/Blogs/Linda
>
> You'd think those fuckers would finally DO something. There's evidence leaking out of every orifice you can think of and then some, and all anyone wants to do is offer a tissue. When I was a young woman visiting England, I remember "spending a penny" in railway station bathrooms – loos, I should say. Back then the toilet paper was shiny and stiff – even had a printed message saying something like "property of British Rail". Couldn't absorb a damn thing, could only shift the shit around

Linda paused, cursed, then deleted everything she had written. This was going too far, but boy, it felt good to vent.

She had found she wasn't enjoying being back home. The house was suffocating her with all the memories contained within its walls. Pushing back her chair she made her way to one of the smaller bookcases, its top ledge a repository of clutter and photos, including one of her family on holiday. She and Ted would have been in their forties, the children still young enough to enjoy family camping trips together. Vermont, perhaps, though she wasn't sure, and couldn't remember who might have taken it. Another camper? None of that was important. She looked at her younger self wearing her usual summer garb of shorts and T-shirt, her white stalk legs next to Ted's tanned muscular ones. He looked so handsome. Despite being an academic he loved the outdoors, and had never become paunchy or flabby even in his sixties. He had always been such a fit man, so his fatal heart attack had been a total shock. In the photo Ted's arm was around her waist. She had been captured brushing her shoulder-length hair from her face, head tilted back, grinning broadly, eyes sparkling. Christ. When had she last been that happy? Really happy. A discomfiting thought.

Ted liked to call her a "corn-fed Christian from Kansas". That was sort of true, but any faith she had grown up with had long since dissipated. Ted liked to call her Lindy-Loo too. Linda smiled remembering how he would stand in the kitchen doing his best Elvis impersonation, giving her a sexy look, bellowing out the Hurriganes song "The Phone Rang" with a girl called Lindy-Loo on the line. That, or his version of Buddy Holly's "Peggy Sue", substituting Lindy-Loo. And he might take her in his arms and twirl her around in a wild jive.

Great songs. Great man.

With the sleeve of her sweater she slowly wiped the glass and carefully placed the photo back on the shelf.

19

THE YOUNG WAITRESS MOVED ASIDE THE PRAWN crackers and Ben lifted his glass of beer to make room for a huge steaming dish: a cone of rice surrounded by an eggy omelette thing with chicken, and the patties must be potatoes. The trouble was, he wasn't hungry.

He had met Yulia the previous evening, but it had been unsatisfactory: a noisy bar, both of them ill at ease, or so it had seemed to him. Now in the restaurant, he realised he was not looking forward to leaving tomorrow. That was on his mind. That, and Linda.

He jumped as Yulia clicked her fingers in front of him.

'A traditional dish, for your last evening.'

'It looks amazing.' He smiled his appreciation and helped himself to samples of everything, half-listening as Yulia explained what each was. A liver dish was the one he had been unsure about. It made him think of ghastly meals his grandmother had forced him to eat. It always seemed to be liver for dinner when they visited. Best avoid that... 'Sorry?'

'I said, I'll come to the airport to see you off tomorrow. I'll take time off work.'

'No, no, you don't need to do that.'

'I'd like to come.'

'I'd rather you didn't.'

Yulia flinched and he was annoyed with himself. 'I hate goodbyes. I didn't mean—'

Yulia held up a hand. 'It's OK.'

They toyed with their meals, sampling morsels, then Yulia put down her chopsticks, reached for her bag and withdrew a CD in a plastic case. 'You can have this now, then.' She handed it to him. 'It's only a small thing...' He saw the colour rise in her cheeks.

It was an Xcalibur album, an image of Rob and the rest of the band on the cover. He smiled, appreciating Yulia's effort to source this. A good job he still owned a CD player.

'Thank you. That's so thoughtful.' Ben was genuinely touched and deeply embarrassed he hadn't got something for her.

'To remember Rob.' Yulia smiled. 'I bought one for myself too.'

Neither of them was likely to forget the Australian, the horror of his death and everything else they had been through together. Those experiences would bond them for life, at some level at least. Yulia reached into her bag again and drew out a large hardcover book: used, well thumbed, its paper jacket torn.

'And I got you this too. Sorry. It will make your baggage heavier going home.'

It was an illustrated version of Grimm's Fairy Tales, an English edition. Why was she giving him a kids' book? He was puzzled.

'I didn't get around to telling you about third sons. They're usually the heroes, you know.' Her smile was warm and her eyes kind.

'Thank you. I'll try to live up to that.'

He absent-mindedly reached for a prawn cracker, crumbling it between his fingers. 'Yulia…' He wasn't sure how to say the things he wanted to.

'Yes?' Yulia looked at him, waiting. She reached across and casually brushed crumbs off his bare arm, then, aware of her gesture, hastily withdrew. Ben caught her hand and held it firmly.

'Yulia. I'm sorry. I didn't think about a gift for you.'

'It's OK.'

'No, it's not OK. I don't know if, or when, we'll see each other again.'

'I know.'

'And this isn't a brilliant time—'

'It's OK. Really. You don't need to…'

Yulia withdrew her hand and sat back in her chair. *Damn!* He had not meant to bring up his divorce. He felt the opportunity slipping away.

After a moment's silence Yulia changed the subject. 'Linda… She's right, you should send it all to her.'

'Can't. I'd be blacklisted from every government department. I'd never get a contract again. That's my bread and butter work. And it's what I believe in.'

'You know, Ben, sometimes we should just think of today. Not worry about yesterday. Not guess tomorrow. Linda could help.'

The moment… *This* moment. Yulia was right. He needed to grab it. He gazed at Yulia sitting across from him and was suddenly determined not to waste more time.

'I don't want to talk about Linda.'

His words were hurried. Reaching for her hand, he drew Yulia forward, raised his hand to touch her head. It was the first time she had worn her hair loose and it hung to her shoulders. He realised he had been longing to do this all evening: to feel the warmth of her skin near her scalp and the silkiness of her hair between his fingers. His breath quickened and he sat back.

'I'm not sure if…' He wasn't sure how to put it.

'If what?' A frown creased between her eyes.

'Well… If a well-brought-up Indonesian woman would—'

'Ben!' Her laughter exploded at his awkwardness. 'I'm a modern woman. My mother despairs of me.'

'Even so—'

'I make my own decisions.'

'I know you do! For sure, I know that!' Ben grinned, seeing a small frown forming between her eyes as she made the humming noise he often heard when she was thinking, or formulating the right words in English.

'Ben. I share an apartment with another woman – it takes ages to get there. But your hotel…?'

He signalled to the waitress and fished out his payment card. Their barely touched meal could be fed to pigs.

Ben's hotel room was just as Yulia expected: a bland décor with easy-to-clean surfaces, harsh overhead ceiling light, softer bedside lamps and a small en-suite bathroom. She hadn't lied when she'd said she was a modern woman, but still, casual sex wasn't her thing. Two serious relationships had flowered then withered, followed by three barren years when she had distanced herself, spurning advances from keen suitors, none of whom interested her.

During the past weeks, witnessing people she cared about being killed or nearly killed, she had reassessed things. Here and now mattered. The feeling inside her was of too many missed meals, and she hungered for intimacy. Getting to know Ben was like peeling away layers of an onion: lots of dry, hard outer layers. She longed to go deeper and explore the softer interior a little more before he left. So little time.

Returning from the bathroom she found the room softly lit. That helped calm her nerves. *Onions, huh?* Her giggle sounded nervous to her own ears. She slipped off her cardigan then reached out to help Ben unbutton his shirt. 'Thanks,' he said, and briefly covered her hand with his. Such an intimate act to unclothe someone, yet such an everyday thing. Hadn't her mother done the same, countless times, when she was a little girl? She focused on undoing a button. Ben had worn a cotton short-sleeved shirt and it was crumpled, slightly damp, giving off the odour of a man. This man. Ben. She breathed in, finding it attractive. Earlier, she had dabbed perfume behind her ears and on her wrists. Might he prefer to smell her without this? She inhaled sharply at the touch of Ben's hand on her shoulder then he slid the strap of her dress down her arm. His face nuzzled her neck. Warm breath touched her skin, then a soft kiss. She sighed, her knees loosening, doubts evaporating. When he raised his head the pupils of his eyes were big pools of black.

She gently touched the large bandage swathing his left shoulder. 'You'll be all right?' She needed to be sure.

He grunted. 'I'll manage.'

Her hand slid gently down his chest, fingers brushing brown curling hair, so different from the Javanese men she had been intimate with. Under her palm his chest rose and fell, and she pressed firmly, feeling his beating heart. Leaning forward she placed her cheek against it to feel the tock, tock, of its regular beat. Ben's right arm encircled her head, holding her close, fingers playing with her hair, lifting strands, inhaling the scent, softly kissing her head. Yes, this would be all right.

Afterwards, she lay encircled in his right arm. They *had* managed and it had been lovely. Not a rocket-to-the-moon adventure, but somehow familiar, as if she had known this man for a long time. Ben's fingers played with her hair. Nice. Reassuring. She was hating the idea of him flying away and out of her life the next day. A pang of anxiety knotted her stomach; she realised it was well after midnight and tomorrow had now become today.

Ben had told her a bit more about Sarah, and when he asked about her own past relationships she said, 'Another time,' but knew there would not be another time for ages. The coming emptiness distressed her.

'Yulia?'

'Mmm?'

'Remember Rob's card trick? With the ace of hearts?'

She nodded, saddened that Rob would never enjoy the game she had just been playing – the game of life. All gone.

'Well, we were the ace of hearts, the good news forest story,' Ben said. 'Maybe the whole Indonesian thing is irrelevant.'

'Huh?' She pulled away and raised her head.

'China's the real prize – what it's all about.' Ben's eyes locked with hers, the pupils no longer big black holes reflecting the desires of his body, but hard and focused. 'I'm not flying back to London. I'm following the money.'

'Ben?' She sat up.

'It'll be easy to find out who Arnott's manufacturers are. Where the timber will be going. I told you what Linda said about "their people" on the mainland.'

'Yes, she will know people who will take risks to look into it for us—'

'Sure, but I mean me. I want to follow up.'

'*You* want to go to China?'

'Have to. Once timber is offloaded it's not their problem where it came from. If it's not been stopped before it arrives, then China treats it as legal. And about eighty per cent of timber landing there is so-called legal.'

Yulia hugged her knees. Ben's fingers began stroking her back, gently but mechanically, his mind no longer on her.

China... She allowed this new idea to play around her mind. 'Have I told you, when I was young, I learnt Mandarin? I'm not very good, but—'

She heard Ben's sharp intake of breath. He sat up and turned her head to face him.

'No way. I... I can't be responsible—'

'For me!' Yulia pulled back and sat up, her arms folded, any notion of presenting herself as a desirable woman gone. She was in work mode. 'I told you, Ben, I take responsibility for myself. We're in this together, OK? How would you get by undercover in China? Are you crazy!' She lightly thumped his good arm, suddenly irritated with him. He needed her. Was he blind to this? Did he think he could enjoy her for just one night?

'I'm coming too, whether you want me or not. I'll get on with the visas and things. Linda can find out where the manufacturer is.'

She dropped back on the bed and curled away from Ben, scrunching her eyes closed, too annoyed to sleep. Moments later his fingers were tracing the knobbly ridges of her spine and she sensed the shift of his body weight then he planted small kisses on her shoulder. Her back muscles twitched and relaxed as his hands and kisses explored. Mmm. Nice. Comfortable. She remained quite still, savouring the moment, allowing another game of loving to begin.

20

ZHANGJIAGANG PORT ON THE YANGTZE RIVER IS THE largest distribution centre for timber in China, the scale of industry enormous. Mobile cranes line the water's edge, and along the port's kilometres of wharves giant open-hold vessels are berthed. The port has over two hundred berths and warehouses and storage yards, spread over two hundred acres. Neatly stacked containers are stored in one area, and in another, stacks of logs waiting for buyers.

A young man, ordinary and inconspicuous – a buyer, he tells anyone who asks – takes a keen interest in a recently berthed vessel, the rusty *Pacific Dawn*. He watches log loaders clamp roundwood logs and deftly lift and place them on a truck; notices the markings – a Z in a circle – on the end of the massive logs; follows the truck to where they are offloaded onto a growing stack. He watches an actual Chinese buyer, phone in hand, scrutinise the roundwood logs with a practised eye, checking for impurities, checking the species. The buyer sees a phone number tagged on the end of the log, keys the number into his phone. 'How much?'

The inconspicuous man is wearing a polo shirt with two buttons in the front. The second button is the lens of a tiny camera. Linda will be interested in this.

It hadn't been difficult to find out about Arnott's suppliers, Sung Woods, and now Ben found himself sitting on the same chair that he imagined Trevor would have parked his backside on. He supposed Trevor must have sipped tea from the same cups. He had never met the British businessman, but Trevor Arnott's shadow hovered near. Arnott had visited recently, he learnt.

Ben and Yulia had concocted a story: a front. They were owners of a company based in Oxford, England, with a convincing website and funky business cards. None of it would bear too much scrutiny, but accessing the internet from China was all but impossible so they were probably safe. In any case, the reference Trevor Arnott would have been surprised to have written seemed to be doing the trick.

Mr Li, the sales manager, perused the letter. 'So… a new company…' His frown suggested he might be cautious.

'But we expect to grow quickly,' Yulia assured him. 'We're ready to place orders. Big orders.'

'Yes.' Ben picked up the narrative. 'We'd like your assurances you can cope with continuity of supply.'

Mr Li bristled. 'Of course, of course.' He folded the letter. 'And please thank Mr Arnott for his kind introduction.'

Ben cleared his throat and managed a smile.

Mr Li rose. 'You want to see the factory?'

'Yes. We'd like to see the process. The scale of what you are doing – as well as your products, of course.'

Mr Li ushered them out and across the yard. It was much as Ben expected: a vast open-plan factory thick with dust and the noise of different machinery competing with itself. He took in whirling blades without safety guards. He watched twenty or more men, none wearing protective earmuffs or face masks, many with cigarettes dangling from lips, working at speed feeding planks into saws, planing to consistent widths, profiling tongue and groove, laminating into engineered wood. Timber from raw planks at one end of the shed, with no markings that he could see, ended up on pallets at the far side of the factory waiting for the next steps. In one area men were gluing chair legs to the seats, dipping brushes into large pots of toxic glue open on a bench. Again no face masks.

'You can see. Supply is not a problem for us.' Mr Li beamed, proud of this industry. 'Come.' Near the yard door he led Ben and Yulia to a man he introduced as a foreman.

Yulia said something in Mandarin and the Sung Wood man laughed. Yulia turned to Ben and said innocently, 'They assure us supply is not a problem. I'm so relieved.' She turned back and engaged them in conversation. Ben watched a forklift driver deftly scoop a wrapped pallet of wood on its front loader, and followed the driver out for some fresh air. It was unbelievable that anyone could work in these conditions. Officials would have visited this factory, likely identified these issues staring him in the face and told Mr Sung, wherever he was, how much it would cost to "fix" it. So Mr Sung would pay up and everything would chug along.

At a far corner of the Sung Woods premises a cluster of ramshackle huts, for the labourers, Ben supposed, showed signs of habitation. A metal drum, cut longways, made a functioning stove. An old man fed the flames with wooden off-cuts, and hanging from an improvised tripod a big bowl of something steamed – no doubt some sort of soup. He approved the ingenuity though he deplored the conditions.

'This way.' Mr Li's smile looked a little tight as he ushered Ben back.

'Absolutely. The sales room?'

Quite a range. Ben's eyes slid past the garden furniture as Mr Li led them to the flooring section. Ben ran his hand along a flooring panel on display and raised a questioning eyebrow. 'Merbau,' Mr Li answered. 'Excellent timber. From Malaysia.' Ben nodded, thinking, West Papua, more likely, and probably looted. He felt his neck heating with indignation. West Papua was in crisis. The eastern reach of Indonesia was a depressing free-for-all with massive merbau trees the prize, each worth hundreds of dollars on the international market while the local people received a handful of cash. Looting, corruption and exploitation was rife. He blew out a breath to calm himself and tuned in to what Yulia was saying. She was playing the charade well, discussing gloss and matte finishes. Mr Li led them to the interiors section, pausing by a coffee table.

'Best quality hardwood from a special forest in Indonesia. Mr Arnott stocks this.'

'You have certificates? Documents?' Ben's voice sounded sharp and Mr Li stiffened.

'You want certificates?'

Ben smiled. 'I mean all the extra paperwork that goes with "special forests". And there's likely to be a problem with a steady supply. That's our concern.'

Mr Li visibly relaxed. 'No, no. Supply no problem. This special forest is magic. Keeps giving. And certificates no problem.'

I bet! Ben tapped the side of his nose, without any idea if Mr Li understood the gesture but the sales manager grinned.

There was no way of knowing if the logs stolen from the protected Indonesia forest and recently arrived at Zhangjiagang would end up here, but this was all part of Agus Zumran's business network, so there was a fair chance that they would.

In the back of the taxi Ben sat slumped next to Yulia as the driver sped away from Sung Woods through the surrounding estate with its endless timber factories. He found it hard to look at it. China was the biggest trader in illegally logged timber, and until they took measures to stop smuggled timber entering the market it didn't bode well. The last frontier really. After China, what then? Hadn't he thought the same thing about the devastated forests and communities in West Papua? Now that same feeling was with him here.

Yulia had been right. He could not have managed without her for all manner of reasons – logistics for a start – and he was totally at sea with the language. On arrival, while Yulia paid the taxi driver, he had found himself at the reception desk rapidly typing into the translation facility on his phone, passing it to the girl on duty, who nodded then typed rapidly into her own phone and passed it to him. In this way they found their booking and were directed to their room.

Practical considerations aside, he could not imagine being without her company. Getting to know her had been a discovery, a delight. A journey that had begun in Connor's London office and seemed a straightforward assessment project was taking him deeper into a complex web of fake permits and business interests spanning continents. And he had not expected this – to find himself loved and giving love. He was changed, in some way he could not explain, even to himself. The other day Yulia had told him: 'You are not as cranky as I first thought.' And he had laughed, happy to discover he wasn't sliding into miserable middle age before his time. She had teased him: 'I've peeled away some tough outer onion skin layers, mmm?'

He turned his gaze from the window, turned away from the world's ongoing problems to look at Yulia. 'Back to the hotel?' He squeezed her hand.

The following morning they had a flight to catch: an internal one. They wouldn't be leaving China just yet.

21

CONNOR REGRETTED HE HAD NOT BEEN AROUND TO experience something of China before the big push to modernise. He would have liked to see it then. The old architecture was all but gone, and cars embraced like they were going out of fashion. Damned Beijing traffic. He checked his watch. He had taken a taxi to arrive early before the official cars rolled up, but found he was cutting things fine.

At Tiananmen Square his taxi stopped at a police cordon. Using an app to pay the driver – and that was another technological change he'd noticed during his recent visits, no more grubby crumpled yuan – Connor hurried towards his destination but found himself kept away by a wall of insistent police officers. 'English? Speak English?' He sped up and down the line of police officers, flashing the identity badge hanging around his neck. One officer jerked his head towards a female colleague, and he made a beeline for her. He fumbled for his passport, flashing every document he had, gabbled far too quickly for the woman to understand, but it seemed to do the trick. After a pat-down and bag search, he was through and he legged it towards the steps.

The press conference was being held in one of the smaller function rooms, but the fact it was being held at the Great Hall of the People spoke of the importance the Chinese were giving it. This was as good as it got in terms of state recognition, and Connor was stoked that they had been accorded the full treatment: UK business delegates given access to the right people in the right corporations, doors opened and Chinese media fulsome in their praise.

Once inside the press room Connor relaxed. Everything was in order; the public relations and comms teams working with counterparts in China had done a great job. On a raised dais stood two speakers' lecterns, their mics being checked by technicians, and a row of chairs behind. The backdrop pronouncing "Shaping the Future" in English and Mandarin looked slick. UK and Chinese flags hung either side of the dais and magnificent flower displays softened the corporate look. In the main hall, rows of forward-facing chairs had glossy branded folders ready and waiting. *Good... good.* Connor caught the eye of their own head of comms, stalking restlessly, his mouth working on the gum he always chewed. He raised a hand, calling a casual, 'All right?' and received a wink in reply.

The limos were due shortly. He texted Simone: *Looking good, all's well. See you soon.* He needed to be at the front steps before the official party arrived, and it was quite a hike in this huge edifice. As he strode through a lobby his phone rang. Simone? He drew up short seeing Ben's name on screen.

'Ben! I've been trying to contact you. Where are you?'

'Here, actually.'

Connor continued walking. 'Here? What does that mean? No time for guessing games.'

'Here. As in outside, beyond the cordon.' Connor stopped in his tracks, momentarily lost for words, his mind whirring. Ben continued: 'We want to meet. Can't get past security.'

Connor guessed *we* must mean Ben was with the Indonesian woman. He let it pass. 'I've got a press thing about to start, more important matters to see to. I'll meet you after.'

'At least let us in.'

Connor cursed softly. He didn't have time for this, but on the other hand he wanted Ben where he could find him. 'Wait there!' he urged, before pocketing his phone and racing back to cadge a couple of visitors' passes from the comms team.

He didn't say a word when he spotted Ben, who looked more rumpled and careworn than he'd ever seen him. Then his eyes darted to the slight Indonesian woman, whose sweet smile he suspected hid a steely resolve.

With Ben and Yulia trailing him, the necessary passes around their necks, he marched briskly inside. Only then could he compose himself to enquire, 'What the hell are you doing here?'

'A post-script. China.'

'The stuff you sent me might best be described as a post-script. At least it was still in Indonesia. China is beyond any definition of your contract.'

'We found *your* contract a little limited.' Ben was dismissive. 'We want assurance our full report will receive attention.'

'I can't guarantee what the minister will do. You know that. Anyway...' Connor's smile was tight. 'Until I actually have it, I can't do anything – useful or otherwise.'

They had reached a lobby, which seemed a good place to deposit his guests. 'Wait here. I'll be back in an hour or so – and don't you dare move.' He could hear the siren of the arriving cavalcade. For the past week he had been wanting to get his hands on Ben, but right now he was the last person he needed. He lengthened his stride to the main entrance.

Simone's eyes were on him as she walked up the steps through a crush of Chinese and UK media people. She was, as ever, a fashion template for a particular type of career woman. Once she had told him laughingly that she favoured the labels the younger royal wives wore. He could well believe that.

'Connor.' Simone acknowledged him, looking like the cat with the cream. This was her moment to shine, and he got a little of the reflected light. 'I can't believe how well the visit's going. The PM's on top form and is optimistic we're making real inroads… Interesting new partnership possibilities.'

'Excellent, Minister.' Connor nodded. 'We've been working hard enough for this.' And that was true. Simone's department, under his supervision, had been working tirelessly behind the scenes with counterparts in China, working with and through their respective embassies. The diplomats had, as always, done a great job of opening doors and keeping conversations going. And he had been back and forth to China the past year or more. It was this – working towards a comprehensive trade deal with China – that had consumed him. And would cement his career.

Connor watched the prime minister make his way up the steps through a phalanx of press. In response to an anodyne question he cheerily called, 'Excellent! We've been most impressed by what we've seen… been so well looked after.' The PM looked grand, his greying hair adding dignity to his pudgy schoolboy face. He had lost a few kilos from his girth and had a surprising choice of jazzy ties, into which the media were always trying to read significance. Today it was a multi-coloured check. Make of that what you will, Connor thought with a smile.

Connor didn't give Ben another thought as the members of the trade delegation trooped towards the prepped conference room. So far so good, and the Chinese could be relied on to manage the occasion to within an inch of their lives.

From a distance, through the bustle of people moving back and forth through the lobby, Yulia eyed two uniformed police officers outside the press room: slender young men with peaked hats shading their eyes, ties carefully knotted, jackets buttoned and pistols in hip holsters. They, along with four bulky security guards, created a solid barrier. Her nerves were jangling but she trusted this tension would not manifest. The tip of Ben's tongue darted out to lick his lips, suggesting he wasn't as composed as he appeared. She caught his eye, he nodded and, notebooks in hand, they rushed up to the security men.

'We're late!' Yulia gasped in Mandarin, wiping her brow. 'Very late. With *The Times*, British paper… press cards stolen. Got given these, last minute.' She flashed her visitor's ID. 'Mr Connor Ahearn, a *senior* British government official, authorised these.' The minders turned and conferred, then talked to the two police officers. 'Please, check with him,' Yulia pressed. 'He's inside. Go. Please go and get him. Check with him.' Again, the security men conferred; again, Yulia pressed. 'We're have a deadline… Ask Mr Ahearn, or find the media co-ordinator…'

She hadn't a clue if there was a person filling that role – if the role even existed. The problem she was causing was outside the security guys' brief – and the police officers'. She and Ben weren't terrorists run amok or – obvious – protestors.

'Please help us.' She flashed a smile, trying to appear like a normal person.

One of the guards stepped forward, arm raised, palm towards her, and it was clear that she and Ben were about to be sent packing. *What to do now?* Just then the door of the press room opened, and two Chinese journalists hurried out, phones in hand. Yulia peered inside and spotted the back of Connor's head. She tugged a security officer's sleeve as he was about to close the door.

'That British man.' She pointed. 'Front row, right at the end. That's Mr Ahearn, our contact. Please ask him to come.'

The security man hesitated and frowned. She was banking that he would not want to walk the length of the hall and risk disrupting procedures.

Again, the conferring. Yulia jiggled from foot to foot, restating they were on deadline, hinting the UK government would be unhappy to know they had been barred. *Very* unhappy. This the men understood. Swiftly the door was opened. She and Ben walked in and one of the security guards stepped in behind them. The solid door clunked shut.

Wow... For a moment Yulia was overwhelmed by their daring, by the room itself and the people in it. She was just an ordinary woman, who until now had never dreamt of doing anything like this. She began to quake afresh.

The security guard indicated two empty seats towards the back, separated by a chair already occupied, and stood just inside the door.

Ben tugged her by the arm. 'OK,' she said. But she felt far from OK.

Ben edged past knees, apologising. He kept his head down and lowered himself into the seat next to someone he took to be a British journalist. The man was slouched in his seat, every so often making a desultory note on a pad resting on his lap. Yulia settled on the other side and shot him a glance, wordlessly telling him, *I've got us in, now over to you.*

The Chinese had fielded their vice premier. Ben recognised him and knew environmental protection was included on his brief. Excellent. The vice premier and his own prime minister were at their respective lecterns. Behind them, political officials from China and the UK sat on a line of chairs. He recognised Simone Bailey. It was refreshing to see a woman – a woman of colour at that – among so many dark-suited men. He brought his attention to the speakers: the prime minister was answering a question about government priorities.

'So, a number of key areas: banking and financial services. We have the brands and China has an expanding market. A perfect fit. And environmental technology. As you know my government is particularly keen to partner initiatives that are good for the environment and good for business.' He turned to smile at the Chinese vice premier, who was listening to a translated version in his earpiece. 'We see interesting opportunities…'

Ben leant towards the bored-looking journalist next to him and asked: 'Forest products from China. Has he mentioned those?

'Nope.'

'Don't you think they're important?'

The journalist shrugged. 'Don't know, mate.' He frowned, taking in Ben's visitor's pass. Forestalling questions of who the hell he was, or why he was here, Ben nudged him. 'Ask him. Go on.'

The journalist shrugged again and shook his head as other journalists raised their hands and were selected. Ben listened to the upbeat replies the PM was a master at delivering, assuring the audience that everything was rosy. He sensed the prime minister didn't want to hog the limelight any longer, wanting to shift questions to the senior Chinese politician. Ben nudged the reluctant journalist.

'Go on. No one's covered this. A new angle. Worth asking.'

The journalist hesitated then raised his hand. Ben had no idea who he was but figured he might be from a British tabloid on a jolly. A man at the front of the room, Ben identified as the UK comms guy, gestured in his direction, saying, 'At the back,' maybe thinking he should give him a break.

'Prime Minister...' The journalist cleared his throat. 'What about trade in forest products? Do they feature in the scheme of things?'

'Of course, I'm glad you asked.' The PM beamed. 'China continues to be a crucial partner and—'

'Prime Minister, what guarantees are there it's all legally sourced?' Ben cut in, calling out, not waiting for some benign spiel, and not caring if he busted this carefully crafted mission. Connor shot to his feet, recognising his voice, but Ben pressed on. 'I mean, timber products making their way to the UK... Doctor Ben Fletcher... we've been looking into this. We want to highlight irregularities—'

He got no further. The security guard, realising his blunder, had hauled his chair back and grabbed his arm – the uninjured one, thankfully – crooking an elbow around his neck threatening to choke him. Heads swivelled. Sharp words in Mandarin from the stage – a Chinese manager taking control – were louder than the surprised mumbles from the gathered audience. He spied Connor's face, frozen in rage, bearing down. Damn! He had wanted to say more.

Christ almighty... what the fuck? Connor couldn't get out of the room quickly enough. He had snatched a glance at Simone, her eyes wide and lips forming the words: 'That's him?' He'd been a complacent idiot – a *feckin' eejit,* his dad would say – to trust Ben.

'What the f...!' He was beyond the thick doors in the lobby where Ben and Yulia were being manhandled. A security fellow had Ben's arm in a tight lock that might well dislocate a shoulder. From Ben's sharp yelp it might have been his wounded shoulder, but Connor didn't give a shit. He jerked his head towards Yulia and hissed to one of the Chinese: 'Get her out of here.' Whether or not they understood English, they got the message, clamped her even more firmly and began marching her away. The woman was shouting Ben's name, and he struggled to get to her, yelling: 'Don't you dare lay a finger on her!'

Connor grabbed Ben by his shirt, thrusting his face close. 'What in hell's name are you trying to achieve?'

'We want to be heard!'

'From inside a Chinese prison? I can assure you that getting you out wouldn't be a priority for our embassy right now.'

'Ben!' Yulia was twisting back. 'I'm OK... *It's* OK... forget about Linda.'

Connor took a breath. He had no interest in what happened to this Indonesian woman and for a moment couldn't think who Linda was. He was aware of frank stares from people around him and of a gathering police presence. This needed de-escalating. 'He's fine... fine... I'll deal with this... Thanks, fellas... It's OK.'

Taking Ben's elbow in a firm grip he steered him away.

'What're you going to do with Yulia?' Ben sounded fearful.

'You should have considered that earlier. But I'm not going to do anything. The first flight back to Jakarta if her embassy has any sense, and your flight out will be the quickest I can arrange. In the meantime, you have my company. Collect your bags, and I'll be right outside the jacks if you need a shit. Understand?'

Boy, this was gutter talk. The kind of talk his dad might have used. The kind of talk he had schooled himself out of years ago. Ben was twisting around, his eyes following Yulia. Connor jerked him. 'Understand?'

Ben found Connor had been true to his word – the man had stuck to him like a leech and was still by his side as they travelled in the back of a taxi to the airport. He had downloaded his report – for whatever good it would do – and watched Connor tuck the memory stick safely in his pocket. He hadn't seen Yulia but they had managed to text. She had assured him there had been no more heavy-handed treatment, only a none-too-subtle nudge to get the first available flight out. This was no way to part from the woman he was just beginning a relationship with. Was he failing in every aspect of his life? He forced his attention back to what Connor was saying.

'...and we can take it your outburst will be expunged from the official Chinese records—'

'Expunged! Nice word. I've just about been wiped out for real. Twice.'

'Did we ask you to risk your life? Would we ever?'

'At least give me the satisfaction of going public with what we've got. You've a duty to tell the truth.'

'Duty?' Connor scoffed. 'If you want to talk about that, then yours is to your country, or least those that pay you. And truth? Get it in perspective. We're talking billion-pound contracts. Look around you.' Connor gestured to the ongoing mega-scale construction projects jostling for space on the skyline. 'We need to be part of this, and all you can think of is bloody trees.'

He lurched across to grip Connor's collar. 'Fuck you! I can talk in billions too. Each year illegal logging is putting billions of dollars into the pockets of the timber mafia. Are you willing to see the entire planet denuded—?'

Connor thrust him away. 'Of course not. I know, I know.'

Ben caught the taxi driver looking back at them. Connor raised a hand. 'It's OK,' he reassured him, before turning back to Ben.

'The Earth's frying. We need our forests. Even so, there are other things at stake here, and what you are doing has the potential to sour relationships with China. We're not going to let this happen. *I'm* not going to let it happen. We need binding trade deals with China.' Connor sighed. 'You have my word I will do everything in my power to get your report before the right eyes. I can't promise more.'

'And perhaps not yet. Perhaps you'll sit on it. Right, Connor? Too embarrassing.'

Connor looked out of the window and they rode in silence a while.

'Here's the thing, Ben. Trevor's a prick. I honestly had no idea he was cutting corners. Not till your little exposé arrived on my screen: the AZTAR logo splashed across everything.' Connor looked him in the eye. 'I swear, I had no idea he was cutting corners. When I challenged him, he admitted "some" timber might have been passed along the chain that shouldn't have been, mixed in with the legal stuff.'

'From the concession next to ours that AZTAR are renting?'

Connor nodded. 'That's the one. A few more trees here and there, and who's to notice? The thing is Trevor was out of his depth. Turns out his business partner—'

'Zumran?'

'Yeah, him. He was using AZTAR machinery to extract in that protected area – all those barges you saw – all those Zs painted on the butt end of logs – and dear Trev was out of the loop. Hadn't a fucking clue.'

'You believe that?'

'I do actually.' Connor smiled. 'You have to understand, the embarrassment isn't just on the international level, it's national too. Trevor's a generous donor to the party—'

'What a surprise,' Ben scoffed.

'...and personal.'

Ben frowned, not knowing how Connor might be involved.

Connor sighed. 'You see, my dad was just another Mick trying his luck across the water – doing hard graft road construction – and it was Trevor's father who gave him a leg-up. My mam worked at the Huntley and Palmers factory in Reading for years. An ordinary life. Anyway, our families became friendly. Before Trevor's old man died, he forked out for me to study in Oxford... You know the politics, economics, and philosophy route so many of our great leaders have chosen to ease their way into public life. And for sure it helped me.'

'OK. But the college fund thing – having Trevor's dad support you. There's nothing wrong with that.'

'Some might conclude Trevor's had access others haven't. Which is correct when you think about it. Others working in business and industry mightn't have managed to promote their schemes in the way he's done. With this Indonesian PPI, I've eased the way for him for sure. No question about that.'

Ben said nothing, knowing this could get Connor sacked. Connor tapped his arm. 'Remember, I'm the one useful contact you still have on the inside. I know money doesn't mean much to you, but you like your opinion to be valued. Call it professional ego—'

'For God's sake!'

'Oh yes, I know I'm right. I know what drives you. Even after this debacle, I can still provide you with access to the inner circle, still provide you with contracts—'

'Even after this debacle, as you call it?'

'If you play your cards right, why not? Just don't bite the hand that feeds you, Ben. Don't be in a rush to hasten my departure from the department, there's more a civil service career can offer me.'

He might be thinking of a Queen's Honours List gong, Ben thought.

'Besides,' Connor was saying, 'there are others in the front line.'

'You'd hide behind Simone?'

'Ministers tend to come and go. She hasn't found a way of shaking up the ministry – not yet – but she wants to. So yeah, I'm still in post, and you know what? I like my job. I'm good at it. I care for the work and for my staff. You'll understand that.'

Ben shot him a look. Why this sudden need to confide? His way of saying "Sorry, I'm human too. I make mistakes"? Connor would know he wasn't the vindictive kind, so he was unlikely to use this against him to remove him from Whitehall. Still, hiding behind Simone seemed shabby.

Tapping his pocket Connor asked, 'You haven't shared it – passed it to outside parties? Guarantee me that. It is our material.'

'Yeah, I mean, no. I haven't passed it on.'

Ben looked out the window. He said nothing till they reached the airport, and very little as Connor waited while he checked his bag: only a terse, 'Bye' as he headed towards security checks.

22

DAE.org/Blogs/Linda

Just to remind you what we're up against, here's a **link** to the latest assassinations of environmental activists. I know it's not a cheerful subject, but don't turn away. The one in the DRC, Democratic Republic of Congo, was one of our volunteers. I never met her but have spoken with her loads. She was a wonderful woman who somehow managed to keep a sense of humour, and however grim her messages were, she always ended her email with a smiley face emoji. That was her all over, the most positive person you could hope to know. Now she's gone, murdered. And who's listening? Who's taking note? Not governments, that's for sure. It's not just Rob we have to mourn – may his soul rest in peace. Everywhere good people are standing up for the rights of communities; the rights of species other than us humans; the rights of the EARTH. And all too often, these good folks are being silenced.

Now more than ever, it's time for Direct Action.

Remember that trade summit in London I've mentioned? Things are shifting. It's going to be a big deal now. The eyes of the world are going to be on London 24/25 September. This is a great opportunity to raise the profile of our cause. We're connecting with others who want to be heard and we are appealing to YOU. What are YOU doing? We'd love you to join us or help in different ways. We have PLANS and they are growing by the day. Remember, we are stronger together; only then can we hope to make a difference. Tell your friends, tell people who *aren't* your friends. Spread the word.

To find out what Direct Action for the Earth is doing to save our planet and how to get involved, go to our **Campaigns**. Check out our **Membership** schemes and don't log off till you've clicked through to **Donations**.

We sure do have plans, Linda thought, and that Jade girl – woman, she should say – was worth her salt. Linda had underestimated her. Prior to meeting the DAE Australian co-ordinator in Sydney, their contact had been via cyberspace, but how much better to meet in the flesh to truly gauge a person's character.

Jade, of Australian-Samoan parentage, was all dreadlocks, piercings and tribal tattoos. Jade had explained the significance of each piece of body art, rolling up a trouser leg to reveal a hefty, ornamented calf muscle; pulling a blouse off her shoulder to reveal a black tattoo with a flower at the centre of geometric shapes and curling black tendrils. 'Beautiful,' Linda had said, and she meant it, wondering if she had her time again whether she might go in for this kind of thing.

'Give me something big to do,' Jade had begged. 'I'm so sick of inputting effing data and chasing up membership fees. Does my head in.'

'Alrighty… Here's what I want.'

Linda talked about drawing Rob's fans into things, particularly drawing their money into DAE's bank account, 'In Rob's name, of course.' Jade's eyes had lit up, and she had rattled off ideas for a social media campaign. Then Linda told her what she had in mind in Indonesia. That got Jade jiggling.

'Linda, if I'm doing more office shit, I want to be in this, and some of the others will want to too.'

'Sure!'

'Will DAE cover our travel costs?'

'You raise the money, you can come. Six max – make them earn their places. They'll need to feed the beast: images and news through social media—'

'Goes without saying.'

'And regular news outlets – Western media in particular. No freebies.'

Jade had given her the strongest hug, lifting her off the ground and crushing her ribs. Muscular arms like this would be a good thing. Jade would be an asset for what she had in mind.

The decibels of Xcalibur's music would surely penetrate the insulation between his ceiling and the floor of the flat above, and Ben hoped the occupants weren't home. The bass guitar reverberated around the walls and bounced off the inside of his skull. He pressed his knuckles to his temples trying to gather the energy to raise himself from the sofa and switch the music off.

The red wine hadn't lightened the despair seeping into the marrow of his bones. Everything depressed him. The room was exactly as it had been when he left – how could it be otherwise? No one had miraculously been in to finish unpacking his belongings or hang some pictures to make the place homely. Apart from chucking a load of dirty clothes into the washing machine, his travel bag lay largely untouched, and his jungle boots needed a good scrub.

What next? was the question playing out in his brain.

He had been back in London three days. The first day he had shut himself off from everything and everyone, not able to face the world except to check that Yulia had arrived home safely. Even then he had only messaged; hadn't mustered the resolve to speak with her, though he felt sick at not having her with him. She was the only person who had shared his experiences, the only person who would understand how he was feeling. And, he understood from their messages, she was going through her own readjustments. 'I'll speak with you tomorrow,' he promised.

Yesterday he had done a few chores and spoken to those he needed to.

Ben groped for the remote control. Before his thumb found the off icon, a new song started, no longer pounding. Gentle. Rob's voice filled the room. A ballad. He recognised the lyrics as the ones Rob had sung when they'd first met: '*The story's in your eyes… can read it in a dream… see we're coming to the end… No, no… don't wanna wake… wan' it all…*'

Rob had been right to call him a Pommy twat. A sharp pain stabbed his heart as an image of those flies swarming around Rob's slashed throat came to mind. He pushed it away, allowing space for an image of Rob as he would have appeared on stage: a sexy, talented man enjoying his music, his undamaged throat the channel through which his breath and voice emanated. *What a waste. What a fucking tragedy.*

Ben rubbed his temples. What had he achieved today? He had talked to Sarah as he had promised he would do. She had been horrified at the extent of things.

'A knife attack! Shit! Ben!' He had held the phone away from his ear, finding she was talking in exclamation marks as well as writing them. Was this a new habit, or was it justified by what had happened to him?

'Ben… I've got it on speaker… Wait, put the visuals on, Mandy's with me.'

Ben duly pressed the icon. Both women, heads close, appeared. Mandy casually placed an arm around Sarah's shoulder.

'Hiya, Ben. Home safely then.'

'Yep. Thanks.'

'Ben.' Sarah peered closely at the screen. 'We can come and visit, check out how you are.'

'Thanks, but no need. I'm OK. The doctors are just as able to stitch flesh back together in Indonesia as here.'

'Eww! Even so. It would be good to have a proper catch-up, and I want to pick up my ukulele. It must be with your things.' Sarah had once played in a ukulele band and it seemed she wanted to get back into it.

'I've no idea where it is. Could be anywhere.'

'It's not that small!'

'I've not really unpacked.'

'You'd been in that flat for weeks before you left. You must've seen it.'

He ended the call, promising he would arrange a time to

meet. 'Sure, a coffee. I'll get back to you soon. And if I find it, I'll bring it with me.'

He had spoken to his parents, downplaying what had happened so as not to freak them out. They had sympathised and tutted about his "spot of bother" and spent the next hour talking about their own activities: what his brothers were up to; a recent visit by the grandchildren. When his father began a rambling story about walking their neighbour's dog while she was on holiday he wanted to yell, *Shut the fuck up!* Listening to their chatter, the disconnect from his family's goings-on was unnerving. This ordinary everyday life was not something he felt tethered to. They talked of surface things, but he had been journeying to places that were deep, and he did not feel able to share those experiences with his parents. Where to start?

Rob's song was soothing. He let his thoughts drift.

Rick had emailed, alerting him to a research position which had just opened up in Vancouver. 'This might be your thing, Fletch. And by the way, how are you? How's Yulia? And when do I get to see the final report? Not that I care much by now, except I'd like to be paid!!'

More exclamation marks. But fair enough, he should be thinking about his team. He needed to settle their fees. He updated Rick and Ardhi, telling them the report had been filed. Connor might ask him to edit it. That was probable. There might be many reviews before it was accepted and payment received. Rick understood that. He told Rick what else had been going on.

'I take it all back, those things I said,' Rick messaged back. 'Truly impressive, my man.'

Perhaps he should take another look at that research position. Ben got up and went to his laptop. Again, he read the proposal from Simon Fraser University. It looked tempting… but somehow this was not the direction he wanted to go.

Enough! He closed the laptop and looked around the room.

With Xcalibur's music ramped up, he began chucking things out for rubbish or recycle and putting other things back into the packing boxes. There was satisfaction in the growing pile of taped and boxes labelled "kitchen", "bedding" and so on. Then he turned to his work desk and began to sort his books.

Sarah would have to buy another ukulele; they were cheap enough, and he was not convinced he even had the thing. He made some phone calls, sent some emails and gave notice on his tenancy. He would lose a month's rent but too bad. In the scheme of things, this no longer mattered.

He contacted Yulia, this time via his laptop, desperate to hear her voice and see her face. He told her lots of things; told her of his plans.

'Ben.' Yulia bit her lip. 'I've passed everything to Linda. You must have figured that.'

'Yeah.' He had been angry at the time – this was not her call – but since then he had come to realise that someone needed to do it as he seemed incapable of taking that step. Linda had pretty much used the same argument. 'It's OK,' he said.

Yulia closed her eyes for a moment. 'Missing you,' she said, bringing her fingers to the screen.

'Yes,' he replied, his fingers meeting hers before ending the connection. The screen reverted to his current screensaver: a selfie Yulia had taken of them both in a Jakarta park a day before they flew to China. He glanced at the time. Linda would be well into her working day by now if she was home. If... She was a busy woman and could be anywhere. He took some settling breaths before pressing the icon for Linda's internet phone. No visuals, audio was quite enough. If Linda saw his face it would betray how low he was feeling, and he suspected she would not hold back from smirking with warped pleasure at his predicament. Was he being unfair? The ringtone went on and on, and he was about to end the call when she picked up.

'Well, well. Who've we here? So Bambi's been losing some of his baby spots, growing up fast.'

'You could say that.' Ben couldn't help smiling. 'I'm up for losing the rest.'

'Atta boy!'

Connor swilled his favourite special edition peaty whisky around the glass – Scottish, not Irish – and inhaled the smoky aroma before taking an appreciative sip. Ahh… If he were told he had only half an hour to live, which would he choose? This, or a fuck with Tess in that silky underwear she kept for special occasions? A dilemma. Both were succulent. Make it an hour and he could fit in both. He took another sip, swilling it around his mouth before swallowing. Received wisdom suggested alcohol should not be drunk before bed, and the ornate fingers of his grandfather clock pointed to ten after midnight. But he didn't hold with that.

His laptop rested on the coffee table, open to a key document for the summit. He wanted to read it through one more time before giving the go-ahead for final papers to be printed out early tomorrow. Many government departments had been hard at it, staff working all hours, including him and his co-workers. Reading it again, he wasn't tempted to suggest further amendments and was satisfied everything was good to go. Yes, this was good. Life was good. Everything was good.

The past two weeks since returning from Beijing had been intense, and the last few days frantic as delegates were hosted, pre-meetings held and arms twisted. Barring a terrorist attack, or some Act of God – he was tempted to cross himself – everything should go smoothly. This was the most comprehensive trade summit his government had hosted for many years. He had been working hard to achieve a good outcome for his department. It was focusing on Asia, showing what Britain could do as a gung-ho, go-it-alone nation at the edge of Europe. Every big cheese from participating nations was here, and security was tight, the Metropolitan Police cancelling all leave.

Simone had collared him earlier that evening, on edge, wanting to micro-manage every detail. He had reassured her: 'Don't worry. Everything's in order, and the displays look great.'

'Yes, I saw them earlier.' Simone beamed. 'The PM popped over with me, and he was impressed. You and the comms team have done us credit.'

Connor nearly fell off his chair at his boss's compliment. But he agreed they did make a splash.

The government was profiling two PPIs, each with well-designed display boards and video loops in the lobby where delegates would congregate for coffee and lunch. His, or more to the point Simone's, was boldly titled *Positive Partnership Initiative. Indonesia, United Kingdom, Forest to Furniture* and had good quality blow-up photos (*thanks, Ben*), the whole sustainable chain showcased visually. There were magnificent photos of lush Indonesian rainforest; guys wearing safety helmets felling a tree in the said same forest; AZTAR logging trucks loaded with marked logs. Another showed branded stacked timber at a sawmill. There was an Indonesian guy bent over a workbench, with a caption explaining he was making furniture. Yet another image showed polo-shirted peaked-cap workers packaging the (he supposed) same wooden furniture into well-labelled boxes, the PPI logos in evidence. And there was Trevor, beaming happily at one of his stores, posing by his furniture, a sign resting on top marked with the PPI logo. Thick green arrows pointed from one link to the other, the chain clear, demonstrating how the business sector, with government support, could make this Positive Partnership Initiative work.

'You and the comms team have done us credit.' Simone's words rang in his ears. Rare praise.

He finished his whisky, glanced at the bottle... No, he needed a clear head in the morning, and he had to catch some sleep as he would be back at the office early. Tomorrow was a big day.

23

THE ANCIENT BUS TRAVELLED A DUSTY ROAD BEFORE slowing and turning onto a smaller, even less well-maintained road pitted with potholes. As the bus juddered deeper into the Kalimantan countryside, farms gave way to patchy scrubland and palm plantations.

Ben passed a bottle of water to Yulia sitting next to him.

When Yulia had understood he would be returning, she had got back to him quickly, saying, 'I've taken more time from work – another week. They're not happy, but we are shuffling my projects with others in our team.'

He had not argued with her. There was no point.

The bus jolted over a particularly deep pothole, drawing a collective groan from all the passengers and a tart American, 'Goddamn!'

He turned to Linda, who was sitting across from him. Her grey hair stood out among the youthful passengers filling the bus: Indonesian men and woman and a handful of Australians. Linda gave him a thumbs-up. He responded by sucking his teeth and raising his shoulders in a "What the hell…" kind of way.

At the back of the bus Jade, the Australian woman he had just met, was intent on partying. She and the other four Australians had brought enough beer to sink a ship. They were rowdy, the Indonesians less so, probably more concerned about consequences. Ben stared at Linda, reflecting… No, she wasn't the one who looked out of place; she fitted right in. It was he and Yulia who had shaken their heads at Linda's 'Sure I can't tempt you?' as she held out DAE T-shirts like everyone else was wearing. Most environmental logos favoured green as a primary colour with caring images: hands encircling the earth or green shoots. Direct Action for the Earth's brand was in your face.

'All right folks. Ready?' Linda pushed herself up from her seat wearing her logoed T-shirt like an armoured breast plate, the orange fist encircled by a blue planet reminding Ben of Soviet-era propaganda.

A young man seated in front of Ben adjusted a bright blue DAE peaked cap, an orange fist punching forward on soft fabric covering the head. He could imagine these caps displaying well on drone footage. He watched men and women pull caps down to shield their eyes, and possibly their identities, while others wore orange and blue patterned bandannas encircling their heads. They looked like marauders and Ben could feel his stomach jigging with what, as kids, they had called "butterflies".

The last time he had been on this stretch of road was with Ardhi and Rick. They were approaching the same sawmill they had visited. He glanced at his watch: 7.30am. The mill would be in full swing.

With one hand Jade hauled a bag bulging with kit from the luggage rack – that woman was an Amazon. All the bags being dragged from under seats or from overhead were jam packed with crowbars, sledgehammers and much else besides. He had a moment of misgiving, fingering the camera and video recorder hanging around his neck. These were his implements, his tools, his weapons. He and Yulia would bear witness to Direct Action for the Earth's protest. That was what they had agreed to. Even so, this was uncomfortable. He was crossing a line: something he could never have imagined himself doing.

As the bus drew to a halt, he looked through the window. The timber yard was exactly as he had seen it weeks earlier. Grapples and forklifts moved between stacks of roundwood logs ready for milling, all marked with the certification logo; and neatly stacked piles of sawn planks also bore the brand. But... he peered closely... the quantity of roundwood logs was double what their audit had seen. He knew the volume of timber passing through did not square with what should have been harvested and had no interest in the rigmarole of even bothering to check. Too late for that.

'Let's go! Let's go! Y'know what you've got to do. Let's get this done.' Linda led the charge, her youthful followers spewing out of the bus, he and Yulia bringing up the rear.

A man hurried from the yard office brandishing a baseball bat. Ben recognised him as the manager he had met during that formal, less hostile, visit. The sawmill boss didn't have eyes for him; didn't notice him. He rapidly assessed the situation before snatching a phone from his pocket and retreating. Before he reached the office door two of Linda's gang had rushed him, knocking his phone from his hand. Even so, one way or another it wouldn't be long before word got out.

Sawmill workers paused, alarm on their faces, when they saw the blue and orange invaders. Others, initially unaware, continued to feed logs into a bandsaw, dust flying. Against the background of whirring machinery the yelling began from saboteurs and workers alike. Ben didn't understand much of what they were saying but he understood chaos.

The electricity was switched off and Ben recorded a chunk of metal being lobbed at the saw blade, flinching at the damage to the expensive machinery. He turned his lens on a crowbar-wielding saboteur levering a mechanism out of kilter, then filmed Linda, sledgehammer in hand, swiping a blade and putting it beyond useful purpose.

He bellowed, 'Watch out!' as a sawmill worker came charging past brandishing an offcut. The man's intended victim dodged and blocked the blow with a crowbar. Three women liberally squirted superglue into finer components. He recorded them too.

'Swap ya.' Linda nudged his arm and held out a sledgehammer. He shook his head. 'C'mon,' she urged. 'You're still wet behind the ears. Don't stand by and let an old lady shame you.' Still he didn't move. That was not his way. Linda grabbed the camera straps around his neck and thrust her face close, voice urgent. 'Do it! Get involved. Just do it!' Her eyes were fierce and determined, urging him to take another step. Her lips began to spread into a sneer, and he thought she might be about to taunt him with Bambi again.

'All right.' Ben inhaled sharply, blew out his cheeks then followed his leader's order. He handed her the video recorder and camera and accepted the hammer. Linda thrust him forward with a shove in the small of his back. He gripped the handle, feeling the heft of the weapon, and like the foot-soldier he had become, he sought a spot in the escalating melee. Swinging his mace sideways he brought it crashing into the edge of a blade.

'I can just see the headlines,' Linda shouted. 'Frustrated bureaucrat turns rogue male. What's that saying? One picture's worth a thousand words? C'mon now, put your back into it!'

'You'd better be right.' Ben glanced up to see Linda recording. He brought his hammer down on the stilled blade with a thwack, raising it again and again, seeing the metal yield and buckle.

Enough! Dodging activists and mill workers, Ben edged away to retrieve his cameras. This sawmill wouldn't be operational for some time and he looked around, grateful that no one on either side appeared to be injured. A sawmill worker was standing back, hands on hips, looking dazed. He would be a local man just trying to earn enough to get by. Ben had a pang of misgiving. What was he doing here? How crazy was this? This was not his way. He hated waste and vandalism. He hurried into the yard to find a group of activists, paint canisters in hand, spraying "ILLEGAL" in huge letters across stacks of wood. Yulia stood nearby, recording.

'Yulia. OK?' She glanced up and smiled tightly. He had not wanted her here, repeating Linda's argument to her: 'Remember, I get to leave; you don't.' To which she had countered, 'And you remember, I'm my own woman.'

'Let's go!' Linda began herding them back to the bus. 'We're done.' She grinned at Ben. 'Talk about throwing a monkey wrench into the machinery.'

'You mean a spanner in the works. That's Brit talk.'

'Ya know,' Linda chuckled, 'I'm beginning to like you.' She gestured to those taking too long to move. 'C'mon! Get moving! We've some way to go.'

At the open fuel tank of a vehicle, an activist dropped an empty bleach bottle on the ground before hurrying away. By the look of other bottles and discarded small sacking bags used to carry sand, Ben figured all the vehicles would be out of action. Hurrying to their bus, guarded by four baton-wielding activists, he had become part of a swarm of blue and orange locusts damaging crops as they moved across the land.

'Where next, boss lady?' Jade's teasing question was to Linda.

'You'll find out. Round up the others. Let's go!'

Jade raced back making wide sweeping gestures to the stragglers. 'Woof, woof. Shift your arses! Get a move on!'

Where next, indeed. Ben had signed up to this thing not knowing exactly what Linda had planned. 'Better not to know too much,' she had cautioned.

Connor decided to walk from his office. Crossing Trafalgar Square he had to navigate the human rights and environmental pressure groups and protestors – thousands of them – who clustered around banners. Greenpeace; Extinction Rebellion; Direct Action for the Earth; Rainforest Rescue; Amnesty International. It would be better if they weren't here, but it was understandable. They were an exuberant lot, colourful, people and banners alike. But it was the orangutan that got his attention.

He stopped to admire the huge puppet, easily twenty feet tall, its orange furry body hunkering down, a cuddly baby orangutan peeping over its shoulder. A strong-looking man supported its main frame, while two others manipulated the arms, each of them holding two long sticks connected to an elbow and a wrist. The massive creature seemed almost real, bending a limb as if to scratch its black face, its dark eyes piercing. *Boy, this was clever.* A good amount of time had been spent modelling this thing and the media were focusing on it. It would make good TV and social media for sure. He brushed aside an attempt to thrust a leaflet into his hand. He could hardly walk into the conference clutching propaganda: a baby orangutan photo, the message screaming loss of habitat and rainforest.

The official route passed this way, so all the delegates could take a gander if they wished, rather than turn away. Good on the London Mayor for allowing this in the name of democracy. Not that Connor shared the more radical views represented by many here: the dreadlocked, tattooed, skin-pierced lot his father might have labelled yobbos and told to take a bath, but Connor was comfortable with the way things could be done in Britain. Kind of messy, but democratic.

He flashed his ID and made his way through police cordons on the Strand to the porticoed Law Society building in Chancery Lane, where the waiting media huddled behind a barrier, long lenses focused, video cameras mounted on tripods or shoulders. And, he noted, a few armed police at the ready. Others would be discreetly held back out of sight, ready if needed.

As he walked through the lobby, he admired the displays. Yes, the PPI forest project looked impressive. All that forest, that industry and proof of international partnerships. Good stuff. He sensed a smug smile lifting the corners of his lips. But why not enjoy small successes?

Inside the sumptuous marble-columned Reading Room, he checked that the rejigged seating positions around the massive conference table had been actioned. Yes, the Chinese delegates had been moved closer to the PM. All good. The room was abuzz with advisers, administrative staff and lesser mortals. Such details were not his brief, but no harm in checking, and he fidgeted, surveying the room. On the central conference table name cards were clearly positioned, delegate packs neatly laid out, headphones and bottles of water at the ready.

Chairs for aides lined the walls, his own positioned behind Simone's at the main table. Looking up to the balcony, on one side he watched translators settling behind desks, while on the opposite side, where the overspill of junior staff had space to sit, there was some jostling for better positions and claiming seats in that time-honoured way of placing bags or jackets on them. Connor rubbed his hands, the excitement and anticipation in the air almost tangible.

A low rumble of voices indicated the limousines had offloaded their valuable cargo and the greets and meets and coffees had taken place. Connor watched the PM stride confidently into the room, a phalanx of delegates and staff from the invited Asian countries behind. Simone walked next to the Indonesian trade minister, engaged in an easy chat, judging by her relaxed expression. Everything was going like clockwork for a prompt nine o'clock start. He settled in his chair near the prime minister and Simone. All forty or so delegates settled in their seats ready to roll. Bang on time. The prime minister stood and beamed his megawatt smile.

'Welcome... welcome, all of you. I'm delighted to be hosting this landmark summit building stronger trade links between *all* of Asia and Britain...' Connor caught the slightest movement of an eyebrow from the Indonesian trade minister – one of the countries shunted back by China. '...and we can be confident our plans for the future are grounded in solid preparation and real partnerships. Partnerships that play to our national strengths, acknowledge our cultural differences yet are mindful of our global responsibilities.'

Looking at the nodding faces listening directly, or through simultaneous translation via their headphones, Connor decided the touch was just right. He settled back and crossed his legs.

The scratched and dusty bus was at a standstill, angled across the forest track, the front overhanging a deep drain. Yulia worried the compacted earth of the badly constructed road might give way and the bus might lurch forward to rest on the axle, then it, and they, would be stuck. At least it was facing the right direction – the way they had come from. A quick getaway was unimaginable, but there was scope to imagine some form of getaway.

All of Linda's disciples were nonchalantly gathered as if they were on a picnic: smoking, sipping from flasks, cans of beer or water bottles, grabbing a bite to eat from plastic containers or munching on bread rolls and fruit. Their numbers had been bolstered by a dozen or so men and women from the village – *their* village – the only village that mattered. Njau was here, and Asung, and Bai… And children. Yulia pressed her lips in frustration watching Asung's two boys cavorting with a bunch of others, excited to be part of this staged drama. Her gaze moved to Asung and Bai, who were talking quietly, Asung's body quite still but her hands worked, twisting the fabric of her dress in a gesture Yulia had come to recognise.

The only place the bus had been able to turn around was at the village. Before setting off back to the point of the planned sit-in a mile or so away, they had piled out for a quick hello: a courtesy call. The villagers needed to know what was being planned on their doorstep.

Everyone Yulia remembered came out to see them, astonished to see her, Ben and Linda back so soon. Back at all. There were hurried hugs and quick chats. It was wonderful to see Asung, and Bai especially. She managed a quick word with the girl and was concerned to find her so withdrawn.

Linda had tapped her on the shoulder, saying, 'You translate,' before stepping up onto the bus entrance to face the gathering, her voice ringing out: 'Join us. Help us make a stand.'

'Wait.' Yulia held up her hand. Refusing to be drawn in. Refusing to translate. 'This isn't a recruitment drive.'

'Sure it is!'

Ben had come running. 'Linda. Get down.' He tugged her but she resisted.

'Uh, uh, this isn't your gig. Where was I?' Then Linda was off again, repeating what she'd said, and again insisting Yulia translate. Ben raised his shoulders, clearly angry, but Linda was right – this was her gig. The American had raised her fist, eyes raking the gathered crowd.

'You need to show the world you exist. Stand with us. You'll be on TV. Important people will see you. What do you say?'

How could she? How could Linda do this? Yulia refused to translate and Ben argued, 'You're not dragging them in.' But Linda was bossy, and she had got her way.

'That road is shit,' someone said. 'No one maintains it. The culverts are blocked, only trucks can get past the parts that are washed out. Can hardly get my bike over.'

'Yes,' another said. 'Maybe they'll fix it if we protest.'

'Maybe that nurse will come back.'

The list of grievances went on and on and there were the dead men, Balan and Ule, to stand up for. Yulia found that the villagers *did* want to come.

Linda had been jubilant. 'Great. We'll put them at the front of the group. It'll look better on camera. You know, locals take a stand, not just a bunch of leftie urbanites.'

Yulia felt used by Linda. She had been tricky. This was no picnic.

'You OK?' She responded to Ben's touch and concerned look with a nod then bit her lip. 'Mmm. I think so. How long do you think we've got?'

Ben would know what she meant: how long before the police

tracked them down after the sawmill people raised the alert. He shrugged. She could see by the tightness in his shoulders and the set of his jaw that he was tense as he joked, 'You never know where things might lead when you sign up for one of Linda's jaunts.' That was so true. Yulia had allowed herself to be sucked deeper into this "jaunt". From being a more or less passive observer, she had instructed two of the older village boys how to use her video camera. She had left them fiddling with it, having fun experimenting with the equipment, and it kept them at a distance. Two disciples were squatting at the side of the road preparing a drone fitted with a camera. They looked like boys with toys playing in a park at the weekend. They couldn't be aged more than eighteen or twenty. Fresh anxiety gripped her.

Someone shouted, 'It's coming!'

Voices hushed, and she heard the change of gear, the driver slowing in readiness for the bend in the track leading from the forest. Linda called out, 'Quick. Positions. Link arms!'

Any moment now the logging truck would bear down on them. She bunched in tight, finding Asung next to her, threading one arm through hers, the other linked with Bai's. She asked Asung: 'You sure? You're all sure? You don't need to be here.' Asung nodded. She had been resolute that her entire family take a stand, even her boys.

A silence fell as they watched the heavy vehicle take the bend twenty metres ahead, the chrome on the bright yellow cab glinting in the afternoon sun. The driver could see them, was leaning on the horn, blaring repeatedly. The vehicle looked so big... It would stop... Had to stop. She tightened her grip around Asung. The headman's family had come to symbolise everything to her: the community she wanted to help, the people she wanted to show the world mattered and shouldn't be shunted aside by industry and government, yet she was doing a terrible job of it and was drawing them deeper into danger. She was confused at how this had escalated. How had she let this happen?

The big tyres of the logging truck rolled forward through the rutted road, bearing down. The truck must stop. The driver wouldn't dare plough into people, and besides, their bus was stationed just metres behind them. They wouldn't ram it...?

Chanting, 'Stand up! Fight back!' Linda pushed her way to the front. Jade, towering over Linda, was at her side, fist raised, bellowing, 'Stand up! Fight back!'

Yulia unpeeled Asung's arm and tried to push her away. 'Go. Both of you.' She looked at Bai, but Asung clung to her with one arm, gripping her daughter tightly with the other. The three of them were in a tight huddle, activists chanting, 'Stand up! Fight back!'

Above them, a drone circled.

She could see Ben, camera ready, positioned off the track a little way ahead to get the best view. She was happy he wasn't in the thick of things. She wanted him safe. He had been through enough, and she knew in her heart he was here because this was her country. He was doing this for her.

The truck wasn't slowing fast enough. Ben could see two men in the cab, the driver blaring the horn. 'Fuck!' His shout merged with everyone else's as they scattered, dropping belongings and diving out of the way. Moments later the driver braked hard, the truck slewed, jack-knifing, threatening to topple with its heavy load.

'Idiot!' Ben raced forward and leapt on the driver's side running board, the truck still moving. Reaching through the open window to grab the wheel he yelled, 'What the fuck? You trying to kill people?' The startled driver elbowed him away, screaming at two activists whose faces crowded in the passenger-side window. Hands gripped Ben's jeans and he was yanked off by an activist. Moments later the cab doors were flung open and the driver and passenger tussled to the ground.

Linda! His eyes searched for her then he raced over. 'Is this what you had in mind? There are kids here. That was dangerous!'

'Should've been kept back. I told someone to do that. Not my fault.'

'But—'

'No buts.' Linda brushed him aside, her attention elsewhere. 'Someone... Jade! Get under the hood, unbolt the injectors.'

'On it, boss!' The Australian loped forward.

'And for good measure, pour bleach in the tank, if you've any left.'

At the sound of another truck approaching Linda scanned the forest road. 'Great! Another one. Bring them on!'

A cheer rose from the young DAE activists and Linda chortled. By the gleam in her eye it looked like the damned woman was enjoying herself. Ben glanced up at the hovering drone camera. It would be getting good images.

Linda had hinted this wasn't the only action happening but had been tight-lipped when he asked what else was going on. 'You'll find out,' she'd said.

He felt he had done enough bearing witness and turned to look for Yulia. The two of them could make themselves more useful keeping the kids out of the way.

It looked like they might be here a while.

The call had come yesterday.

'Are you up for it?' DAE's London co-ordinator asked.

'Course!' he'd scoffed.

The activist had rallied ten volunteers, enough to look good on camera, and he was satisfied their placards looked good too, with images of forests and orangutans. He had rooted around a drawer to find a favourite mask, a gorilla one, and found himself cavorting with a fox and a pig among black balaclava-covered heads. Naturally, everyone wore their DAE T-shirts.

'Let's do it!' He gave the order and walked purposely towards Arnott's shop, a brick in one hand and a sledgehammer in the other.

It was opening time at the London retail park when he drew back his arm and hurled the brick with all his strength at Arnott's plate glass window. The brick bounced off. The toughened glass had shattered into a web of cracks but hadn't caved in. He gripped the sledgehammer and went for it. With a few good bashes it yielded. The shattered pane knocked over a sale sign and sent shards over a display of garden furniture. He kicked at the glass with a sturdy black lace-up ankle boot, roaring, 'C'mon!' Four of his mates pushed in more of the glass. He was conscious of running feet, and watched as a store manager, or someone in charge, raced to the door and bolted it. He grinned, yelling, 'That won't keep us out.'

The activist barely registered a woman yelling from the car park, 'You bastards!' as she turned tail and hurried away with a pushchair. Others yelled shit at him too, but he was immune, had been for years. Some recently arrived customers peered out of their parked cars, one with a phone to her ear, another holding hers out, filming. He crawled through the smashed display window.

No one stopped them as they tossed wooden chairs and dragged heavy furniture out onto the pavement. No one stopped them as one of his group poured petrol over the growing heap. The provocateur tossed a lit match, stood back and grinned as the bonfire caught alight with a satisfying "whoomp".

'Green-wash... Green-wash...'

He joined in the chanting, roared, beating his chest, playing to the gathering crowd and especially to the phone cameras.

'Get going. Get outta here.' He herded his band of anarchists towards two parked white vans with their number plates covered. *Good old white vans, what would you do without them?* It would be a while before the police responded: those understaffed bastards didn't give priority to shit like this. When, or if, this did come to court – well, it was more publicity. All good. He didn't mind spending time at Her Majesty's pleasure. Meanwhile, he speculated, these happy customers who had turned up early for the sales at Arnott's or come to buy a new toaster, fridge or TV from the electrical goods outlet next door, would have something to talk about when they got home. And filmed footage would be passed to the media or uploaded on social media. That was what this was about.

He jumped in the van and joined in a clamour of, 'Shit, that was fun!' Burnt rubber left a streak of black on the tarmac as they accelerated away. Job done. He wasn't sure what else was going on, but it was all happening. He checked the time: about now, actually...

24

When Ben had casually asked the Australians why they were so far from home, one bright-eyed guy answered, 'Same reason as you: for Rob. I'm here to support his cause.' Ben had been taken aback. Linda's cause, yes, but Rob's? The musician had had a romantic notion of saving rainforests, but he couldn't imagine Rob's enthusiasm extending far beyond his next album.

Another Aussie, a young woman, had shrugged. 'I've never travelled abroad. So why not? Anyway, I'm with him.' She nudged the bright-eyed guy. Were all young people so facile? He was about to walk away, more uncharitable thoughts swirling in his head, when the young woman continued. 'We usually stick our necks out for our own people's rights, you know: indigenous Aussies. They've got it rough. We're campaigning to get their history onto the school curriculum.'

After that, Ben found he enjoyed talking with them, learning more about what drove them in their lives. And Jade had been more thoughtful than he'd given her credit for. 'Dad's from Samoa,' she told him. 'When he came to work in the mines, he was treated like shit. He'll tell ya plenty of stories, and I've got a fair few. Everyone should be respected, aye?' She gestured to more villagers approaching on motorbikes, navigating past the two disabled logging trucks. Each bike had bundles of food lashed onto the back seats – meals to sustain them.

That had been an hour earlier, when the atmosphere had been, as Yulia had put it, "like a picnic".

The picnic was over.

The orange sun dropped towards the horizon. In half an hour they would be pitched into darkness save for torches, and – Ben turned to the parked police vehicles – headlights.

It hadn't taken long for three police vehicles to turn up, each with a bunch of armed officers. Among the police were those who had been with Sartano on the "courtesy" visit to the village – and on the barge. Bai's face had crumpled when she saw them arrive. He had watched a heated family exchange, then Asung pushed Bai and her older son away.

'Asung's sent Bai home,' Yulia told Ben. 'Her brother will look out for her.'

'They're the ones, aren't they?' Ben stared at the police officers, his eyes moving from one to the other, wondering which two of them had raped the girl. He was freshly appalled at the gross act of violence, yet unless Asung and Bai could be persuaded to act there wasn't a thing he could do.

It hadn't taken long for the police to push the bus over the edge of the drain, its rear end skyward. Now police vehicles and officers formed a barrier one end, the immobile logging trucks the other. The truck drivers had been set free, but as Linda had gleefully shouted, 'You ain't going anywhere!' True enough. One truck was out of action and the other, parked behind, couldn't get past, as the rutted track gave way to deep drains either side.

Between the massive logging trucks and intimidating police vehicles, the ragtag of humans taking a stand were small and vulnerable, Ben thought.

'Stand up... Fight back...'

English: the language chosen to reach throughout the world. Ben wasn't chanting, but villagers who didn't speak a word of English had learnt the phrase.

Many of DAE's most ardent Indonesian activists were "busy in Jakarta", Linda had told him, so the ones here had come from this region – students in the main. They looked as if they'd be more comfortable sitting at computers, exercising their minds rather than their soft bodies. He worried for them.

Jade and her four countrymen and women looked like they could hold back a truck, legs astride, arms linked. Jade had mentioned she played rugby sevens in any of the forward positions. Seeing sturdy legs emerging from shorts, and the breadth of her back, he could imagine her in a scrum.

'Stand up... Fight back.'

Linda was at his side looking beyond him. 'Well, well. Lookie here.'

An armoured police van manoeuvred on the narrow road, back and forth, back and forth, till it faced in the direction it had come. More officers leapt out. The back doors opened to reveal an arsenal of shields, batons and protective head gear: equipment known to Ben only from TV news coverage of police containing civil unrest. If chanting slogans wasn't his thing, then being in the line against charging police was definitely not. He turned to Linda, voice hopeful.

'Is this where you call a halt? Have you got enough news footage to satisfy you? Point made?'

Linda didn't deign to respond and began to walk away.

'Then when? When is enough, Linda?' Again, she ignored him. 'Well, how about calling it off for the night? I don't know how these things work. Can't you call a truce? Get some sleep? Resume battle stations at dawn?'

Linda laughed. 'Nice plan. No, we'll stick to where we are... still some daylight.' She turned to the police getting kitted out and raised her voice, crowing: 'The world's watching, boys.'

A couple of activists were filming on phones. If sporadic internet reception was available, those images along with drone footage would be on DAE's social media sites at any moment, and their comms people would be whisking things through to media feeds. This was not a shambolic, amateurish stunt. Linda had contacts in many countries and all of them were ready to receive and pass on. And ready to act.

Ben looked uneasily at the Indonesians and Australians blocking the road: young men and women in bright orange and blue get-ups, and Njau, Asung, and other local men and women. And children – far too close. He was seriously worried about the kids. And Yulia. He made his way towards her.

The long transparent shields, each with yellow POLISI written across in bold letters, had been handed out, and helmets with protective visors were being strapped to heads. Until now the local police had kept their distance. Ben had been surprised – and grateful – as had Linda. They hadn't confiscated cameras or tried to intervene, but every so often one of them would be on a phone. So why the riot gear? He watched the van, now empty of protective equipment and weapons, its back doors wide. 'Like open arms waiting to embrace us,' Yulia whispered. That was his fear also, as he calculated how many people could be squeezed into it.

At Yulia's, 'Ahh,' he followed her gaze.

Another vehicle had drawn up. Its tinted windows and heavy black body suggested that this SUV was discreetly armoured. Ben imagined it had a blast-protected floor, and other special features. It had that look about it. The driver got out and opened the back door. Yulia's second, 'Ahh,' was barely audible.

Inspector General Sartano stepped out, pistol holder in full view. He stood, hands on hips, and took in the scene.

'Hey, we have our important visitor dropping by again.' Linda spoke quietly, then turned to her activists, urging, 'Sit tight,' before turning back to the police. 'The world's watching. Just remember, boys.'

An officer, the senior one, perhaps, walked up to Sartano. Ben could see their mouths working, a head dipping, small hand gestures. Their gazes turned towards the activists then back to each other. The officer stepped away and raised his hand.

It happened fast. The police clustered in tight formation, shields held in front of them with one hand, batons in the other.

Then they charged.

Ben pushed Yulia into the middle of their group, trying to shield her, saw Asung cowering, her hands over her head. Moments later a baton thudded across his back. His grunt was more of shock than pain, and he instinctively tucked his injured left shoulder down. Hearing a yowl, he twisted his head and glimpsed a baton strike repeatedly over one of the Indonesian activist's shoulders. He couldn't bear it. His own screams of, 'Stop! Stop!' mingled with whatever entreaties the DAE protestors and villagers were yelling. Raising his arms to protect his head he spotted Asung gripping one of the shields, shaking it and yelling. A baton caught the side of her head and she dropped like a stone. Yulia was at her side screaming something Ben couldn't understand, but he understood Linda's: 'Fucking animal!'

Linda was in the fray now, a buffer between the police and Yulia, who was shielding Asung and her youngest son, who had rushed to his mother's side. Asung was scrunched into a ball.

'Uhh!' Another blow caught him, his ribs taking a pounding, his neck whiplashed. Shit that hurt! He suspected they had orders to go light with him, but they weren't holding back with their treatment of the Indonesians. A young woman was dragged along by her long hair, her hands clawing at the officer's arms, feet trying to get purchase on the ground. Ben started towards her, only to be shoved aside.

'Pigs!' Jade tackled the officer doing the dragging. He was down. She was down. Batons beat on her back. Ben could barely see in the rapidly falling dusk and was no longer sure what was happening. If this was a scrum only one side was wearing the correct kit and his side didn't stand a chance.

Linda was tussling with an officer's visor, clawing it upwards. In her other hand she had a pepper spray canister, and squirted it in his face, shrieking, 'See how you like this!'

'Linda!' Ben squeezed between police and protesters in a bid to save Linda from herself. He was some steps away from her when a baton whacked down on Linda's upper arm with enough force to smash a block of concrete. Ben heard the bone crack, heard Linda's horrified shriek. Before Ben could reach her, a young activist swung a sledgehammer into the legs of the attacking police officer, who crumpled. Above the screams a gunshot rang out. Ben instinctively ducked. When he looked up, he saw the hammer-wielding activist had been targeted. The young Indonesian dropped to the ground, writhing in pain. That young man should be back home, playing a computer game or some such. Not here. Definitely not here.

In the pandemonium Ben became aware of a village kid screaming, tears running down his cheeks, small hands clawing his way into the mass of bodies, trying to reach his father. He recognised the boy as Njau's son. Ben struggled through arms and legs and tugged at the young boy, grabbing him, and ejecting him like a hatchling from a nest, gesturing and yelling, 'Run!'

Ben found himself being manhandled by a young Indonesian guy, as slender as a whippet, and pushed into the centre along with Yulia and men, women and children from the village as the DAE activists attempted to form a shield. A fat lot of good. Ben resisted the young man's attempts to safeguard him. 'Look after yourself!'

Beams of light sliced through the gloom. Sartano's driver had switched on the vehicle's headlights and additional powerful spotlights. Ben glanced up to see the police chief illuminated, cigarette in hand, impassively watching.

And Linda? Her pain didn't bear thinking of. She was struggling with two officers who were intent on getting her to the van. She clutched her broken arm, screeching, sobbing, kicking out, spitting – whatever it took. Ben tried to reach her, elbowing aside those intent on keeping him safe.

Before he got to Linda, Yulia barged past – not to Linda but away from the melee. 'Good, go, go!' he urged. But instead of heading out of danger she was racing towards Sartano, her face full of hatred, screaming: 'Murderer! Murderer!'

'Yulia!' What was she clutching in her hand? A stone? A small rock? Was she trying to take out an armed officer with a fucking rock?

Sartano reached for his pistol.

'Stop. Don't shoot!' He raced after Yulia.

Sartano levelled his gun.

Ben flung his arms wide. He heard the crack of the shot as he hurled himself at Yulia. They both landed heavily, him on top of her.

'Sorry. You OK? You OK?' His words were urgent. Basic.

Yulia looked stunned.

'Get off! You're hurting me!'

A baton thumped across his back. This time his injured shoulder took the brunt and he yelled. Arms yanked him to his feet. He tugged to free himself, wanting to lift Yulia. Something wasn't right. The front of his T-shirt was soaking. Even before he touched the stain he understood it was blood. But he hadn't been hit, had he? For a moment this puzzled him.

Yulia lay on the ground, staring at him, eyes surprised, hands clutching her abdomen, whimpering, shaking. She tried to raise herself but fell back.

'Oh, God. She's been shot! Help her… Please…' Ben's knees gave way and the officers jerked him upright. Hands are practical things, can provide comfort and aid, but his wrists were grasped behind his back, cuffed with plastic ties.

'Let go, for fuck's sake… Yulia!'

All the police car lights were on now, like a harshly lit black and white Hollywood B movie, Ben would think later, but at that moment his imagination did not kick in. The woman he loved was dying before his eyes, the T-shirt that had started the day crisp and white oddly patterned with a red splodge. Sartano was standing above Yulia, staring at her, puzzled, maybe wondering where he had seen her before.

'Help her! Don't stand there. Help her!'

As he was being manhandled towards the van his last glimpse of Yulia was of her head dropping to the ground, her body still.

Air could not reach Ben's lungs quickly enough. He was still screaming Yulia's name when he was shoved into the police van, tripping over his own feet and colliding with others already loaded. More followed, men and women. He heard Linda's curses and shrieks and twisted to see a hand on her head as a police officer pushed her lower and into the van. Sweaty bodies pressed into him, his pinioned arms were useless, unable to offer comfort to Linda or bind her broken arm to her body. He could only yell: 'I'm here. I'm here.' She seemed unaware of him, wrapped in her own pain, eyes wild, foam at the corners of her mouth. She shrieked, 'Pigs. Fucking pigs!'

A police officer – the one she had pepper-sprayed – was about to lock the door. He hesitated then jumped onto the tailgate and thrust Linda down. Not satisfied, he forced her head to the floor. Still not satisfied, he brought a booted foot to rest on her neck. The other foot, resting on the tailgate, was barely taking any weight. The boot on Linda's neck kept a steady pressure. The officer's eyes were still streaming. Linda begged him to stop. The boot pushed more. The officer squeezed his eyes shut. Linda was wheezing. It was an image Ben would remember over and over.

He kicked out, but it was too crowded. He bellowed, the cords in his neck fit to pop. Still the thick-soled boot did not budge from Linda's slender neck. Others tried to help, throwing their weight forward, hurting Linda more by falling on top of her. From somewhere a police baton warded them off. Was this the same officer, or had another leaned in from outside? Who could say? Still Ben kicked out, trying to make that boot go away, make that murdering mother-fucker cop stop. Again he roared, 'Get off!'

A fixed light in the back of the van barely illuminated the tangle of bodies. It was a standard internal vehicle light, the kind a tradesman might use to see what they were doing when stowing or retrieving tools: a basic internal fixture. It was enough for Ben to see Linda's face turning purple as she continued to wheeze and plead.

'Get off! You're fucking killing her!' Ben lurched again, throwing himself forward.

The hard surface of a baton connected with the side of his skull and he pitched into darkness.

25

CONNOR SIGHED AS HE FLICKED THROUGH THE document with its scribbled insertions, crossed-out sentences and closely fought over phrases. The Chinese had been a pain in the arse. Just when all the delegates had been on board with the direction they were travelling, objections were raised. Now here was another. He watched the Chinese speaker, face inscrutable, and listened through an earpiece as the politician's words were translated in fits and starts.

'...clause forty-four, second sentence... must state more strongly the, er, prominence we are giving to environmental controls... So, we propose the following amendments...'

There were so many words and phrases in the English language, Connor reflected, that could be substituted for a word like "goal". Broad-brush objectives and vague aspirations – dreams, even – could replace specific statements about purposeful ambitions or hard targets. His heart sank. The slide had started. This summit was about trade and if the environment got in the way as it always did, the terminology would become vaguer or tautological. It took him back to his student days, living with a bunch of slackers, forever negotiating on what "clean" meant when it came to the shared bathroom and kitchen until they settled for an uneasy compromise somewhere between messiness and outright filth.

Connor's attention was drawn to muffled sounds from beyond the closed doors. In the adjoining room catering staff would be trying to be discreet as they offloaded crockery and cutlery from trolleys onto buffet tables covered in crisp white cloths. Good, nearly one o'clock: lunch time. The entire room felt in need of recharging; the air had grown stale with endeavour to achieve some outcome.

Documents strewn across the conference table showed hastily written notes and doodles in the margins. Everyone was flagging, some slumped or leaned back in their chairs, hands clasped behind heads, ties loosened. A woman near him had surreptitiously heeled off her shoes. Not Simone. Not her. She was sitting with her back straight, as immaculate as ever.

'It is vital we seize the many opportunities in expanding markets. We must grasp this chance to work together,' the prime minister was saying. 'We are a trading nation. Trade between us and our international partners is the cornerstone of our economy, always has been...'

The adjoining door opened. Connor glanced up, expecting to see an efficient event manager signal that lunch was ready. But no, disappointingly not. Connor's eyes followed a woman from the Indonesian delegation as she made her way to one of their aides sitting near him on chairs lining the wall. She handed over a note and whispered something before leaving. He heard further whispers between the aides, then one of them stood, tapped the Indonesian trade minister's shoulder, spoke softly next to his ear before handing over the folded paper. The minister's lips pressed together and he brushed away any further attempt to talk. The aide discreetly retreated. Connor focused on what the PM was saying as he sought to keep them all singing from the same hymn sheet.

It was a working lunch, a buffet, the kind of affair designed to help people circulate rather than sit down, especially next to people you didn't want to be stuck with. This midday break was a chance to stretch legs, go out to the enclosed back garden for a smoke. Connor noticed the Chinese, Vietnamese, Japanese and Indonesians, the male delegates particularly, hurry away, fingers reaching for packets or cigarettes already between lips, itching to light up. The tobacco trade had its claws deeply into the Asian market. He balanced his full plate in one hand, his glass resting in one of those clip-on glass holders. This buffet set-up sort of worked, but eating on the move, seeking out people you needed to talk to while avoiding others, was tricky. Where was his junior staffer? He wanted a word…

'Connor!'

The nudge to his elbow almost upended his plate. He turned at the sharpness in Simone's voice, her face equally sharp-edged as she jerked her nose towards the almost-empty conference room. He followed her, sweeping past a steward keeping watchful guard on who was entering.

'I've been badly advised. This whole thing lurches from bad to worse. An absolute disaster.' Though she spoke quietly Simone's voice was vibrating with anger.

While two conference assistants refreshed water bottles and glasses and a handful of diligent aides went through notes, Simone quietly but comprehensively ripped into him.

Remaining standing, she opened her tablet and scrolled through Direct Action for the Earth's newsfeeds. He looked at shaky footage of a stand-off in the Indonesian forest – *their* forest project – with AZTAR trucks right in the middle of things. And a sawmill put out of action. *Shit.* These were the very locations that had been trumpeted in the displays no more than six metres from where he stood. 'Look!' Simone paused a video. 'That's him, isn't it? Your damned Indiana Jones fellow. Right there.'

Connor sat down and brought his eyes closer to the screen. Among the orange-fisted peaked-cap protesters filmed by a drone, he spotted Ben's bare head. Simone was right. Hadn't she said his own professional instincts were a little blunted? *Fuck! Beyond blunted.*

Moving on to the BBC news he learnt there had been deaths, Linda Smith among them. He was sorry for her family, of course, but this was a big deal. First that rock star, Rob, now her. There was no hiding her importance. The media were making a meal of it. Under one link the headline read: "Veteran activist dies in police custody while protesting illegal logging near a British-Indonesian-sponsored project..."

What had happened to Ben? Was he injured? Dead? There was no mention of him. The first flush of news was about Linda's death and the scale of the protests. Direct Action for the Earth had gone global. Hundreds of thousands had taken to the streets in cities – Jakarta and London, among them – and there seemed to be sea chases going on. Just off a coast an inflatable dinghy was cutting through the water, activists on board unfurling a big banner, with the message ILLEGAL spelt out. They seemed to be heading for an anchored vessel... Hong Kong? China? Vietnam? Connor wasn't sure about the police boat in hot pursuit... *Was that Trevor's store?* His neck craned forward at the sight of a bonfire blaze with placard-waving protestors linking Arnott's businesses to rainforest destruction and loss of habitat. 'Oh, crap,' Connor managed to say. Direct Action for the Earth had been extremely busy, and all their locations, banners and actions linked directly to the summit. Central America and the Amazon basin seemed to have been spared. This time.

'Clever bastards,' Connor whispered as the massive orangutan puppet filled the screen, one hand to its sad-looking face. He peered closer at the baby. It was not just a stuffed toy; it had some automation: its eyes opened and closed, looking cute, then alarmed. 'Clever bastards,' he repeated, feeling no small admiration for the co-ordinated effort.

'I'm not sure there is anything to salvage with our forest project PPI.' Simone looked crestfallen. 'It will be contaminated'.

'I'm sorry. No quick fix. No instant solution.'

'Nothing in time for this.' Simone snatched up a summit agenda from the table. 'How's it possible to keep things balanced? Keep everyone on board?'

One of the water-filling attendants paused and glanced at them. Simone lowered her voice. 'We get beaten with a stick for not doing enough about the climate crisis, but the crazy thing, the really crazy thing is, if we did push through truly radical legislation—'

'You'd be voted out. The business sector wouldn't stand for it. They'd complain they couldn't keep up with environmental changes forced on them.'

Connor looked steadily at Simone. It was his job to support her. 'I'll get someone on to this. Check out the stats. Find out how many are dead, detained, nationalities and so on—'

Simone placed a staying hand on his arm. 'And find out if your Doctor Fletcher is among the living. One martyr's enough.' She glanced past his shoulder, her nails biting his skin.

The prime minister was making his way back into the room surrounded by his comms team, a phalanx of delegates and advisors following. Minutes earlier they had been balancing plates or glasses in hands that now held phones and tablets, eyes glued to the screens, barely caring who they bumped into.

There were bigger things to keep balanced. The PM's eyes locked on Simone's. 'Ah, I was looking for you. A moment...' Connor ducked away and hurried to search for one of his junior staffers who might be lingering over lunch.

It did not take long for things to stall. The afternoon session had barely commenced before the Chinese delegates excused themselves. Not quite the dramatic walkout the North Koreans were famed for, Connor thought, but still. They were clearly discomfited by the coverage, and "needed to take stock", as the translator put it. When the Indonesians followed soon after, the summit fell apart quite quickly.

At the front entrance, a large group of protestors had gathered. How they had got so close Connor didn't have time to find out, but there they were. Possibly the London Mayor had exerted his authority over his domain and allowed it. And the media were all eyes and ears, human and mechanical. The limousines whisking away the Chinese and Indonesian delegates would make the news for sure, and now the PM was bustling forward, looking harassed, straightening his tie. Connor flinched at the colour combo: orange and blue. The media would be sure to pick up on *that*. But the man could not have foreseen this added public relations disaster. One of the aides should have spotted it and offered his own tie before sending him out to face the cameras. Someone would get their knuckles rapped, for sure. For now, the PM was putting on a brave face for the crush of journalists.

'We are committed to positive environment actions – to work with international partners, playing an active part to save rainforests. We're pushing forward legislation, as you know, for CO_2 emissions, with plans—'

'But the summit, Prime Minister,' a journalist interrupted. 'Can you talk about what's gone wrong with this showcase

PPI, the forest one? It was meant to show the way. Has there been a cover-up?'

'Absolutely not. I assure you—'

'But surely this is an embarrassment?'

And this was the thing, Connor knew, as the prime minister struggled on. This protest had been timed to maximise embarrassment. He wondered if the summit would even resume the next day. Suddenly forests were the hot topic. Indignation was stoked by each new story coming in of brutalised local people and activists. There were graphic accounts, currently being verified, of what happened to Linda Smith. She had been lucky until now, risking her neck over and over. He flinched. It *was* her neck that had been crushed. Didn't bear thinking of. He couldn't imagine what cause might inspire him to put his own head above the parapet like that. He flinched again. Direct Action for the Earth could expect a surge in membership.

He needed to get back to the office, take time to absorb the facts and decide how best to advise Simone. As he headed towards the Strand, he skirted past a journalist speaking to camera and paused to listen.

'We understand at least eight British citizens are in detention in China, and we believe that Doctor Ben Fletcher was with Linda Smith when she died. He seems to be the only British citizen involved in the Indonesian forest confrontations, and we understand he's in police custody...'

So Ben was alive. One fewer martyr for the cause. He hurried on.

Even as Trevor parked his car, the damage was clear to see. Six yellow-helmeted, black-uniformed fire brigade officers were rolling away hoses, their fire engine ready to leave. A police vehicle was parked nearby, with two police officers keeping curious onlookers away from the incident cordon tape. He waited a minute or so, summoning his courage to face the mess, then heaved himself out of his comfortable cocoon.

He made his way towards the soggy ash and charred wood – his furniture, his stock, his business! And the smashed display window. 'Bastards!'

'Dad!'

He was startled to see Sean running towards him.

'Mum told me you were on your way over. I just thought, you know, you might want me…'

Trevor took in the array of badges on his son's sweatshirt: pinned-on buttons proclaiming "Fight Climate Change Not Wars", "Save Earth" and vivid stuck-on patches with all sorts of stop this or that slogans. If Sean was wearing a Direct Action for the Earth emblem, he might be tempted to thump him.

Sean grinned. 'They kept offering them, so hey, I thought why not? I'll be democratic. They're all worthwhile.'

Trevor was seething. How could his own flesh and blood support something like *this?*

'You approve?' His voice was shaky as he spread his hands to the nearby scene.

'No!' Sean looked taken aback. 'I didn't know this was happening. I was hanging out in the centre with the others.' Sean hesitated. 'But I understand.'

A fresh sadness settled around Trevor's heart. Was he so out of touch with his son? He took a second or two to collect himself. 'Come on.' He placed a hand on Sean's back, steering him towards the shop. As he lifted the cordon tape and was about to duck under a young woman police officer hurried over.

'Sorry, sir. You can't go through.'

'I'm the fucking owner!' He jabbed his finger at the Arnott's sign above the store.

'Ah. Sorry. I didn't recognise you.' She backed off.

Sean sniggered. 'Be happy they didn't damage this one, Dad.' He gestured to the sign. Trevor grunted. He had seen a photo of another of his outlets, where a graffiti job had amended ARNOTT's, to read "Am not a wanker... Sure?" with a crudely sprayed fist gripping a dick.

He was angered by Sean's cocksure – oh, bad choice of word – sassiness, but didn't trust himself to speak right now.

'It's OK, Dad, let's go in.' This time it was Sean's hand on his back.

Trevor stepped into his store, pausing to thank two store assistants vacuuming up glass chips, then his shop manager was at his side.

'Mr Arnott. I'm so sorry. I couldn't stop it.'

'What's so wrong that people would do this?'

His manager shrugged. 'I don't know.'

Trevor looked at the man; Polish, maybe. He liked to employ people from outside Britain, found them to be hardworking. That scored points in his book, and showed he wasn't a "Little Englander" as well. Wasn't he doing something right? It pissed him off that people put him down, found reason to find fault. Even his kids.

He watched Sean take a broom from one of his assistants and begin to clean up the glass. Sean wasn't a bad lad, he knew that, but just not on the same page he was. Few people were, so it seemed. Tears pricked the corner of his eyes and he repeated, 'What's so wrong...?'

Am not a wanker! That stung. So crude. Such bad publicity. And yet...

Strolling around his shop he allowed his mind to settle. His fingers brushed the surface of a rosewood chest of drawers. Touching the silky wood comforted him. His brain began whirring as he looked around at the rest of his stock.

The majority was undamaged. He felt another sale looming. Not a smoke damage kind of fire sale – there was nothing to salvage here from the furniture that had been hauled out and made into kindling, but maybe he could find a marketing angle: a business-as-usual kind of fire sale. He liked that idea. A kind of "fuck you" fire sale. Customers would see he had a sense of humour, was resilient, could bounce back.

He turned to his manager with a tight smile. 'Let's get this cleaned up. Arrange for fresh stock from the warehouse and open for business tomorrow.'

'We could do with shifting last year's outside loungers. We've a lot left.'

'Good. Good!' He slapped his manager on his shoulder. He was getting his mojo back. 'I'll speak with marketing. I've got some ideas about how to handle this.'

The ministerial office where Simone had shut herself away that evening offered somewhere to hide. She kicked off her shoes and turned to the muted TV news. Shaky video footage, camera lens splashed with spray, showed a small boat whooshing towards a massive timber-carrying open-hold vessel. She watched two men wearing DAE T-shirts clamber onto a huge anchor chain and hook a banner on it. With the movement of the camera and folds in the banner the image of deforested land wasn't clearly visible, but the message splashed across it was: 'Illegal. The world is watching.'

The world would have to be quick, Simone thought, as moments later those on the container vessel turned powerful water jets on the protestors and the force of the water ripped away the banner. Even so, the message had made international news, and would probably be repeated over and over with the need to fill twenty-four-hour news coverage. This footage wouldn't be hidden away on an obscure website. A political correspondent was now on screen, standing in the dark street outside the law courts. Simone could see her mouth working, so she switched up the sound.

'...British nationals are among others who have been detained by police in Hong Kong and mainland China. Clashes between protestors and police in Indonesia include staged events in the city of Jakarta and in Kalimantan. Three deaths at a forest location are reported, among them Indonesian campaigners and veteran campaigner Linda Smith. We can reveal that shortly before she died, she leaked information about irregularities in the government-supported business initiative...'

The screen showed Linda at the front of a huddle of protestors blocking a forest road, raising her arms, fists clenched, to ward off an oncoming logging truck. This, Simone supposed, was just before the shit hit the fan. The news package cut to a close-up of a teary-eyed British environment personality being interviewed: a man who had mellowed with age and was adored by his TV public.

'We claim her too, she was as much of a national treasure here as in America. We argued, of course.' The interviewee smiled sadly. 'Everyone argued with Linda. But, my goodness, she was someone you wanted on your team. I can't believe she's no longer with us.'

Yes, yes, yes! Simone frowned. Enough of Linda. She wanted the political analysis. She watched impatiently as footage of new demonstrations emerged – ones she hadn't seen online... Ah, so there *had* been action outside Asia. Thousands had been marching, waving placards to save the Amazon, in Rio de Janeiro and Brasília. Good on them! Their government was doing shit-all to stop destruction; even endorsing it, while in Britain they had been *trying*... The political correspondent was on screen again, and Simone focused on what she was saying.

'We don't know yet whether the Chinese and Indonesian delegates will return tomorrow.' The correspondent pointed back over her shoulder with a thumb. 'There's no doubt the timing of these protests will have impacted on the summit, and no one from the government is available to talk with us right now. We are waiting for an update from the secretary of state for international trade, Simone Bailey, and from the prime minister's office...'

Simone snapped off the TV. There would be no update from her. The PM's people could deal with it. It was only a matter of time before she received a call to his office. She expected it but was grateful he had allowed her, as he had put it, "time to reflect".

And she had reflected.

Connor had surprised her. He had knocked tentatively then poked his head around the door. 'Minister. Would you like company? Like to chew things over?'

Or maybe chew you. She had been tempted to toss a shoe at his head, but decided to retain some dignity and beckoned him in.

Connor sat on the edge of a chair, ready to bolt by the look of him.

'I swear, this was well-intentioned. I thought – we all thought – it was a small project we could get behind. Who could guess it would snowball as it did?'

'Who could guess?' She mirrored his small shrug. But damn it. That was the job of civil servants, *his* job, to look at all the angles. Had he done so? Too late to go down that line.

'I'm truly sorry,' he offered.

They watched the news together, made small talk, then she asked him to leave. Tears were pricking her eyes and she did not want to blub in front of him.

She lifted the framed family photo perched on her office

desk: her, her husband and their three children, the youngest two in pyjamas ready for bed. It had been taken the day she had been called into the PM's office and offered the ministerial position. Later, back home after the press interviews, her husband had swung her around giddily. 'Hey, babe! So proud of you. That's my girl!' He was cock-a-hoop. And in the photo he did look proud, grinning as he held the camera phone at the end of a selfie stick capturing them in a tight huddle.

She had loved being at the heart of power. But now she was out. She packed the family photo in her bag. From a drawer she withdrew a sheet of thick writing paper with the Parliamentary crest at the top, and took up a pen.

26

Massive bruises covered his back and it hurt to breathe deeply. Ben leaned his back against the paint-flaked concrete wall trying to get comfortable, momentarily diverted by patterns of mould blooming in the corners and around the iron-barred window. To his right, metal bars separated him from a dismal corridor. He was locked up, suspended in time, along with nine Indonesian male activists, all of them injured but not enough to require medical attention. And where were the women? The Australians? He had given them a passing thought, but it was Yulia who consumed him. Her name throbbed, resonated. He wondered if he sometimes shouted her name out loud.

He ran a finger around the stain on his T-shirt, now dried to a dull reddish brown. Yulia's blood.

Images played over and over like a looped film. Yulia pressing her hands to her abdomen; a bloom of scarlet against her white shirt; her eyes widening in shock; the shape of her mouth forming his name.

And Linda.

He was haunted by those hours in the pitch dark, bumping along in the police van, his wrists swelling around their plastic restraints, knowing Linda's body was right by him. He could not reach out to hold her so instead he had squatted, bent over till his face found hers. Her cheek had still been warm at first, but when he next made the gesture, her skin was cool. He discovered this happens rapidly. Later he was aware the muscles in her jaw and neck had hardened as rigor mortis set in.

The stench of sweat and fear had closed around him. They were thirsty, all of them. Three of the Indonesians spoke some English, but they weren't interested in him. Rightly so. He applauded their courage taking this stand, knowing their future was more uncertain than his own.

In the back of the van he had sensed dawn arriving, or perhaps imagined he could see a grey light creeping between the door seals. When the doors had been flung open, he had blinked rapidly, blinded by the sun's sharpness.

Linda's face had set into a hard death mask, her body scrunched up, limbs curled and fingers clawing. It reminded him of the time he and Sarah had holidayed in Naples, taking in visits to Pompeii and Herculaneum – those ancient towns devastated when Mount Vesuvius blew its top. He recalled the casts of people that had been caught in a pyroclastic flow, bodies of men, women and children captured at the horrifying last beat of life. He turned away, preferring to remember Linda as a powerful life force.

Balan, Rob, Ule, Linda… death had stalked them, claimed them, and he had been in their shadow.

And Yulia? What of her? Always Yulia.

Two wardens strolled along the corridor. Ben pushed his way to the cell door and reached through the bars. 'Hey…

Hey! Wait!' He swung back to one of the Indonesians who spoke English. 'Ask them! About Yulia!' Before the activist could yell his question, the uniformed officials had moved on, impervious to everyone's shouted pleas and arms reaching through the bars of this cell and others lining the length of the building. Then the men were gone. Nothing he had attempted had worked out and he was wretched with grief.

Another day passed. Every time a warden came by the cell, he got the same answer: *Nanti*. Later. Where was the British consulate when you needed it? Did they care? His phone had been taken; no one would have any idea where he was. Questions and uncertainties tumbled over each other.

The reek in the cell was ripe. He longed for a shower; longed to get out of his bloodied stinking clothes with the ever-present reminder of Yulia's lifeblood draining away. He ran a hand over the stubble on his jaw knowing he must look a wreck.

'Hey, Ben! I'll win this time.'

Ben grinned at the young man challenging him to yet another game of paper, scissors, stone. It took his mind off things, sharing silly games and sharing stories. They had time. As his flat palm was trumped by V-shaped fingers, he heard his name.

'Fletcher!'

He looked up to see a prison warden standing outside the cell, gesturing to him, saying something. He caught the name "Yulia" and his heart contracted.

An explosion of clapping and whoops broke out around him and he was dragged to his feet.

'Go, go, man! You're being released. No charges!'

'And Yulia? Did he say—'

'Yes. Yes… He says she's in hospital.'

Ben clasped his cellmate in a tight embrace, dizzy with this news.

'Go!' The activist pushed him away, the look in his eyes changing from happiness to concern. 'And don't forget us.'

As he shook hands with them all, he promised he would do what he could; promised he would stay involved. He had memorised everyone's name, age, home town. He would write everything down so he wouldn't forget. No, he assured them, he would not let them down. Yes, he would contact the Jakarta DAE office immediately. *God, he hoped someone was there.* And yes, DAE would have a legal team on to it.

Then he was out, the noise of the street reminding him that people were going about their lives. Living.

DAE.org/news

May the force be with you, Linda Smith. Many of us plan on being with you for your send-off, but don't doubt that ALL of us will be there in spirit, to farewell our Warrior Queen. Whether you like it or not, that's what you were to us – YOU, the founder of what's now this ginormous global movement. It's impossible to list what you've achieved and the many ways you'll be missed.

Members, or anyone, can share their **memories** of how Linda touched their lives. We'll keep this page live for a month or two. Please share your favourite Linda stories – no shortage of those – or offer your thanks and condolences to her family. The best way you can honour Linda is to **JOIN**. Pay as much as you can. We've got some hefty legal fees coming up. But if you are strapped for cash you may like to give us your time. And, if you'd like to donate to something specific, then her family suggest the **Orangutan Sanctuary** that Linda visited a few months back. Donations will go towards a visitor's centre and improving walkways. Keep an eye on our news for updates.

Rest in Power, Warrior Queen.

27

The hospital reception staff seemed to think he was an emergency patient, then someone tried to shoo him away thinking he was a vagrant. Ben was panicking, hands flapping, talking too loudly and slowly like some idiot tourist thinking everyone must understand English. It took some effort to explain his bloodied T-shirt and dishevelled looks, and further effort to convince them he wasn't a danger to them or their patients. He gratefully accepted a plastic gown to cover his filthy clothes and they pointed to the men's toilet. Seeing himself in the mirror he understood their reaction and did his best to wash his face and hair and regretted not showering and changing before racing over. Knowing Yulia was alive had pushed every other thought aside. In any case, he had no idea where his belongings were. Only his phone and wallet had been returned.

He almost trotted along a corridor, urging the nurse accompanying him to walk faster, ignoring the glances of staff, trusting no one would challenge his right to be there. The nurse pointed and he followed her into a busy open ward of female patients, some curtains screening beds, others left open. He scanned the ward of mostly older women, sleeping or leaning propped against pillows chatting with visitors.

Where was Yulia? He couldn't see her. Had there been a mistake? He shrugged, hands out, palms up. The nurse indicated a curtained-off bed and led him to it, hesitating with her hand protectively on the fabric. Any manner of things might make her decide it was a bad idea that he was here, so he didn't wait, but impatiently pushed past her.

The patient was sleeping, attached to a drip, her face puffy and grey-looking, and… and… He hesitated. Yulia? Of course it was her. In two strides he was at her bedside, aware of the nurse hovering, keeping an eye on her patient.

He drew up a plastic chair to the side of the bed and gazed at her, adjusting to this new Yulia. She looked unbearably fragile, her eyelids quivering, her breath laboured. Gently he reached across and stroked a strand of hair from her face. Yulia started; her eyes flickered and met his. Ben expelled a breath he hadn't realised he had been holding. 'Oh, Yulia!'

The nurse was at the foot of the bed, speaking to Yulia. She said something back, her voice small, a shadow of what he remembered. He kept his eyes on Yulia as the nurse moved away, her shoes squeaking. She left the curtain open, no doubt wanting to keep an eye on him.

Leaning forward he gently stroked Yulia's cheek. She smiled and he almost melted. He kissed her lightly then reached for her hand lying on the bed cover, turned it over and stroked her palm.

'A rock? Little more than a stone…?'

'I was angry… He's a bad shot. He missed most of my important bits.'

Yulia withdrew her hand and carefully pushed back the bed cover to reveal a large dressing on the left side of her abdomen.

He swallowed. 'Yulia!'

'You know something?' Her voice was small and dry. 'He'll die one day, and he'll come back as a cockroach. Next life.' She managed a small smile.

'He's got to be charged. Someone senior to him must charge him for shooting you, and for everything...'

'Ben...' Her voice trailed off and a frown gathered.

'Yes?'

'I hate to tell you, but after trying to kill me that man helped me live.'

'Sartano?'

'His guys told him he'd shot a government contractor, so he had me bundled into a car. Expected me to die. I don't remember a thing after that, but I'm told there was a helicopter ride.'

'God, Yulia.' How he hated that man. And now was he supposed to thank him? He stroked her hair and cheek.

Yulia scrutinised him. 'What's happened? Why are you wearing that gown? You look terrible.'

'Hospital garb. I'll have to buy new clothes and a shaver... Sorry. I couldn't wait.'

They were quiet for some minutes and Ben noticed Yulia had closed her eyes. He sat back, thinking she was snoozing, but he saw a crease forming between her eyes.

'Tell me about Linda.'

'If you want.' He cleared his throat. 'Her arm was shattered – perhaps you knew that – then afterwards... afterwards...' He bowed his head, unable to describe the horror of those minutes and hours in the police van. How honest should he be?

'It's OK. Another time.' She opened her eyes and after some moments spoke again. 'I'll miss that crazy woman. People in the future had better look out. Her next life will be quite something.' Yulia wagged a finger. 'And no more action-man stuff from you?'

'I've had enough for a lifetime. This lifetime anyway.' He stared intently into her eyes. 'And you. Promise?'

'Mmm.' She nodded and he sealed the promise with a kiss.

Out of the corner of his eye he saw the nurse was hovering and he was conscious that Yulia needed to rest. But he wasn't ready to leave just yet. Leaning closer he whispered, 'I love you.' There was no awkwardness about it. It had been easy to say. He had grown to love this woman and he needed to tell her so.

'Thank you,' she whispered back. 'I knew that really, but it's nice to hear. And you know, you've been sneaking up on me. I love you too.'

He sat holding her hand until she had drifted off to sleep. He listened to her regular breathing then gently disengaged his hand, rose and nodded to the nurse.

'Thanks.'

Close by Ben found a guest house. And shops. He showered, shaved and, wearing new clothes, he set out for the hospital, feeling reborn. He bought flowers, juice and fruit he hoped Yulia might like.

She was awake when he arrived and smiled her approval at how he looked, joking she would allow him to kiss her properly without "that sandpaper chin". He plumped her pillows, helped adjust her position, asked how she was, if he could do anything for her. 'Just be here,' she told him.

That was something he could do. He settled in the chair.

'You think it worked? Linda's plan? All those demos everywhere…' Yulia's voice trailed off.

'Maybe. A little. We might be flavour of the month before some new catastrophe strikes or people get bored. Or forget.'

'Push your advantage, Ben. While attention is still on the forests.'

'How? I won't ever get another government contract, and I'm not risking my life again—'

'Oh no. Definitely not!'

He hesitated. 'But, you know, these past days – in the moments I wasn't out of my mind worried about you – I kept on thinking of Trevor Arnott.'

Yulia looked at him, too surprised to speak.

'I know. I know.' Ben raised his hands. 'But the thing is, he had a great opportunity. He could've shown how things could be done, but instead he cut corners—'

'Another bad man. What might he come back as next time around? Another beetle?'

'Bad? I dunno. Let's say limited vision. Greedy. Shortsighted. The thing is businessmen always think things like this are easy, and the reality is they are very complex.'

'You should sort him out.'

'That would be interesting… Yeah. I could phone him.' He brought a thumb to his ear, little finger extended to his mouth. '"Look, Mr Arnott, I know I'm kind of responsible for bringing your business into disrepute. The thing is, Mr Arnott, I may be the one who can help you become a market leader…"'

Yulia looked serious. 'Good idea.'

'You think I should begin to convert Trevor. A personal crusade to make him see the errors of his ways?' He grinned.

'Umm. Him, or others. There are plenty of Trevors in the world who need people like you.'

'And like you too.'

'Do it then. No harm. He might surprise you.'

She gestured to a bottle of water on the cabinet and he helped her drink. He dreaded the moment the nurse might appear and tell him it was time to leave, that he was tiring her, that it was time to rest, or eat, or something else, and he was mucking up a strict hospital routine. Yulia settled back on her pillow.

'Did you read any of those fairy tales I gave you?'

'Not yet. Third sons: they always get the girl in the end, right?' He looked at her meaningfully.

'Mmm… Sometimes. But sometimes it's just an old farm he inherits, or he surprises people.' Ben raised his eyebrows. 'They come to see he's not as stupid as they thought. He's really quite smart. He earns their respect.'

'Respect. OK, that sounds pretty good. But I like my version too.' He smiled.

Yulia sighed. 'So many wonderful people have died. We have to keep trying.'

Ben nodded.

'Promise?' Yulia squeezed his hand. 'Promise you won't go off, and… I don't know, get an easy job.'

'Will you help me?'

'Yes.'

'Promise?' He waited for her nod and kissed her lightly.

Yulia closed her eyes. 'I'm tired. Enough talking. But stay here, heh? When I woke up before I thought I'd dreamt you'd been here. These drugs I'm on do strange things.'

He promised he would stay and hoped the new nurse on duty fell in with Yulia's idea of what was best for her recovery.

Connor had been a kid when the Berlin Wall fell. If he remembered it at all, it was because he saw his parents jumping up and down and hugging while watching the telly. They were left-wing Labourites, but as his dad had said: 'Time this was swept away, time to move on, time those eejit dinosaur politicians faced facts.' Later, studying politics, he could appreciate the groundswell of dissatisfaction, the tipping point that opened the borders and led to the Wall being demolished. It might be a fanciful comparison, as there was nothing to suggest such a magnitude of change in Britain, yet the way the trade summit had ground to a halt had given pause. Ripples *were* being felt.

The prime minister was bending over backwards to demonstrate his government were committed to climate-change initiatives, promising to strengthen "even more" import regulations, and that at the next climate action summit Britain would put pressure on Brazil, Indonesia, China "and others" to emphasise the importance of a healthy ecosystem. Ecosystem services. He noticed the PM using that term over and over like an electioneering mantra, banging the message home. 'Together we can do this, together we can make the world healthy,' he might say.

Connor found his position was safe. There was many an occasion when he resisted the urge to cross his chest and whisper a Hail Mary. No one had come gunning for him. He was just a bland civil servant doing his job, supporting his minister. He had searched his conscience to see what he might have done differently with this forestry PPI. But he genuinely had hoped it would work out for all partners. Perhaps that was his error? *Hope* was fine if it was on the top end of the spectrum meaning aim, ambition or aspiration with a fair chance of success, but they had found themselves sliding into the dangerous zone where hope was no more than a vague yearning for something to work out, and they had ended with egg on their faces – or Simone had.

Connor's new boss appeared at the door just as he was leaving for the minister's office. Harry Blythe, promoted from the Department for Environment, Food and Rural Affairs, was a youngish man keen to grab this chance to make his mark.

'Ah, Minister, I was about to—'

'Stay, stay. I was passing.' Harry waved a folded *Guardian* and placed it on his desk. 'Seen this yet?' He tapped the article in question and settled in a chair across from Connor.

Connor's eye was caught by the headline:

OIL PALM ESTATES PROHIBITED

The Indonesian government has bowed to pressure from the Australian government to prohibit further expansion of oil palm plantations in the Malinau Regency, Kalimantan. It is believed this is connected to the death of Australian citizen Robert Gilmore. Investigations conclude that the probable cause of the rock musician's death was that he and his local guide disturbed men working for a palm oil company scouting for suitable areas to clear...

'Interesting.' Connor looked up. 'Though *probable cause* is rather hedging their bets. They either know or they don't know.'

'The most interesting thing is to see how these things work.'

'Minister?'

'We're a more or less Christian nation, our culture driven by guilt. Not so the Indonesians. Losing face is their thing. Shame. I would imagine they know very well what has happened, so this is their way of acknowledging it. And how wonderful to see they have finally taken steps to curb this creeping menace.'

Connor indicated the article. 'I'm pleased to read this. You know, if it takes a rock singer's death to bring about change, then great. And there's the American government influence at work here too, I imagine.'

'I imagine so.' Harry beamed and Connor beamed back. He was looking forward to this new relationship. A meeting of minds. They both understood the death of Linda Smith had played a part in this decision.

'By the way, I've been looking at Doctor Fletcher's report,' Harry said. 'Putting aside what he did afterwards, his recommendations are sound. Our problem was we wanted to shout about this too soon. You know we're about to announce changes to our aid policy: aid linked to trade—'

'Indeed, it rather narrows the aid focus, but our department gets to benefit.'

'So let's make the most of it before there's another change!' Harry's voice oozed enthusiasm. 'And this, of course, is what the Dutch have been providing in Borneo – aid to support sustainable trading practices. I don't see why we shouldn't use it as a model, as Fletcher is suggesting. Don't you think?'

'We might, for example, work with existing logging companies to improve training and standards. But we'll need to stay in for some time, you realise that?' Don't be tempted to want instant results, Connor's eyes warned Harry.

'National support for a local plan. Sure. In fact, I don't see why we shouldn't pick up where we were with Indonesia, but get better partners on board. What do you think?' Without waiting to find out what Connor thought, he hurried on. 'Oh, and let's get some input from WWF and so on.' He clicked his fingers. 'Let's do it!'

'Minister.'

His new boss knew his stuff, and if Connor was to advise him he needed to raise his game. He was stimulated by the challenge, by the stakes. If any new initiative was to have a chance of competing against the illegal logging and supply chain, it would require substantial investment from many partners, both government and business. Voluntary agreements between partners could only do so much. A pity he couldn't reach out to Ben again. As an economist, he more than anyone knew how interdependent ecosystems were, how fragile or failing ecosystems impacted on the entire world. Connor had gleaned as much from Ben's recent report; in fact in all the reports Ben had written for him he banged on about this. But Ben had burnt his bridges, at least for now. Maybe in time he would reach out, invite him for a drink or something...

28

THIS BAR WAS NOISY, BUT IT SERVED GOOD DRINKS and Ben had downed a few. He checked his watch. Again. OK... OK, it was time. He had saved the number he had been given and now touched the dial icon on his phone, his hands shaking a little. Odd for a grown man to be nervous about putting in a call. With the dial tone ringing, he risked another sip. Whiskies today.

'Arnott's. Can I help you?'

'I'd like to speak with Mr Arnott.'

'A moment.'

The line went quiet and Ben felt his hands getting clammy. Pathetic!

'Mr Arnott's office.' Another female voice. Brisk. Efficient.

'Yes. I want to speak to Mr Arnott, please.'

'Is he expecting your call?' She was one of those gatekeepers, excellent at keeping pesterers away.

'No, but please tell him it's Ben Fletcher... Doctor Ben Fletcher.'

'He's busy. If you give me your details, I'll see—'

'No, no!' He gripped his phone. 'Please. I'm phoning from abroad. This is important!'

'Who did you say you were?'

'Doctor Fletcher.' He was sounding impatient. Worse, he might sound aggressive.

'Will he know who you are?'

Oh God. Ben pressed the phone to his ear as if he were pressing this bloody woman. He explained, and finally, he heard the words he wanted.

'I'll see if Mr Arnott will take your call.'

A group of men and women walked into the bar chattering loudly, so he sought a quieter corner, glass in one hand, phone in the other. This was taking ages. Had the connection been lost?

A growling voice: 'What the hell do you want?'

'Mr Arnott. Good morning.'

Ben looked through the window at the street lamps and people strolling, enjoying the cooler tropical evening air.

'Well?'

He took a breath. 'I want you to try harder. I want you to—'

'What is this?

'—visit the village we were at, and—'

'Are you drunk?'

'A little, perhaps a little.' He heard Trevor mumble, 'Fuck off.' Panicking, Ben called out, 'Don't hang up! Don't hang up... Please!'

'Damn it, man. I'm busy. I haven't time for your games.'

'Wait! Give me a minute.'

'Seconds are counting down.'

'I want you to dump Agus Zumran, find a better partner; dump your Chinese suppliers too, I can point you to certified suppliers in China – there are plenty. But first I want you to go to the village. See how they live, learn what's important to them. Get the Health Centre operational – that will win you friends. I want you to see the forest; be in the forest, experience it—'

'And hug a fucking tree?'

'Yes, maybe. Why not?' He heard Trevor blow a raspberry so he galloped on. 'I want you to see the possibilities. My friend, Yulia, she's fantastic. Has all the local knowledge and contacts you need. Her colleague is working with a community forest project we'd like to take you to – in the Malinau district, quite close by your project. It's doing well. Goddamn it, I want—'

'That's a hell of a lot of "wants".'

'Yes, a long list, a very long list. I want you to get back out here and see how it can be done. Mr Arnott, I want to help you. Do you hear me?'

He heard a snort of derision at the other end followed by silence. Had the businessman hung up? He detected a soft humming, an expelling of air, and Trevor cleared his throat.

'Mr Fletcher, to my knowledge you and I have never met—'

''S'right—'

'Yet you and your people have done your damnedest to bring me down—'

'That wasn't *my* people—'

'So why should I listen to you? More to the point, why should I trust you?'

'I'm not a frigging activist.' Ben took a breath and tried a fresh tack. 'You and I want the same thing—'

'Huh!'

'I can help. I'm offering to work with you. Show that what you started can be made to work—'

'It didn't, did it? Work out?' Trevor sounded sulky.

'You broke the rules you agreed to – a little here and there – figuring it wouldn't matter.'

'Don't lecture me!'

Ben could imagine the businessman's face getting redder and redder. Agus Zumran had had more than his fingers rapped. He'd been fined – nothing his family couldn't afford – but more importantly he had lost his right to log the concession. Trevor would need a new business partner in Indonesia if Ben could only persuade him. He took a gulp of whisky and changed tack.

'Look, Mr Arnott, let's flip things around. Don't think about rules and regulations. They're important, we know that, but let's look at *outcomes*. You want to be a market leader? Then what would be a good outcome for you, for your customers, your shareholders? And what would be a good outcome for the community here? All the people living here who rely on the forest. And can we talk about the environment?'

'This sounds like a lecture.'

'OK… OK.' Ben had to agree it did.

'And you've had more than a minute.'

He clutched his phone, willing the man to stay with him. 'And you've not hung up.'

'No. I've not…' Trevor sounded surprised. 'Not yet.'

It was Ben's turn to release a humming expulsion of breath.

It took further phone calls and lengthy emails to persuade Trevor to take him seriously. Ben talked about the advantages if he gave his customers the clear message that he only stocked certified chain of custody products. 'No mixed messages,' he warned Trevor. 'Go green and stay green – all your lines. Work towards certification by the Forest Stewardship Council.' Each of his emails had contained links to websites he wanted Trevor to look at, and benefits he could expect to see. Over and over he coaxed the businessman. Then one day he received a text message direct from Trevor.

How many seats does that small plane have? My son Sean will be with me.

Ben didn't enquire further but assumed Sean wasn't coming along for a holiday. It took further days to schedule time to meet. 'He'll slot you in between Sydney and Hong Kong,' Trevor's PA said. 'You'll have three days.'

'Not enough,' Ben had begged. 'A week at least!'

After a hasty consultation with Trevor the woman returned to the phone with a tart, 'Three days, and Mr Arnott says not to try his patience.' She named dates a few weeks hence. They should just about manage to get where he wanted before the rainy season set in and forest roads became impassable.

Yulia was being discharged. Ben wheeled her to the hospital entrance in a wonky wheelchair, then helped her stand and walk to the waiting taxi, each step a tentative exploration. They would stay at the guest house for the coming weeks.

Jade was keeping him and Yulia up to date with all things relating to Linda.

'Gotta laugh,' Jade's voice boomed down the phone. 'Her kids expected to repatriate her body – had a plot lined up next to their dad's – only then they discovered she had left a will tucked away in a filing cabinet among some old junk.'

'Oh?' Ben was curious to know why Jade was chuckling.

'You're gonna love this. These were her words. "No fuss. Wherever I die, incinerate me. I'll be done with my flesh and bones. Period." And she'd underlined the word period.'

Ben laughed too. He could just imagine Linda sitting at a desk, forcefully drawing that black line, the ballpoint all but going through the paper.

The Indonesian embassy had wanted to get rid of Linda's

body as soon as possible, only too happy to see an end to the diplomatic embarrassment and eager to comply with anything the Americans wanted. Relations between the two countries were being stretched by the Americans demanding action against the police. But just as arrangements were being made to fly Linda's body to Washington DC, this new complication arose.

'I'm flying back out,' Jade told him. 'Gotta be there.'

So in a country where cremation was not the norm, Linda was cremated. Neither Ben nor Yulia attended, but they watched a video of the ceremony posted on Direct Action for the Earth's website.

'Some party, heh.' Yulia smiled at the procession, Linda's coffin held aloft by six of her supporters, one of them, fittingly, Jade. A Gamelan orchestra followed, along with a crowd of mourners who had flown in from all parts of the world. The Indonesian government had insisted on a send-off.

'Not so simple after all,' Ben agreed, squinting at the screen to see if he could identify any of the other mourners. Men and women wearing the DAE T-shirts all merged. He had a pang of conscience, thinking of those activists still being processed through the courts.

DAE's website had plenty of updates. 'They're reporting a spike in membership and donations for legal fees,' Ben read. Wherever protests had taken place, DAE were throwing themselves into organising legal representation for those who had been arrested.

'And Linda's money will help,' Yulia said.

'Yep!' He laughed remembering what else Jade had said about the will.

'Oh, something else... Really funny... Linda's kids are left her house and her fifteen-year old Honda – a rust-bucket – but we get the rest.'

The majority of Linda's estate would go to Direct Action for the Earth.

Little by little Yulia found her strength returning. She had not enjoyed being stuck in a hospital bed, dopey with all the meds dripped into her blood. Her own fault. It had been crazy to go after that man. She had had masses of time to reflect on it, and still couldn't find a satisfactory answer to why she'd done it. 'Caught up in the moment,' she would shrug.

Ben traced a finger around the puncture wound in her abdomen. 'We'll be able to compare scars,' he said. The pucker, still an angry purplish wound, would be with her for life, as would the raised welt across his shoulder. His scar would fade; so would hers. In time the trauma of her ordeal would fade and leave only a trace, but she refused to allow herself to be emotionally scarred by that man, Sartano.

She was like bamboo, bending and swaying and very strong.

'Ben, I want to go to the orangutan sanctuary – the one Linda's left money to.'

After everything they had gone through, she was determined Ben should see what was being done to educate people, and to rehabilitate orangutan orphans and others made homeless. She longed for them to experience something positive together. 'Please,' she said.

'Not yet,' he countered. 'You need to get stronger.'

'Walking's good. Builds strength.'

'Another time,' he said.

But she got her way.

The rainy season had started, leaving the ground a quagmire with paths half submerged. Ben placed a steadying hand on her elbow as they picked their way along the wooden planks. Ahead, two women carried woven plastic baskets on their backs full of fruit and vegetables.

She drew Ben's attention upward. Five adult orangutans, one with a baby clinging to her side, were swinging along a rope stretching between trees in no rush to reach the other side. One tugged playfully at a tempting limb of the ape in front, another tried to steal a chunk of durian fruit its neighbour was munching.

'Nice, heh. Ordinary things. Family things.'

Side by side they stood and watched.

A mist hung through the canopy, and above the sky was soft grey. Minutes later metal grey clouds rolled in, thunder rumbled and rain pelted down. Their fold-up umbrellas were useless. She should have been quicker to find shelter. Stupid.

'Come… come…'

But she couldn't run – not yet – as she headed with Ben to shelter under a tree. Seeing them, one of the women sanctuary workers laughingly offered massive banana leaves.

'Thank you. Traditional umbrellas,' she told Ben.

'And environmentally spot on.' Ben grinned.

Huddling together, they waited for the deluge to pass.

Those orangutans, their shaggy fur matted, didn't look like they wanted to be wet either. But the little ones weren't in a hurry to take cover. She watched a baby orangutan getting into mischief, taking fruit meant for another. An adult, the mother, she supposed, grabbed an arm. The baby shrieked, resisting, then Mum casually slung the youngster onto her side and sloped away.

Yulia had a sudden vision of herself with a little one on her hip: her own baby…

Sartano's bullet had done damage. How could it not? On learning that one of her ovaries had been mashed, the floodgates had opened and she had sobbed and sobbed.

'But,' she had been assured, 'you can still have a family, the other ovary is functioning normally.' The doctor, an earnest woman, had checked her age – thirty-three – before adding, 'But don't leave it too long.'

And Yulia did want a family, wanted to get on with this game of life. She watched the orangutan mum taking the little one firmly in hand then glanced at Ben, hoping her inner thoughts were not written on her face. She mustn't get ahead of things and Ben wasn't one to be rushed. She reminded herself she must live for the moment. Hadn't she said as much to him? But still... She slipped her arm into his.

'There's hope, don't you think?' What did that mean? For her and Ben? These animals? The forest? The world? Would he understand she meant a future for all of it?

'Without hope we die.' He kissed her lightly and tightened his hold around her waist.

She nuzzled in. Even getting soaked, this moment, this very moment, felt good.

'Let's go,' Ben said. 'You need to rest, and no argument.'

'Rest sounds good.'

It was the same Cessna that Ben had flown in with Ardhi and Rick and the same cheery pilot at the controls. Now he shared the small plane with Yulia, Trevor, Sean – a young man Ben was still getting a feel for – and... Ben glanced further along to the head of black hair... Mr Marpuah from Jakarta. It was quite a party.

Mr Marpuah was friendly, relaxed, quite different from the cautious civil servant he and Ardhi had met with in Jakarta. Before boarding the large man had spoken earnestly with Yulia, and Ben had watched her hands fly to her mouth at something he said.

Yulia rushed over to him. 'He was asking if I've recovered. And Ben...' A broad smile lit up her face. 'Sartano's gone!'

'Gone?'

'Been retired from the police force.'

'I'd rather he was charged and put away, jailed, rather than free to dip into his stash for luxury holidays or—'

'Spend his evenings singing karaoke,' Yulia cut in. 'Was that what you were going to say?' She grinned and he responded in kind. If she was happy with this outcome, he was too.

Nearly there. Palm plantations were giving way to forest.

Mr Marpuah twisted around in his snug seat and called to Ben. 'I've never been anywhere like this. Quite an adventure. My central government has fresh enthusiasm. Your new international trade minister's energy is, er, infectious.'

'Infectious!' Trevor looked up. 'It must be catching.' He shared a look with his son, who added, 'I hope so, Dad.'

Perhaps Trevor had a sense of humour. He would have time to find out.

'Ben?'

'Trevor?' They were on first-name terms now.

'I take it this is it?'

Trevor pointed through the window. Ben stood and leaned over to share the view as the small plane descended, the outline of a landing strip – their landing strip – ahead. Sunlight glinted on the windscreens of two SUVs waiting to collect them.

Three days wasn't long enough to set the world to rights but it was a start, and Trevor had agreed to return next season. For the second trip, Yulia and he planned to accompany Trevor to a community forest project that was prospering so he could see for himself how things might be done. But this first visit was to *their* village, the village that had been compromised, and badly hurt.

'I've offered them compensation,' Trevor had said.

'That's a start. But you need to go there yourself. Get to know them, understand what they want, what is important. Getting a nurse to them, *regularly*, will win you friends.'

'Do they have proper toilet facilities? Decent food?' The businessman had seemed worried about that.

Ben gave him what assurances he could, talking up the delights of the Shack, deciding discussions about cultural values could wait. He had tried to persuade him to break ties with the Zumran family altogether. Nothing good could come of that connection.

Time. Everything took time.

Ben reached across the narrow aisle for Yulia's hand. 'So glad you're with me.'

'Partners.'

He squeezed her hand in confirmation. Yes, partners, and together they would hold the businessman's hand too – in a manner of speaking.

The Cessna dipped for approach.

Ben reached over and touched Trevor's shoulder. 'Buckle your seatbelt. The ride's just beginning.'

Author's Note and Acknowledgements

Blind Eye began life as a screenplay in 2008. My partner Hubert Kwisthout was – and remains – involved with Forest Stewardship Council (FSC), promoting responsible management of the world's forests. At that time, he had a company supplying FSC timber and I assisted with marketing. Through his contacts I accessed specialists to advise on the story and Film Agency Wales supported me with development funding. The finished screenplay had some forays out, then remained on file. In 2019, having written my debut novel, *Wayward Voyage*, I considered whether *Blind Eye* might have a new life in novel format.

2020 was a difficult year with the coronavirus pandemic disrupting lives but it provided me with time to write. I worked on *Blind Eye* novel, updated *Blind Eye* screenplay and submitted it to Green Stories screenplay competition, where it was awarded joint first prize, judges saying, *'A great success of this script is locating the plight to save forestry in a global context and showing how interdependent we are as a community.'*

In the eleven years between 2008 – when I first wrote my story – to 2019, using figures compiled by Global Forest Watch (GFW) of the World Resources Institute, the area of primary humid forest lost was about the area of Sweden. If you include tree cover lost to thinning of forests by logging, mining or cattle grazing but not resulting in complete loss of canopy then the area is about five times larger: roughly the area of Indonesia or Mexico.

Preservation of the world's forests is more important than ever.

I am indebted to specialists who have assisted. Special thanks to a tropical forester who has been committed to forest certification for decades but wishes to remain anonymous. Thanks to professional contacts in Indonesia who wish to remain anonymous. Thanks to Chris van der Goot who has been involved with FSC from early days. Thanks to Lord Jonny Oates, Liberal Democrat Lords Spokesperson on Energy and Climate Change, for checking political scenes pass muster.

Thanks to early readers Vivienne Hamblin and Jane Scroxton; book coach Ruth Bullivant; my sons Luther Kwisthout and Matt Kwisthout, for their feedback. Thanks to my Slack Writers group and to my line editor Lynne Patrick.

Thanks, in particular, to Hubert Kwisthout. Without his real-life commitment this story wouldn't have emerged from my imagination.

Anna M Holmes
www.annamholmes.com

WAYWARD VOYAGE

Anna M Holmes

*

PROLOGUE

Spanish Town, Jamaica
November 1720

MILITARY DRUMS AND FIFE NOTES SLICED THE morning air. Anne jumped onto a bench under the high window, gripped the iron bars and peered out.

An Admiralty Marshal, ceremonial silver oar in hand, marched into view, head erect, a fifer and two drummers keeping step. She spat as far as she could. A futile gesture that fell short, but she didn't care about the pompous-looking official, it was those following she was impatient to see.

She yelled above the drums, 'Godspeed! Godspeed!'

A man's voice reached her. 'We go to the devil if he'll take us.'

Let the devil take him.

A second voice responded, 'And God be with you, lass.'

These weren't the ones she wanted. Perhaps he wasn't there? They were moving too fast, the Marshal already passing out of sight... Yes! He was at the rear, head bowed, wrists lashed together. Standing on tiptoes, she pressed her face as far as she could between the bars and shouted, 'You!'

His head jerked up and twisted to face her.

'If you'd fought like a man you wouldn't have to die like a dog!'

He smiled and gave a quick shake of his head. Smiled! She had more to say – words she had rehearsed over and over the past days and nights when sleep wouldn't come, but it was too late. Craning her neck, she watched till they were out of sight, listening to the footsteps and fife and drums fade. The gates thudded shut but still she could hear the drums – faintly – then not at all.

Resting her forehead against the wall she waited for her breath to steady.

'I won't be next.' Her words emerged as a croak. She cleared her throat and spoke forcefully. 'I'll not die.'

'Anne...'

Anne turned to meet the gaze of the woman sitting slumped against their cell wall in blood-encrusted seaman's clothes.

She stared into the raddled face.

'Neither of us are going to die. You hear me?'

She was not ready to die and could not bear to think of what was unfolding beyond the gates.